TRIGGER TIME

When you looked at Sam Tollin, you didn't see a
gawky sixteen-year-old kid anymore. You saw a
lean, hard man, his body coiled for action, with the
tied-down six-gun on his hip looking like it was a
natural-born part of him.

Forty days alone in the mountains had done that. Forty
days practicing drawing, aiming, and firing the six-
gun from dawn to dusk. Forty days of blisters on his
hand turning into calluses, forty days of muscles
turning into steel-like sinews.

But now those forty days were over.

And now as Sam Tollin faced the two gunmen heading toward him with hate in their eyes and death
in their holsters, he knew the time of testing had
begun. . . .

THE SEARCHER

F. M. PARKER

A SIGNET BOOK

NEW AMERICAN LIBRARY

PUBLISHER'S NOTE

This novel is a work of fiction. Names, characters, places, and incidents either are the product of the author's imagination or are used fictitiously, and any resemblance to actual persons, living or dead, events, or locales is entirely coincidental.

The Making of the Desert— A Prologue

In the beginning there was no man.
In the beginning there was no desert.

The great continent won the battle. It beat back the attack of the two salty oceans that tore at its flanks. After uncounted millions of years of warfare, the pounding waves and ripping currents had retreated a very long distance, and the land surface exposed to the yellow sun was greater by threefold.

However, the seas had played a devilish trick upon the continent. The world had grown cold while the conflict raged, and as the level of the seas lowered and drew back from the shores, the waters that no longer filled the deep basins to overflowing were thrown down upon the plains and mountains of the continent. Most of the moisture fell as snow. Much did not melt during the short, chilly summers, and frigid glaciers were birthed.

For thousands of years the glaciers grew, merging together into one colossal ice sheet more than a mile thick. The white mantle of ice, its solid water crystals turned to plastic by its own immeasurable, crushing tons, flowed outward, slow and cold, to smother the land for more than a million square miles. It overrode the hills, filled the valleys, and depressed the rock crust of the earth into broad basins.

Forests grew on all the land not hidden by the ice. Into the far northern reaches of these woods appeared an alien, upright creature with a thin-haired pelt and a brown skin. Migrating at three to four miles a year, and with his female and sturdy offspring in tow, the man moved south along the western shore. He searched for a warm land, close to the sun.

One generation after another was born and died during the long trek. At last, the man reached the lowland on the southern portion of the continent. Yet here, too, cold rain and heavy snow fell in superabundance.

The snow never fully melted from one year to the next on the tall mountains of this new country. Small glaciers came to life in high valleys, to slip slowly, like ice tears, down the face of the mountains.

Then a change occurred; the earth began to be less cold. The continental glacier shrank, and as it melted a deluge of unimaginable quantity flooded across the land. Rivers became vast cataracts charging headlong for the seas.

At one latitude on the sphere of the earth, the sun had burned directly down for billions of years. In this equatorial zone, the air became heated as in a furnace and surged heavenward in an unending tide. As the torrent rose and cooled, downpours cascaded out of the cloudy, tormented skies.

At tremendous heights, this stupendous updraft split, half dashing south and half north. The northern segment, rushing through the frigid atmosphere at speeds exceeding two hundred miles an hour, hurried toward the top of the world. However, it grew weary before it reached its goal and plunged down toward the earth and the great continent.

During the glacial epoch, these dry, descending south winds would have mixed with the damp, cool surface air blowing from the north. Now, however, the land was warm and the equatorial wind, growing hot, and parched with a mighty thirst that could consume ten feet of water in a year, sucked up and stole away the mere five inches of moisture the land was given.

The glacier continued to wane. Finally, it shrank to nothing. The desiccating south wind grew stronger. The forest died except on the very highest peaks of the mountains. Countless species of animals died. All the lowland became barren. Sandstorms raged.

Rainstorms rarely fell. When they did pour down their floods, the land was scarred and cut, and the soil that had taken thousands of years to form was flushed down from the highlands to create broad floodplains along the rivers.

A few species of plant and animal life adapted to the harsh

land of the desert mountains and valleys. The brown man adapted. He was as one with the desert for fifteen millennia.

A new clan of man came upon the desert. His skin was white and his numbers many. He and the brown man pursued each other across the land, and they fought savage battles. The victor slew the vanquished without mercy.

Beneath the burning sun, the desert lay mute and uncaring of the dead that rotted upon its breast.

CHAPTER 1

The Indian war party, twenty Comanche and two Kiowa strong and mounted on fast mustangs, crossed the Gallinas River just south of Mesa Cuatas. The Comanche chief led, wading his long-legged pony through the belly-deep current of the ford. At the far shore, he halted and twisted in his blood-stained U.S. Army saddle to watch the progress of his fighters.

They were lean, sinewy warriors armed with Winchester and Henry rifles, nearly half of them repeating weapons. Most of the braves also carried their old familiar war bows tied behind their saddles. A few had long battle lances.

The chief's eyes paused on the two Kiowa. They had arrived in the Comanche camp in Palo Duro Canyon in the land of Texas at the time the band was preparing to leave to steal horses in the valley of the Rio Grande. The Kiowa had been returning from a sojourn in their village in the Oklahoma Territory, north of the Red River, and were heading for Santa Fe. With the same destination, the two groups made a pact to ride together and join forces to fight any battle they might fall into along the way.

The Comanche wore breechcloths, elk-hide moccasins, and leggings tied above their knees. Except for moccasins, the Kiowa were dressed like white men, in cotton pants and shirts, and had six-guns in holsters strapped around their waists. The chief believed the two men sometimes rode with renegade white men and had acquired that habit of wearing pistols from them.

The Kiowa's association with enemies of the Comanche made them suspect. Still, the chief had heard the two were

8

brave warriors, and that was sufficient for now. If a battle started and they faltered, or gave any sign they did not want to kill white men, his braves would slay them.

The band had been riding for three days, pressing swiftly onward from morning's first graying of night until the next darkness overtook them from the east. They had crossed the grassy prairie of northwest Texas and driven deeply into the hilly desert of northern New Mexico. Twice they had spotted distant riders and circled widely around them. Until the Indians reached the valley of the Rio Grande, every contact with white men must be avoided. The chief's war cry as he hurled his warriors into the attack would be the first and only warning to their foes.

The Comanche were now entering the stunted pine on the rolling eastern foothills of the great mountains, the two-hundred-mile-long chain called Sangre de Cristo by the Mexicans. In one more day, they would be near Santa Fe and taking the excellent horses from the *ranchos* of the Mexicans and *gringos*. Any man that tried to stop them would be killed.

With good fortune, the Comanche would take hundreds of ponies with them when they returned to the Wintering Place, Palo Duro Canyon. The chief was anxious to go back to that beautiful place, invisible from the flat horizon, a curving chasm slashed into the plains, an oasis of sweet springs, streams and waterfalls, willows, and buffalo grass tall and nutritious. It was all sunken below the flat prairie and hidden from the frigid winter wind that would soon blow down from the north. It was entered only by a few trails beaten out by buffalo herds. Best of all, his people would be safe there, for few white men knew of the existence of the deep river canyon.

It was late in the Yellow Leaves Moon, October, and yet the sun had unnaturally retained much of its fire. Several of the swarthy riders bent down from the backs of their cayuses as they waded the river and scooped up handfuls of the cool water to splash onto their hot faces and bare chests.

The warriors did not speak. The only sound was the current of the stream swirling around the legs of their mounts and the hard hooves of the animals grating on the sand and rock as they climbed the bank.

The Comanche chief turned his square brown face to the

west. His black, piercing eyes scanned ahead, missing nothing as he examined the series of ridges that climbed ever upward for the next half-day ride. The land finally culminated in the two-mile-high volcanic crest of the Sangre de Cristo, pine-cloaked and dark against the opal sky.

The chief knew that beyond the high skyline the terrain fell away steeply into the valley of the Rio Grande. There lay the town of Santa Fe. Five years before, he and other fighting men of his people had made a raid to the very outskirts of the town. They had stolen three hundred horses, and taken sixteen scalps.

The chief's burly body sat his mustang with tense wariness as he surveyed the route ahead. The moments slid by as he searched for danger. That danger was the white men who were spreading like some loathsome disease, suddenly appearing in a dozen unexpected places.

The Comanche saw the mule deer doe watching them from a patch of brush on a distant ridgetop. At the extreme limit of his vision, he noted the eagle pumping long black wings slowly, moving south across the flank of the mountain. Closer in, he heard the call of a mountain quail, and a covey came out of high grass and, with quick, nervous starts and stops, went down to the river to drink. Everything was as it should be.

He kicked his pony forward. Another ten miles could be put behind them before it grew dark. In the early morning, they would cross the Pecos River just below its beginning, then go up and through the pass that cut the backbone of the massive mountain, and down into the distant, unseen Rio Grande Valley.

The remaining warriors hastened to fall in behind their chief. They passed beneath the tall rock escarpment of Mesa Cuatas and onward. Each man and his mustang, like one fierce animal, lean and hungry, hurried forward on the savage hunt.

The sun slid down the last arc of its warm trajectory. Its rays turned golden and bathed the land in a mellow light like wild honey. It plunged lower, dropping behind the peak of the Sangre de Cristo. Shadows invaded the deep gullies, grew swiftly beyond those narrow confines, and crept out to consume the entire pine-rimmed Pecos River Valley.

No wind stirred. It rested quietly in the short span of equilibrium between its daytime climb up the mountain and its nighttime tumble into the valley.

Here the Pecos River was a small stream, being only a few short miles from its birthplace in a high cove on the Sangre de Cristo. A horse trail made its way out of the timber on the west, entered the grassy valley, and forded the river at a shallow riffle. A log cabin of one large room sat on the bluff above the crossing.

A tall gray horse, bridle reins tied loosely over its neck, grazed on the edge of the meadow some quarter mile east of the cabin. In the fringe of timber near the horse, a man and boy worked in perfect unison, pulling a long crosscut saw. They did not speak, each knowing exactly his portion of the task before them.

This was high country and deep snow accumulated in the winter. In the forenoon, they had cut grass hay in the small meadows along the river. Then they had built brush fences around the stacks to save it for the hungry cows when all other feed was buried by the deep white drifts.

Later in the day they had felled a large dead pine. Now the two-man saw, with a muted rasp of sharp teeth on wood, flashed back and forth, cutting downward through the dry body of the tree.

The youth watched the yellow spray of sawdust spring from first one side of the log and then the other as the saw bit deeply with each stroke. He felt good cutting the winter supply of wood. Better still, he found great pleasure in working with his father, feeling the solid contact with the big man through the metal length of the saw.

A trickle of sweat found the tip of the young man's nose and he blew it away with a puff of air. He looked up from the saw to his father's face. Without slowing his stroke, he said, "Dad, let's saw the log clear up before we stop."

Tom Tollin met his son's gaze and smiled broadly. The boy was tall and lanky, nearly as tall as he and still growing rapidly. In his youthful thinness, the freckled planes of his face were sharp and angular. He would be a large man one day.

"You called it, Sam, so we'll do it," said the father. His son's red hair was sweat-plastered to his head, but that was just a normal working sweat.

Sam concentrated on his grip on the saw handle and listened to the cadence of the rough, purring whisper of each stroke. One length of wood fell free after another as the two labored along the log. Finally, man and boy finished the task and straightened their backs.

"You're a stout sawyer," said Tom.

Sam knew the praise was truly meant and smiled his pleasure. "I ought to be, I turned sixteen last month. And I'm going to be a stout eater at supper, too. I'm starved."

They turned to look at the cabin. A woman was kneeling in the woodyard and filling her apron with wood chips. A girl three-quarters grown carried a pail toward the spring behind the house.

"Your ma is getting kindling to start the evening fire, and Sarah is after the water. By the time we get the chores finished and washed up, it'll be time to eat."

Still the two remained standing together, each enjoying the companionship of the other. The valley bottom cooled. A slow, invisible stream of wind began to slide down the mountainside and fan their sweat-dampened faces.

Tom ranged his view over the valley. A half dozen good horses and several cows grazed along the river. The balance of his one hundred and forty cows were out of sight, scattered in the pine or in other meadows up and down the river. His herd was small, but it was of good quality and paid for. Given time and good luck, he would make it grow into a very large herd.

On the flat above the river sat the solid log cabin Sam and he had built. It had a steeply pitched roof shingled with pine and small square windows with heavy shutters. Gunports were cut through each shutter. The nearest cover for an enemy, the woods on the north side, was nearly three hundred yards distant. The structure was a fair fortress. Tom hoped he would never have to use it for that purpose.

He savored the pleasant feeling of owning property. For many years, he had worked for wages hauling freight between St. Joe and Santa Fe. He had saved his money and waited to see if the peace between the Indians and white men would endure. It had for several years. The Comanche and Kiowa had stayed on their lands in Texas and Oklahoma. The Navajo were peaceful on their reservation far to the northwest.

This was the year 1871 and the second summer since he had led his family and the herd of cattle from the safety of St. Joe. They had made the long trip across the dry prairie and then the pine-covered mountains to finally settle upon the grass-rich valley of the Pecos River.

Tom's gaze wandered off to the east to evaluate an area of second-growth pine in an old burn. He had promised his wife to add a room to the cabin after the summer work was finished. Those trees were of the correct size to supply the logs.

From his elevation, he could see over the tops of the pine trees and into a small grassy opening beyond. He jerked with surprise and alarm as a band of Indians rode into that meadow and crossed toward him. They entered the woods on his side.

"Sam, listen to me carefully," Tom said in a tight voice. "A bunch of Indians are just over there in the timber. They will be where they can see the house in a minute or two. You run for the house fast as you can. I'll get the horse and catch up with you. Now, boy. Run for it! Run!"

Sam raced full tilt, his legs driving and feet reaching for distance. He snapped a look over his shoulder and saw his father vault into the saddle and spur after him. Suddenly, fierce war cries and the rumble of speeding ponies erupted behind them.

Bullets spanged from the ground around Sam, kicking up dust and whining away. Ahead he saw his mother, skirts billowing and long red hair blowing, dashing for the cabin. Sarah sped down the hill carrying a splashing bucket of water. Good girl, thought Sam. Bring the water, for we may badly need it.

His father flashed past on the horse. Almost immediately, the horse slid to a stop at the cabin door. Tom sprang down and, dragging the animal after him, vanished inside.

Sam dove through the door, spun about, and slammed it shut. He grabbed up a heavy wooden plank and dropped it into place to bar the entrance.

The Indians split into two streams of riders and, screaming and firing their rifles into the walls and windows, poured past the cabin.

Tom jerked his pistol as he jumped to a window. A spotted

pony, with a brown man leaning forward low over its neck, dashed past. As the white man drew aim, he was looking directly into the Comanche's eyes. He fired.

The Indian held to his running mustang for two strides, then fell off to the side, sliding and bumping loose-jointedly on the ground. The horse raced after its mates, a blanket saddle flapping in the wind.

A bullet punched through the chink between the logs near Tom's head and whirred angrily across the single room to thud into the opposite wall. The gray stallion squealed in fear and spun about, striking the table and knocking it against the fireplace. Yet, even in his fright, he avoided kicking or stepping on the four humans crouched near the walls and drawing the thick shutters closed.

Mary Tollin finished barricading the window and took up a rifle. She caught Tom's look upon her.

"Are you all right?" he called across the shadowy cabin.

"Yes. Thank God we all made it inside."

Tom nodded. He spoke to Sarah. "Quiet Smoke down. Talk to him. Pet him a little. And you, Sam, climb up to the loft and watch toward the river and the woods to the north. They'll be back, so get ready. Take good aim."

"What kind of Indians do you think they are?" asked Sam hurriedly.

"Comanches, I think. Now up in the loft with you."

Sam draped a bandoleer of shells over his shoulder and jerked himself hand over hand up the pole ladder fastened to the rear wall.

Sarah caught the dragging reins of the horse and, talking softly to him, tugged the big head close to her. She began to stroke the long, bony jaw of the stallion.

A bullet rammed through one of the shutters, spitting splinters like a handful of darts. In the attic, Sam shot quickly in reply. The rifle crashed like an exploding cannon in the confined space of the cabin.

The stallion screamed and began to shake. He wanted to break away from the thunder that hammered his ears, tear free of these narrow walls, and run—and run. In his fear, he emptied himself, his urine splashing and puddling on the dirt floor.

"Missed him, Dad." Sam's voice, shrill with excitement, came down from above. "He ducked behind a tree too fast."

"Keep shooting. Let them know we're ready for them."

Tom moved to another gunport. He smelled the heavy odor of gunpowder, urine, and horse dung that hung like a pall in the dead, still air of the cabin. He glanced at the stallion. The frightened animal must not hurt himself, for soon all of his strength and speed would be needed.

The man scrutinized the territory outside through the tiny opening in the shutter. His family was in a bad situation. Three or four Indians could be beaten off from the strongly built cabin. However, the twenty-five or so braves in this band, with a determined effort, could capture his family's small stronghold.

He probed for Indians in the gloom of the fast-settling darkness. In the night shadows growing in the trees above the cabin, a wink of red fire appeared and a bullet from a long-range rifle thunked into the outside wall. The Comanche were biding their time, but they were here to stay.

Mary came to him and took him by the arm. He felt her tremble as she clutched him.

In the deepening darkness of the cabin, her eyes were barely visible in the blurred whiteness of her face. He sensed her fear at the danger that had come so quickly upon them. She leaned close. "Tom, we must not let the children be harmed."

He caught her face between his hands. "I know. Now, please go back to the window and keep watch."

"Sarah, Smoke is quiet now," said Tom. "Go to the window facing up toward the spring. Now, watch close and yell if anything at all looks strange."

She did as told, peering cautiously out the opening. "It's getting dark, Dad. Soon I won't be able to see anything."

Tom surveyed the approach toward the river. He ran his glance along the horse trail, carefully examining the bank by the river and the fringe of brush edging the water on the far side. Beyond that, he could dimly make out where the trail crossed the open meadow before entering the forest.

Night was almost upon them. With the night, the Comanche would tighten their ring on the cabin, and the trap would be closed.

Tom faced away from the window and called out, "Sam, come down here."

"Right, Dad," answered Sam, and dropped down from the attic.

Tom unbuckled his spurs and jerked them off. As Sam came near, he thrust them out to him.

"Take these."

"But why?"

"No questions and no arguments," said his father firmly as he unstrapped his six-gun and handed it to Sam. "Put this on and pull it tight."

Sam did as directed and then looked closely at his father, only faintly visible in the heavy, dark shadows of the cabin.

"Now, get up on Smoke. Sarah, you up behind Sam."

"No. We're not leaving you and Ma," exclaimed Sam, backing away from the horse.

"Oh, Dad, please don't make us go without you," pleaded Sarah in a trembly voice.

"Now listen, Sam, and you too, Sarah, with you two riding like demons and drawing the Indians after you, your ma and I can slip off and get away. You know someone must go to the fort in Santa Fe for help."

Sam tried to see his father's face, but all he could make out was the dark outline of his form. He felt terribly strange at the thought of abandoning his father and mother. Terribly guilty.

Sam said, "It's forty miles to the nearest help in Santa Fe."

"More like forty-five and it's best you get on your way," said his father in a rough voice.

Sam knew that tone meant his father's mind was set. "You can depend on me," said Sam in a choked voice. "I'll get the soldiers and be back tomorrow afternoon." He swung astride the tall horse.

"I know you will," responded Tom. "Come here, Sarah."

She came hesitatingly forward. He caught her under the arms and lifted her astride behind her brother.

Mary rummaged briefly in a trunk in the corner. There was a clink of metal on metal as she handed Sam a leather pouch. 'You may need some money, so take this."

Sam knew the few gold coins in his hand were all the money the family possessed. He almost objected, but this was not the time to argue with his two beloved parents. He shoved the pouch into a front pocket. "Hand me my rifle," he said.

"That'd only add weight. Your best hope to escape is to outride the Indians. Old Smoke can do it. If you have to do some close-in shooting, use the pistol." Tom gripped Sam by the knee. "Now listen, your sister's safety is in your hands. Spur Smoke in a flat-out run clear across the river and through the woods until you come to the steep grade that starts to climb up the mountain. Do you know where I mean?"

"Yes, I know."

"Good. Then once on the grade, watch and listen in back of you. Keep moving, but not so fast as to wind Smoke. Sarah, you help Sam watch behind."

"Yes, Dad." Sarah's voice was a whisper. She wanted to cry.

Tom stepped to the gunport facing the river and measured the blackness of the night.

"May I kiss you, Sammy?" asked his mother.

He bent far down, saw the faint white cloud of her face, and felt her soft lips on his cheek for a second. Then she kissed Sarah and drew away.

Sam heard his sister sob. Then she was quiet. Still, he sensed her struggle to control her anguish.

"It's dark enough," said his father, and went to the door. "When you are outside, point Smoke in the direction you want to go. Then give him his head, for there's less chance he will trip and fall that way. Get your head down so you won't hit the door jamb. Both of you ready?"

Sarah's arms tightened their encirclement of her brother's waist.

"We're ready," said Sam.

Tom heard the dull thud on the shingles of the roof. And yet another, and a third. Fire arrows. The dry pine shingles would be a bright blaze in a few minutes.

He lifted the bar and yanked open the door.

"Hang on, Sarah. Go, Sam! Go! Ride! Ride!"

Sam jabbed the sharp rowels of the spurs into Smoke's flanks.

The big brute of a horse plunged through the doorway and into the darkness. Where the Indians waited.

CHAPTER 2

The gray mustang bolted through the blackness. His hooves were thunder on the hard-packed ground. Sam felt the powerful muscles of the beast moving between his legs, knotting and stretching with each great stride as the stallion surged forward. They crossed the river in three long, splashing leaps and rushed up the far bank.

Sam's eyes wrestled with the darkness. The shadowy outline of the woods grew visible on the distant side of the river bottom. On his right, ghostly horsemen came into sight racing over the meadow, speeding to cut him off before he could reach the opening where the trail entered the forest.

Ahead, in the edge of the trees, Sam made out the silhouette of a lone horseman blocking the path. Even as he discovered the Indian, the man fired his weapon and a red flame lanced out. There was a tug on Sam's right ear, a sting, instantly becoming a searing pain.

"Hang on!" he cried to Sarah. He leaned low along the neck of the horse. Sarah held fast, pressing her face to her brother's back.

Sam thought of swerving aside from the menacing dark figure in the woods and gripped the reins to make the turn. Then the loud tattoo of running horses closing fast on his right changed his mind. He had to avoid these men, had to stay on the course, for the trail before him was the only way through the thick forest in the night.

He pulled his father's six-gun from its holster and screamed into Smoke's ear, encouraging the stallion to give his all to make the escape.

He fired two shots, hastily aimed, and charged straight at the Indian.

The Indian's gun flashed brightly in return and a bullet zipped past. Then Sam was within a few feet of his enemy and the man's pony was spinning to the side to escape the large horse boiling headlong upon him.

He was too slow. Smoke's broad chest rammed him, slamming him aside, rolling him into the brush beside the trail.

At the collision, Smoke stumbled a step. He caught his feet quickly and rushed into the dark tunnel in the wall of the forest.

Shots crashed in the rear as the other Indians came within range. The trail curved away among the trees and the shooting ceased.

The only sound in the woods was the thud of the horse's racing hooves and the swift suck and blow as he pulled his breaths.

Sam turned his head and spoke over his shoulder. "Are you all right, Sis?"

"Yes, Sammy, but I'm so afraid." Her voice was a weak whisper in his ear.

"The worst is over. Hang on to me tight."

Sam felt of his injury. Beneath his fingers, the ear burned and ached, and blood oozed out wet and sticky. He found where the hot, speeding bullet had cut the outside rim of his ear, leaving behind a little half-circle notch. He wiped his hand on his pants and tried to ignore the pain.

The horse ran free, the reins hanging loosely. Excited by the race and the thunderclaps of the guns, he plunged along the winding path, attacking the slopes of the Cristo with mighty lunges.

The trees swept past in blurred shapes. Sam clung to the saddle horn to keep from being thrown by the swerve and dodge of the horse avoiding rock and brush on the trail. Obstacles that only the night-seeing eyes of the mustang could detect.

Miles dropped behind. An almost full moon, like a silver plate with one side of its rim broken, crept up over the eastern horizon and cast feeble rays of light down through the limbs of the pines.

The grade turned up more steeply and Sam dragged hard on the reins. The gray came to a halt, his breath rushing with a hoarse sawing sound through his throat and into the hollows of his lungs.

The pace had been a full, all-out run. Too fast, Sam knew. He touched the horse's neck. Sweat was a thick lather on the heated body of the faithful and willing animal.

Sam twisted around and aimed his ear for any noise from a pursuer coming up the mountain. He could hear nothing above the strained breathing of the horse.

In a break through the trees and in the far distance, there was a faint yellow spot flickering. Sam caught his breath. That was a fire and just about exactly where the cabin should be. The Indians were burning his family's home. Fervently he hoped his mother and father had escaped.

He watched for only a handful of seconds and turned sorrowfully away. His father was a good fighter, and just maybe he had gotten to the woods. Once he was there, the Indians could not catch him in the dark. But daylight would soon come.

A sharp stab of guilt cut through Sam for deserting them. He must get help quickly.

"Sarah, the grade is very steep here," said Sam. "I'll get down and run for a while and take part of the weight off Smoke. You ride. Now, listen behind. You should be able to hear better than I can up front. Do you understand?"

"Yes, Sammy. I'll listen carefully. I won't let anyone come up behind. But doesn't Smoke need more time to catch his breath?"

"He can get his wind and still keep up with me."

Sarah moved up into the saddle. She turned her head half to the side, cocking her ear to the rear.

Sam sprang off along the path. The horse followed close behind on the heels of his young master.

An hour later, sweat-drenched and with his lungs burning, Sam stopped.

"Sarah, I'm going to ride with you again. I'll run some more later. You stay in the saddle and I'll get up behind." He crawled up on the back of the horse.

Sam thought he heard a rock rattle somewhere down the

trail. He listened intently. The sound did not come again. He spoke to Smoke and the horse stepped out smartly.

In the middle of the night, the crest of the Sangre de Cristo was reached. With Sarah leaning back and sleeping in his arms, Sam urged the valiant stallion to a faster pace down the west-facing slope of the mountain.

"You cleaned me out," said the gambler, and threw his cards down onto the felt-topped table.

"Took us all night to do it," said the soldier, glancing up briefly at the gambler. The fool had drunk too much and had made reckless bets. Damn poor example of a professional gambler. The soldier began to pick up his cards as a new deal started.

The gambler staggered slightly as he stood up. He patted his pockets and growled to himself. Two Mexican sheepherders, an army private, and a cowboy had beaten him. Had taken every thin dime.

He left the lighted card room and entered the barroom of the cantina. The big room was dark, and he stumbled into several chairs before he gained the bat-winged door and pushed through to the wooden sidewalk. He looked both ways along the main thoroughfare of Santa Fe.

The street was a shallow canyon between rows of flat-topped adobe buildings, jammed end to end except where the short side streets made a break. The way extended for more than a mile along the Santa Fe River. The westering moon, sinking fast toward the peak of Jemez Mountain, threw a frail light upon the dusty road. Daylight was only a fainter tone of black in the east.

Already the industrious were astir. Five large freight wagons piled high with goods and covered with canvas were lined up in the street. Three teams of mules, harnessed and hooked in a place astraddle the long wooden tongues of each wagon, stood waiting patiently. Two spare animals were tied to the tailgate of the lead wagon.

The gambler knew that would be the Mexican wagon train that had arrived two days before. Now it was ready to strike out back along the El Camino Real, The Royal Highway, for Chihuahua.

Just beyond the last wagon, a reddish glow shone from the

open door of the blacksmith shop. The smith must have been using his forge. Probably some last minute repair for the wagon train.

Across the street from the smithy, Falina's Cantina spilled light onto the sidewalk. Two horses were tied to the hitch rail in front.

The gambler badly needed a cup of coffee, and he was hungry. He shrugged the thought away. Falina's husband gave no credit.

The gambler put his hands into his empty pockets and cursed his luck. He needed a stake and had absolutely no idea how to get one.

The dark form of a horse plodded in from a side street. It stopped and stood a minute with its legs splayed, gathering strength. Then it continued in the direction of the gambler, its steps muffled to soft, almost inaudible, thumps by the deep dust.

The gambler saw the slumped figures astride the horse and stepped out to catch the reins. The horse halted and spread its legs, and its muzzle drooped to almost touch the earth.

"Say, are you all right?" asked the gambler, peering up at the young boy and girl.

"Need help," muttered Sam. "My folks need help. Indians attacked our place over on the Pecos."

"What's that? Indians on the Pecos? When was this?"

Sam shook himself, trying to clear his head, fuzzy with exhaustion. He looked at the gambler through bleary eyes. "I must get help. Which way is it to the army camp?"

"About a quarter mile up that way on the edge of town," said the gambler, pointing. "Here, let me help you down and you can rest while I go roust out the soldiers."

Sam lowered Sarah into the man's arms. She sagged against him and he held her upright.

Sam slid from the saddle. The world swayed and began to spin slowly around him. His legs shook with weariness. He would have fallen had not the gambler caught him.

"Let me help you to the sidewalk where you can sit down," said the man.

"I've got to get the soldiers right away," mumbled Sam. He fished the bag of gold out of his pocket. "Will you help me, please? I'll pay you five dollars." He fumbled a gold coin out.

The gambler took the coin and at the same time evaluated the weight of the pouch with a practiced eye. He estimated there could be three to four hundred dollars if all the coins were gold. His mind raced to develop a plan, for here was his new stake if he played his cards correctly.

A dog barked somewhere in Burro Alley just beyond the row of houses north of him. The woodcutters were stirring and would soon be going into the woods with their little pack of animals. The cardplayers could come out of the saloon at any time. The sky was brightening and the teamsters might leave the cantina. He had only a minute to act.

"Come with me," said the gambler. "Rest in one of my wagons just over there and I'll get the soldiers in a hurry."

Mostly carrying Sarah on one arm and supporting Sam on the other, he shuffled them along the street in the direction of the wagon train.

A warning that he should be after the soldiers himself nagged Sam's tired mind. His father had often told him to be wary of strangers. However, his body, worn to numbness by a full day's work and then the nightlong travel by horseback and on foot, was not up to further movement. And the man had promised to rouse the soldiers.

The gambler unfastened the canvas on the tail end of the last wagon and spread it open. "Climb up in here and rest a few minutes," he urged. "Here, let me help you up. There you are. Now, lay down and take it easy. We'll be moving out soon to go help your folks."

Sam sank down on something soft. He reached his hand to touch Sarah. Must keep her safe. He succumbed to sleep.

The gambler tied the canvas back into place. He went to the horse the youths had ridden, led it into the side street beside the cantina, and fastened it to the hitch rail at the side door beside the mounts of the cardplayers. He climbed upon his own steed and, without a backward glance, hurried into the darkness. It was far past the time when he should be shaking the dust of Santa Fe.

The gambler had hardly disappeared when one of the Kiowa who had ridden with the Comanche band came trotting in from the same direction the horse carrying the boy and girl had arrived. On silent feet, he stole into the gloom at the corner of the street. Holding his rifle ready, he cautiously scanned both ways.

The Kiowa stood stock still in surprise, for he had expected to see armed men noisily preparing to ride to battle. However, all was deserted and quiet. Even the mules at the wagons waited, dozing and unmoving. The only sound was the barely audible murmur of voices in the restaurant.

He listened to the stillness of the town for several moments. All night he had pursued a rider, trying to catch him to prevent an alarm being given to signal the presence of the Indian raiding party. His favorite horse, an excellent animal, had died on the mountain in the fruitless effort. Now there was absolutely no sign that the rider had ever reached Santa Fe. Yet, the Kiowa knew the man had gained this destination, for he had trailed the smell of fresh dust to this very point.

Hanging in the deeper shadows near the walls of the buildings, the Kiowa slipped up to the window of the restaurant and peered in. A plump woman was clearing dishes from a large table full of Mexican teamsters. A pair of Americans sat off by themselves in a corner. They were bent over their food and eating without talk.

The wagon master arose and spoke to the teamsters. They paid for their food and filed out the door. The Indian stepped back around the corner of the restaurant before they could see him. From the darkness, he watched the men go to the wagons, climb up in the high seats, and pick up the reins of the mules.

The leader of the caravan mounted his horse and took up position in front of the lead wagon. A second horseman stationed himself at the rear of the line.

With the call of the drivers and a few sharp cracks of long bullwhips, the wagon train lumbered into motion. A little cloud of dust, kicked up by the wheels of the vehicles and feet of the animals, rose up to mix with the darkness.

The Kiowa watched the departure. His gimlet eyes paid special attention to one of the teamsters. The Indian's hand fingered the long skinning knife in his belt.

Leaning his rifle against the wall of the building beside him, the Indian sprang up to grab the edge of the flat-topped roof. He hoisted himself easily up and stood to look to the northeast at the white soldiers' fort. Once he had been a prisoner there for six months, locked up in one of the guard-house cells. That had been a very bad time. Never again would he allow himself to be captured and taken to such a place.

The Kiowa knew where the barracks were located across the parade ground from the guardhouse. The officers' quarters occupied the high ground on the far side of the compound. The Indian also knew where all the other parts of the fort lay.

He scrutinized the dark bulk of the structure silhouetted against the late night sky. One light showed in the extreme west end. That would be the mess hall. All signs indicated that just a normal, routine day was beginning for the soldiers.

The Kiowa swung back down to the ground. Retrieving his rifle, he padded past the window of the restaurant, glancing in briefly at the Americans. They sat reared back and sipping their coffee.

The two mustangs tied to the hitch rail twisted their heads to watch the Indian as he circled them with a measuring eye. Good animals, as near as the man could tell in the half dark. Both had a bedroll, grub bag, and canteen. The rifle scabbards were empty, the weapons most probably inside with the Americans. The ponies were ready for a long trail.

Let the white man ride double, thought the Indian. Selecting one of the cayuses, he stepped astride and wheeled the animal in the direction the wagons had taken.

At the card game, the Mexicans folded their cards and shoved them away. They looked at each other across the table. The older man nodded and they began to pick up the money stacked in front of them.

"Leaving winners, eh?" said the soldier.

"Yes, señor. That is always the best way," said the older Mexican. "But we win only a little *dinero*, not enough to brag about."

"Well, stick around. I've took the gambler's money and I think most of this cowboy's. I'll get to you two fellows in a little while."

"No, thanks, señor, we must leave. A busy day is almost here and we have had no sleep."

They walked away and out through the side door.

"Leaves only you and me," said the soldier, looking down at the small stack of change before the cowboy. "Do you have more money?"

Keesling smiled. He pushed his hat to the back of his head to expose a broad face. "I feel my luck has just changed."

"Then haul out your cash and let's get to dealing the cards."

"No need for that," responded Keesling. His eyes narrowed as he stood up. "Just give me all your money."

"You'll have to win it," said the soldier. Then an alarmed look of understanding swept over his face. He started to quickly rise.

Keesling's hand darted down and came up with his six-gun. He swung, and the steel barrel of the weapon cracked wickedly against the soldier's head before he was fully erect. The unconscious body slumped sideways to the floor.

"I knew I would win tonight, one way or the other," Keesling said to the deaf ears of the man.

He raked the clutter of bills and coins from the table into a hand and stuffed it into a pocket. Quickly he searched the limp form. He grinned when he found a wad of paper money hidden inside the man's shirt front. "Banking some *dinero* as you went along, eh?"

One strong puff blew the coal-oil lamp out.

Keesling left by the same door as the Mexicans. He stepped into the leather of the horse that had waited the night for him, jerked the lead rope loose on his pack animal that had been equally patient, and rode toward the Santa Fe River.

He forded the stream, pausing in the center to allow his animals to drink. On the north side, he took a course to the southwest. Sixty miles away, he would rendezvous with his gang and tell them of a grand plan he had to make them all rich. If they were brave enough to help him.

CHAPTER 3

In the drought of late summer, the dust lay deep on the heavily used El Camino Real. The thick softness of the pulverized dirt dampened the jostle and bump of the iron-rimmed wheels as the wagons marched with good speed along the Santa Fe River. A plume of brown dust trailed the train, hanging in the air for several minutes before it settled back to the roadway.

Sam's exhausted body rested and his sleeping brain did not take alarm at the movement. Sarah slept with her hand lightly touching her brother's arm.

The sun came up yellow and hot. The heat began to build. The mules sweated. In the water of the river, the fish sought the shade beneath the overhanging banks.

Bastamente, the wagon train leader, pulled his horse to a halt and sat waiting for the lead vehicle to come up to him. The road had led through a series of low rocky hills on the east side of the Santa Fe River for several miles. Now the river curved away from them to the west. The next water for the animals would be the Rio Grande, some twelve miles distant to the south.

Joaquin's wagon came abreast and Bastamente spoke to the man. "Water your teams and pull up in the shade of those cottonwoods. We will eat and take a short siesta."

"Way past time," growled Joaquin. He wiped sweat from his forehead with a curved finger and flicked it away onto the rumps of the nearest mules. "I have never seen October so hot." He yanked on the right reins to guide the mules down the bank and into the river.

The animals trotted, gradually increasing speed to stay ahead of the wagon gaining momentum and threatening their heels. In the middle of the slow, shallow stream, they stopped and began to slake their thirst with long, noisy pulls at the cool water.

The remaining wagons followed, one after the other, iron wheels grinding on the gravel and rock and splashing the water. The last vehicle lurched down the grade and out onto the stony river bottom with a crashing rattle.

Inside the wagon, Sam jerked erect with a cry. He flung a look around just as they came to a stop with a bone-jarring bump. Sarah rose up beside him, her eyes large with fright.

"Sammy, what's happening?" she asked, sweeping her eyes over the strange surroundings. "Where are we?"

"Quiet!" he whispered sharply. "Keep quiet until we figure this out."

He looked about in disbelief at the inside of the covered wagon. Sarah and he were resting on a stack of dozens of rolls of brightly colored cotton cloth. In the center of the wagon, ten or fifteen moldboard plows were tied down with strong rope. Farther forward was a wood-burning cooking stove, with warming oven, and water reservoir. Several large boxes of pots and pans sat to each side of the stove.

Sam hurried back through his memory, trying to recall what had happened to put them in this odd place. From outside came voices of men talking. Sam did not know the language. He judged it to be Mexican.

He pushed the canvas flaps apart a crack and poked his head through to the outside. The rear guard, sitting his mount as the animal drank, saw the movement and spun to face Sam.

An expression of astonishment flashed over the man's face. He swung his rifle around to point the open bore of the barrel straight at Sam's heart.

"Bastamente! Come quickly. See what I have found." He raised his voice louder. "Bastamente, I have caught a *gringo* thief."

Bastamente spurred his mount and came splashing around the wagon. His hard black eyes caught and riveted on Sam.

"What are you doing in there?" he demanded.

"I . . . I was sleeping," stammered Sam, staring at the

threatening Mexicans. "A man said I could rest a minute while he went to get the soldiers to help my folks. You see, Comanches attacked our ranch."

The wagon train leader ran his disbelieving eye over the redheaded *gringo* youth with the bloody ear. "A very poor lie. Is that the best you can do?"

"It's the full truth," exclaimed Sam.

"There is no Indian trouble," snorted Bastamente. "Now get down out of there." He pulled the knot loose on the rope tying the canvas flaps shut.

"Where are we?" asked Sam, looking past the Mexican riders and out across the brush-covered hills and up at a tall pine-covered mountain. He recognized nothing. "I got to go help my folks. I must get back to Santa Fe and find the soldiers."

"Move when I tell you to," roared Bastamente. His hand snapped out, grabbed Sam by the shirt front, and flung him into the water of the river.

Sam lit on the rocks of the shallow current. A sharp pain sliced at his left knee.

"Get up," ordered Bastamente.

Before Sam could rise, the Mexican leader leaned over, caught him by the hair of the head, and yanked him to his feet.

Hurt and angry, the youth struck out, knocking the man's grip loose. The Mexican jabbed his horse with iron and it lunged forward, upending Sam roughly backward.

The Mexican walked his horse up beside Sam and dragged him upright by his hair. Bastamente continued to firmly hold the red mane, and his eyes bore into Sam, daring him to strike out.

"Lost some of your fire, eh?" said the man with a mocking grin.

Sam did not reply, glaring through the river water and his own tears of anger and frustration at his tormenter.

"Don't hurt my brother anymore," cried Sarah, peeking out from the rear of the wagon. "Please don't."

Bastamente looked with amazement at the golden-haired girl that had appeared so suddenly and unexpectedly. Her eyes, large and wide with pleading, were sky blue. To the mahogany-colored man, her face was startlingly white.

The leader twisted in his saddle. "Leos, do you see what we have found?"

The guard edged his mount closer. He spoke in awe. *"Sí, muy bonita. Ella será una mujer hermosa."* She will make a beautiful woman.

"She is almost a woman now," said Bastamente.

Sarah did not understand the men's conversation. She spoke imploringly to them. "My brother hasn't done anything wrong, and he's telling the truth. Please let him alone."

Bastamente continued to hold Sam by the head. For a full minute he examined Sarah. She flinched at the intensity of the eyes staring out from the black, bristly hair of his face.

At last, Bastamente shifted his attention to Sam and released his grip on the red mop of hair. "Go up there," he said and motioned toward the cottonwoods on the bank. "If you try to run, I will shoot you."

"Leos, go with him," ordered the leader. "Lasso and drag him a little if he doesn't behave."

Bastamente guided his horse up to the tail end of the wagon and turned it sideways.

"Get on behind me," he directed Sarah.

She hesitated, but only for a moment, for she remembered how quickly this man had grown angry and struck Sam. She hoisted the long tail of her dress and swung astride behind him.

As a signal from its master, the horse pivoted and splashed for the bank. Sarah almost tumbled off and had to grab the man around the waist to keep from falling. She did not like the feel of him.

The teamsters finished watering the mules. Yelling and popping their long whips, they drove the heavy wagons up the bank and into the shade under the trees.

"Sit down there and don't move," Bastamente told Sam and pointed to a spot of the ground by the side of one of the wagons. He took Sarah by the arm and lowered her to the ground. She hastened to her brother and sat down very near him. She drew some comfort from his closeness.

One of the teamsters, Carrasco, dug food from a grub box and spread it on the tailgate of his wagon. But no one came to eat. Instead the men drifted together and began to talk among themselves. All except Bastamente, who paced back and forth with his face strained and furrowed. Now and then he cast a look at Sarah, or to the north, as if watching for someone to come into sight on the El Camino Real.

He believed the boy's story. It was a strange tale, but it was told with the conviction of truth.

He stalked up near Sam. "What did this man look like, the one that told you to get in my wagon?"

Sam desperately wanted this brutal man to believe him and let Sarah and him go free. "I can't remember very well. It was nighttime and I was tired and sleepy. But I recall him wearing dark clothes. Had a coat on. And yes, he had a mustache."

"*Gringo* or Mexican?"

"American."

"These wagons belong to a man in Chihuahua. I am the wagon master. So you see that man in Santa Fe lied to you. Now why would he do that?"

Sam worried that thought around in his head. He had given the man money, some of his father's gold. As that remembrance struck Sam, he quickly felt of his pocket. It was empty.

"He stole my gold," exclaimed Sam, his voice rising in anger and dismay.

An audacious thought excited Bastamente. The golden girl, one who would be a beautiful woman in only a very short time, was worth thousands of pesos in Mexico. The chance to make a fortune was suddenly his. Such an opportunity was given to a man only once in a lifetime. Should he challenge the hazard, the risk?

Bastamente knew the very man who would buy the girl, with no questions asked. His lips grinned, pulling back to show coarse teeth in his black beard. There would always be a buyer for a pretty woman. He grinned more broadly.

The wolfish expression on the man's face sent Sam's heart racing. He had unwittingly given the man the information that no one would be coming to search for Sarah and him. In fact, no one even knew where they were.

The boy was a problem, thought Bastamente, recalling the look in the young *gringo's* face when he had landed in the river. He was too old and spirited to ever accept the rule of another man. Also, he would cause the girl to be difficult to handle if they remained together. However, there was an easy solution to that.

The wagon master had made his decision. He called out loud enough for all to hear. There was the hint of a sharp edge of a challenge in his voice. "We will take her with us to Mexico," he declared bluntly, knowing full well that was the question on all their minds.

He spread his legs and let his hand fall near his tied-down six-gun. These were hard men, bandits and ruffians, hired by him for their toughness. Not once had they lost a cargo to thieves. But that willingness to fight could now be against him, for some of them might not agree with his plan.

All stood silent, digesting that idea. They shuffled their feet and glanced furtively at each other. This was a very dangerous scheme.

"It is not a good plan," said Joaquin. He shook his head several times for emphasis. "We are hardly fifteen miles out of Santa Fe, probably the place where her family lives. Mexico is two hundred miles away. It will take us nine to ten days to get across the border. Eight days if we push hard from daylight to dark."

"Joaquin is correct," said Carrasco, the driver of the wagon where Sarah and Sam had ridden. "We should turn them loose. They can walk back to Santa Fe by the time it is night."

Two other teamsters, Fragoso and Leos, nodded in agreement with Carrasco. The remaining pair said nothing.

Bastamente saw the greed in the expressions of these last two, and the doubts, but mostly greed. They just needed a little push and he would have them on his side.

Bastamente examined the faces of all the men as he spoke. "Nobody will be coming after them. They were tricked into the wagon and their *dinero* stolen. They are just brats of *gringos*. What do they mean to us? How many of our people have the North Americans killed and taken their property? Didn't they steal all of Nuevo México, all this very land we stand on, from us? Didn't they?"

All the dark faces nodded in the affirmative to that question.

"What's the payment if we go along with you on this?" asked Joaquin.

"I will give each of you a bonus of two hundred American

dollars. What do you say?'' Bastamente rested his hand on the butt of his pistol. To gain his fortune, he would kill.

"Five hundred dollars American," said Joaquin. He had noted Bastamente's hand. The man was very fast, but still there was room to negotiate. "I know she will bring a high price. Especially if you take her to Ciudad de México and sell her to one of the rich *caballeros* there."

"Four hundred dollars American," countered Bastamente. It was not wise to give in too easily, for then the men would think they had been cheated and try to get even.

Joaquin pivoted to sweep his sight over the others. "I'm for it. How about the rest of you?"

"For four hundred dollars, I agree," said Leos. "For that much *dinero*, I would fight the whole American army."

"And the rest of you?" questioned Bastamente.

Fragoso spoke. "That amount of money is more than I make in a year whipping those mules along this dry road. I will do it."

The two that had not yet spoken nodded affirmatively in unison.

Carrasco shook his head in a doubtful manner. "You have all made a very great mistake. But I am with you."

"Then it is done," cried Bastamente. He raised his head and began to laugh at his good fortune.

The blood red sun vanished into the bottomless hole behind the rim of the world. In the deep dusk of the evening, the wagon train halted where the El Camino Real crossed a grassy meadow beside the Rio Grande. The vehicles were drawn into a crude circle. The weary mules were unhitched, front legs hobbled, and turned loose to water at the river and graze the tall sedges and grass along the bank.

A flock of ducks, resting in their nighttime bed in a quiet eddy of water in the river, became alarmed as the mules stomped noisily down the bank to drink. With loud quacks of complaint, they took to wing, speeding away swiftly to vanish in the heavy gloom.

Carrasco kindled a fire, and soon the aroma of frying tortillas and bubbling stew spread throughout the camp. The other men finished their chores and came to squat in the light of the flames. No one talked as the darkness closed in.

Withdrawn into themselves, they gazed into the fire and pondered private thoughts. One would sometimes throw a short look at Sarah where she sat near Sam beside one of the wagons in the edge of the firelight.

Sam had not understood the long discussion between the leader and his drivers at the noon stop. All had been spoken in their native tongue. Still, it was obvious the talk had been of Sarah and him, and that some plan had been proposed and accepted.

Sarah had been hoisted into the middle wagon. Joaquin took charge of Sam, forcing him up into the front of his vehicle. There, he tied the youth's hands and feet. He pulled his knife and cut a chunk out of the wooden seat to show Sam how sharp the blade was. Sam understood the unspoken message.

Once during the afternoon, travelers were met. Bastamente called a warning, and Sam was gagged and the canvas front of the wagon dropped to hide him until the people passed.

At every chance during the day, Sam had examined the land they crossed over. He tried to memorize every unusual detail, paying particular attention to those of the land they crossed over that might be visible at night. When the Mexicans slept, he would somehow take Sarah and flee.

Carrasco lifted the lid on the stew and stirred it with a long-handled spoon. "*Está listo,*" it is ready, he called.

Bastamente filled a metal plate to heaping and, with a large bottle of wine under his arm, found a place where he could watch the yellow-haired girl. He sat down with a grunt and began to eat, washing the food down with long swigs of the dark red wine.

"Get your own food," said Carrasco, gesturing toward the steaming kettle and pile of tortillas.

Sam went to the fire and put food on two plates. Sarah accepted one, but she ate little. She kept her eyes down. The presence of the swarthy kidnappers, with the unreadable black eyes, often probing in her direction, frightened and overwhelmed her.

The men finished eating. With stomachs full of food, and blood warmed by the wine, they began to converse among themselves. Carrasco brought a guitar from his wagon and began to softly, and with some skill, strum a melody.

Bastamente arose and walked to Sarah. "Dance for us," he directed.

The girl remained seated, her hands clasped tightly together and eyes fastened on the dusty ground.

"Dance, I say," the dark man ordered in a loud voice.

Sarah cringed at the threatening tone, but did not move. Bastamente grabbed her by the hand and jerked her to her feet.

"Leave her alone," yelled Sam furiously. He sprang up and advanced upon the big man.

Bastamente whirled and quickly struck the thin youth in the chest with a hard right fist. Sam was stopped dead in his tracks and he lost his breath with a swishing expulsion of air. Bastamente's left lashed swiftly across, catching the dazed boy on the side of the face. Sam's eyes spun out of focus.

Stunned, he fell backward, crashing onto the ground. A tornado of stars sprang to life and swirled and danced in his addled brain.

Sarah cried out in torment and clutched at her breast. She started toward her brother. The Mexican caught her, whirled her about, and shoved her into the bright firelight. He circled his hand in the air, indicating a pirouette. "Dance for me, or I will cut your brother's ears off."

The frightened girl believed the man. Yes, knew he would do precisely as he said. But she did not know how to dance.

Her heart pounded with her dilemma. She would do anything to keep the man from hurting Sammy again. Then she remembered that once in Santa Fe she had looked in the open door of one of the cantinas and a pretty woman had been dancing for a roomful of men. She had danced barefoot.

Standing first on one foot and then the other, Sarah hastily removed her shoes.

Carrasco had ceased playing when Sam challenged Bastamente. Now the wagon master snapped his fingers to get the music maker's attention. "Play," he said. "She is ready now."

The young teamster began to pluck the strings of his instrument, producing a strong beat. A second man took up two short lengths of wood and started to tap on the iron rim of a wheel in rhythm with the guitar. All the time his eyes remained on the girl.

Sarah felt the dust, still warm from the day's heat, under her feet as she began to sway to the music. Her mind hastened back to the dancing woman in the cantina. Her hands had moved like this and this. But the gestures seemed so awkward to Sarah as she made them. A fool, that was what she was, a fool trying to dance. Better to let them beat her. No! They would cut Sammy's ears off.

The men had to be pleased. She looked into her memory and imitated the woman's movements.

Sarah's natural grace guided her hands and feet and the gentle sway of her hips. She went beyond what she had seen that time long past, improvising spontaneously, discovering within her young woman's mind the movements and artful timing that responded perfectly to the music.

The vortex of stars in Sam's head cleared. There was the salty taste of blood in his mouth, and he wiped a red smear from his lips and chin.

He looked about. In the firelight, Sarah danced, turning with elegant steps, and her arms and hands made wondrous, fluid motions.

Every man intently watched the girl's body as she interpreted the music.

Sam viewed his young sister. The flames were caught in her tousled hair, turning it into woven gold about her face. More of the golden hair shimmered on her shoulders. She pivoted and her dress umbrellaed out, exposing her feet and calves etched white by the background of brown dust. Her jutting, half-mature breasts surprised Sam.

For the very first time he really looked at his thirteen-year-old sister as a female almost grown. He noted the exquisite curve of her cheek, the delicate straight nose, and the eyes, large, set far apart, and almost round. He knew all men would find her truly beautiful.

He noticed something else also. There was a tinge of fear in her big, wide eyes. He did not like that. In this place and time, Sarah was a very great danger to herself.

A dark figure, a mere shadow, stole in noiselessly from the night. It moved through the deep grass to the very edge of the firelight. Not a long pebble flip distant from the dancing girl, the shadow stopped.

The Kiowa scanned the men, found their total attention concentrated upon the feminine movements of Sarah. They were foolish men. The Kiowa believed he could kill most if not all of them with his repeating rifle before they could defend themselves.

The young woman drew the Indian's eyes. He lay his chin on his arm and marveled at her flawless performance.

The fire burned down as the half woman-half child danced. More fuel was fed to the flames, and they flared up, shining like splinters of the sun. And they pressed back the encroaching night so the men could plainly see the young woman.

The music of the guitar and the cadence of the wood stroking iron mixed with the firelight, and floated beyond that to become part of the darkness lying on the river and the nearby hills.

Sarah danced in the dust of the ancient, three-hundred-year-old El Camino Real. Where invading armies had marched, priests had traveled preaching their harsh religion, and the Indian warriors had raided.

She danced. And danced.

CHAPTER 4

The broken-edged moon cast a thin silver light down upon the Rio Grande. In the meadow beside the river, the circle of five wagons crouched like strange humped-backed animals grazing the moon-gilded grass.

The Kiowa rose from his hiding place in the shadows of the grass and stole inside the ring of wagons. A gust of wind swirled past him to flap the canvas on the vehicles. He froze as it fanned the bed of red coals of the dying fire and a yellow flame candled up.

His view swiftly ranged the camp. He had earlier seen the dancing girl shoved into one of the wagons and confined there. The white boy was trussed on the ground beside a wagon on the opposite side of the encampment. A rope led away from his bound hands, a second from his feet, stretching him between the front and rear wheels.

The Mexicans slept on their bedrolls around the fire. All except a hairy-faced one the Indian knew was called Joaquin; he prowled the darkness on sentry duty outside.

The weak flame died, and the flickering shadows that danced on the canvas coverings collapsed abruptly. The Indian slipped forward, directly toward the boy.

Sam muffled his labored breathing as he struggled to tear free of his bonds. His wrists were raw and bleeding. Still the bindings were as tight and firm as when first tied. He ceased his struggle, resigned to not breaking loose this night, and conserved his strength to wait the morrow.

Something moved, with a slithering sound very near Sam. His pulse jumped to a throbbing hammer. One of the Mexicans had come to kill him. He started to hurl himself away from the person.

A strong hand caught him by the chin, clamping his mouth shut. An ugly, distorted visage bent close over him. A face hideously painted.

"Quiet. Make no sound," hissed the Kiowa, and he shook Sam's head sharply twice for emphasis. "I will return and cut you free in a moment. Do you understand me?"

Sam nodded his head as best he could under the firm hold of the man. The words were wonderful. But why would an Indian help him? It made no difference—he would accept assistance from anyone.

"Good. Don't move."

The grip of the hand was removed. Sam saw the icy glitter of the moonlight in the Indian's eyes as the man rose to a stoop and glided away between two wagons. He could still smell the strange, pungent odor of the man's war paint.

Sam felt a glow of hope as he waited. He raised his head slightly and listened intently. What was the Indian up to? If he was truly going to release him, why did he not do it now instead of later? What pay would he want for his help?

A long half minute later, Sam thought he heard the sound of a muted thud on the ground. Though he strained to hear more, all was silent.

Bastamente, in the center of the circle of wagons, sat up on his blankets and surveyed the camp. He called out in a cautious voice, "Joaquin, where are you? Is all safe?"

No answer came.

The Indian, stooped low, appeared at the rear of the wagon where Sam was fastened. He dropped to the ground and crawled up beside the youth.

At the fire, Bastamente stood up, his pistol ready in his fist. "Joaquin, answer me. Is everything all right?" The leader's sight raked the area enclosed by the wagons and then through the openings to the outside.

The Indian moved his hand. Sam almost cried out as the moonlight sparkled on the steel blade of a long knife. With one slice of the sharp-edged steel, the thongs binding Sam's hands fell loose.

The Indian vanished under the wagon and into the night.

* * *

Hastily Sam began to pry at the knots that held his feet. He had to get to Sarah and set her free before the whole camp was aroused.

"¡*Alerta!* ¡*Alerta!*" called Bastamente in al anarmed voice. "*Hombres*, get your guns. Be on guard."

At the shouted warning, the teamsters sprang from their beds and grabbed up their weapons. They squatted in the shadows, their eyes sweeping the darkness all around and out beyond the wagons for the enemy.

"Watch closely," ordered Bastamente. "I'm going to look for Joaquin." He slid quickly through the gap between two wagons.

Sam fought the hard knots. At last they parted. Hunched low, he crept across the camp toward the wagon that held Sarah. He would not leave without her.

"Joaquin is dead!" Bastamente roared loud and angry from outside the wagons. A moment later, he ran in and stopped in the middle of the encampment.

Sam made it to Sarah's wagon. He pressed his face to the canvas. "Sis, are you there? Can you hear me?" he whispered.

"Yes, Sammy. Oh, yes!" Sarah's whisper came back.

"Come to the rear of the wagon. I'll have it open in a second."

"Sammy, I'm coming. Don't leave me. Please don't. They will hurt me," her voice was a half sob.

Bastamente swiftly surveyed the moonlit enclosure. He made out the forms of his men with their rifles braced for battle, and he spied Sam working on the lashing that held the canvas of the girl's wagon.

Bastamente did not know who had killed Joaquin. The *gringo* boy could have done it. Somehow he had escaped and crossed the camp without being stopped. The Mexican leader pulled his six-gun. This was an excellent time to rid himself of that problem person.

"Shoot the redhead *gringo*. He killed Joaquin," yelled Bastamente, and snapped a shot at the youth.

The bullet struck the wooden hoop holding up the canvas covering of the wagon. A second shot roared, and lead shattered against the iron rim of a wheel, ricocheting off at many angles. One metal sliver pierced the flesh of Sam's chest.

He recoiled at the sting of the wound. He whirled around and leaped behind the wagon.

A chunk of lead tugged at the heel of his shoe. Another ripped through his pant leg. The Mexicans were trying to cripple him, to shoot away his legs where they were exposed beneath the wagon. The poor light was all that had kept him from already being dead. Soon someone would make a lucky shot.

Sam sprang away from the vehicle and bolted into the night. He raced north along the river bed.

He crossed the meadow in long, driving strides and climbed a low, brush-covered hill. At the top, he stopped, his heart pounding, and faced back toward the Mexican camp. Toward the prison where he had left Sarah a captive.

The Mexicans yelled out in raging voices, a blood roar of a hunting pack, deep and savage. Only the darkness that hid his footprints kept them from boiling out in pursuit.

Above the clamor of the men, Sam heard Sarah's scream, high and shrill. The terrified cry was suddenly cut off at the top of its crescendo.

In despair, Sam listened down toward the wagons. What were the men doing to her? Was she being punished for his escape?

He was a coward and had abandoned his sister to cruel, vicious men. His chest cramped as shame burned like a hot iron within him. He fiercely wished for a weapon to kill them, every one.

A light came to life among the wagons as a fire was built up. The long flames reached high and Sam saw the Mexicans gathered close together around them. Their angry voices rumbled and growled.

It was dangerous to be so near the camp. The men might slip out and find him in the moonlit night. Sam walked to the north, moving through the brush into a deep ravine and up to the top of the next hill.

He dropped down on the ground and sat watching where Sarah was held prisoner. The fire was plainly visible, but no sounds of the camp reached him.

The moon drifted across the vast, black heavens. A slow wind droned over the hill and talked in ragged sounds in the sagebrush. Down the hill in the edge of the river, a bullfrog began a low, dismal croak in the autumn night.

Sam's weariness bore him to the ground. He dozed off and on during the night. Toward morning, the wind shifted around to the north and started to blow cold.

Sam was awake and shivering when the sky changed from black to gray in the east. The outline of the tall mountain took form to the north. Then the first rays from the sun, still hidden below the edge of the earth, caught a high, thin cloud and turned it fresh blood red.

He arose and faced the new day being born. With guilt, he recalled his failures. His father and mother had been deserted to fight an overwhelming number of Indians. The man in Sante Fe had tricked him as if he were a child—had stolen his gold—and no soldiers rode to aid his embattled parents. Now Sarah had been forsaken to save his own skin.

He clenched his hands at his sides. Never again would he show fear. Any man's offer of friendship would be doubted and harshly judged.

What should he do now? His parents were either dead or safe by this time and he could do nothing for them. However, he could still help Sarah. He would follow the Mexican wagon train—dog it for days or weeks. Sooner or later, the opportunity to strike back and rescue his sister would come.

The promise to himself made him feel better. He turned to look at the circle of wagons to find two horsemen racing from the camp directly along his trail.

Sam dashed from the hilltop and charged along the river-bank. The bulk of the hill would hide him for two or three minutes. Before the riders crested the ridge, he had to find a place to hide.

Beneath his feet, there was loose, sandy soil. His trail would be so plain a man could track him from the back of a running horse.

A meander of the Rio Grande swung in close to Sam's route. Without hesitation, he jumped down the head-high bank into the bed of the river. He labored to maintain his pace, now splashing in ankle-deep water, now running on the looseness of a sandbar. The unstable footings took their toll of his speed.

The fresh tracks of a horse came down from a gash in the bank and cut across in front of Sam. He threw a quick look to the left along the sign. It went directly into the water. On the far shore it emerged, the soil still dark with the dampness from the water the horse had splashed.

The imprints had to have been made during the night to still be wet. The Indian who had set him free could have come this way. That man had weapons. Just maybe he would give one to Sam if he understood his great need to save Sarah.

The boy veered abruptly to follow along the hoofprints. The bottom of the river was firm sand and the water hardly waist-deep. An easy crossing, and then the boy was scrambling up the bank.

Behind Sam, the Mexicans yelled out in full-mouthed glee as they spotted their quarry. They aimed their mounts straight for the running youth.

Above the pounding of his feet on the hard ground, Sam heard his pursuers. He looked backward. The mustangs of the men were stretched in a flat-out run a few hundred feet away on the opposite side of the river. In only a minute they would cross the stream and ride him down.

Sam desperately scoured the land for a hiding place. To the left and ahead lay flat terrain covered with grass and patches of short brush. Off to the right beyond a broad boulder field was the fringe of the stunted pine on the lower slope of the mountain.

The distance to the trees was too long for him to run before the horses caught and trampled him. Yet, that was all that held any hope at all. He spun toward the beckoning woods.

His breath ripped in his throat as he tested the limit of every muscle. He twisted and turned to skirt the waist-high rocks. Though the going was difficult, stones should slow the riders. Otherwise they would break the legs of ther ponies. Sam hoped they would.

A pistol crashed and a gray splotch of lead suddenly appeared on a lava boulder beside him. Broken fragments of rock exploded, slapped Sam on the side, and pierced his clothes to burn him. He staggered under the impact, but did not slow. Run! Run! Just a few more steps to the protective shield of the pine.

Sam darted to the side to go around a tall chunk of lava. A bullet zipped past his head. Then he gained the pines and plowed into the green boughs.

Sam selected the rockiest slope of the mountain and the densest thickets and scurried upward. There was a chance now that he could throw the men off his trail.

He climbed for a quarter hour and then, maintaining his elevation, angled west around the flank of the mountain. Once he reached the south face, he would descend and try to again locate the tracks of the Indian.

As he warily stole through the pine, he thought it strange that an unknown Indian should be the only man to show him any friendliness at all.

Sam made it to the boundary of the woods and peered cautiously out. Nothing moved within the range of his vision. He trotted into the open, heading southwest. As he dropped downward, an ever-larger bulge of the mountain rose to obscure him from the last place he had seen his pursuers.

He was weary and soaked in his own sweat. Still he ran.

Half an hour later, he found the tracks he sought. With a surge of fresh hope, he fell upon them, following them due west.

The morning sun rose, an orange-red ball inexorably mounting the eastern horizon. Pinned like some tiny, struggling insect against the bright, round face was the dark form of a running man.

Two Foxes, the Kiowa, spotted the figure silhouetted on the distant ridgetop. It took only a moment of measuring the movement of the man for the Indian to know he was exactly on his trail.

There had been much gunfire in the wagon camp as the Kiowa had made his getaway in the dark. Then in the early dawn, as he had been breaking camp in a hidden cove west of the river, more shots had sounded from that direction. Had the white youth been discovered twice as he tried to escape? Was this strange, unidentified person the boy? Two Foxes believed so, but why was he following?

The Indian put his pony into a ground-devouring gallop. Soon the fellow would be lost far behind, and that was good, for Two Foxes had no time to waste on him.

When the sun climbed to the top of the sky, Two Foxes saw the stranger was still coming. He was far away, but continued to run. The Indian felt a stir of interest at the endurance of the white pup.

But there was a long piece of the day remaining. That would lose him.

In the late afternoon, the Kiowa reined his mustang to a halt on top of a small juniper-capped hill. He sat for several minutes leaning on the pommel of his saddle and watched along his back trail. He felt the person still followed, somewhere out there too far to see.

It bothered him that he did not know for certain who the man was or his intentions. He did not want to go into the night without finding out those things. He stepped down. The pony was hobbled, the bit slipped from between the big teeth, and the brute hazed away to graze on the north side of the hill where the wild grass grew the tallest.

Carrying his rifle and canteen, Two Foxes found a seat at the edge of the juniper on the point of the hill. Then, motionless, he ranged his sight to the east.

The wind that had drifted in from the north all day grew more boisterous and began to tug at the thin, worn shirt of the Indian. The sunlight was strong. It overrode the chill the wind tried to bring and gently bathed the hilltop.

Two Foxes rested, savoring the pleasant minutes he knew would be very short. For he saw the storm cloud starting to poke its thick gray snout over the crown of the mountain range to the north.

The sun floated down another half a hand width and the shadows grew long. The cloud increased in size until it dwarfed the mountain and began to spill into the valley. Borne on a fast wind, the dark curtain beneath the cloud moved swiftly to darken the land.

The Kiowa made out the form of a man among the rocks and brush on the crown of a far hill. Then the figure vanished as the masking shadow of the cloud obliterated it.

The sunlight dimmed where the Indian sat, and the yellow rays moved off ahead of the cloud. The wind instantly turned chilly. It whipped the limbs of the juniper and sent the coarse black hair of the Indian dancing and flicking. He did not notice, intent upon locating the man that hunted him.

CHAPTER 5

Mile after weary mile lay stretched behind Sam as he pursued the Indian. He moved with a shambling gait, and his legs trembled with exhaustion.

He knew it was crazy to be chasing an Indian to ask for aid. Yet, that man had been the only person to give any help and had done so without being asked. He must be overtaken this day and a gun gotten from him. Then Sam would hasten back to the river and pick up the tracks of the wagon train. He had to hurry and kill the cruel man and save Sarah from great danger.

The trail of the Indian led Sam deeply into a wild region of low, broken hills and lava rock. The mountain that had been close in the morning had receded to the northeast. Another strange mountain was piling up to the west.

He had found no water since leaving the river. His very survival could well depend upon catching up with the man—a man on horseback, who, if he desired, could easily ride off and leave him.

Sam's vision probed the land ahead. The sign of the Indian's pony was difficult to detect on the stony ground. His passage was scantily marked here and there by a disturbed clump of grass or a soft zone of earth where a hoof made an indentation or broke the crust to leave a spot of crumpled soil.

The course began to climb one of the numerous hills. The dark cloud that had ominously lowered and drawn near scudded in the last, short space and severed the sun from the earth. A dense gray shadow fell.

At the disappearance of the sunlight, Sam looked up from

his intense scrutiny of the Indian's trail. He saw the man sitting in the fringe of juniper on the top of the hill directly ahead.

Sam broke stride and stopped. The range was no more than a moderate rifle shot. Still, the man did not raise the weapon that lay in his lap.

Sam continued to move up the grade. He was completely defenseless and at the mercy of the Indian. The man had cut him free to escape. Would he now kill him?

Half the distance was closed. The Indian gave no indication he was aware of Sam's approach, merely staring past him at the dark landscape.

The boy walked steadily forward. He kept his hands at his sides where the man could see them. He climbed the last of the slope and halted in front of the seated Indian.

The Kiowa focused his sight on Sam. He evaluated the white youth with his black eyes, like a panther watching. The fellow was a nuisance that wasted his time. At some half-conscious level, the Indian sensed he had made a mistake and would regret having ever cut the boy free. The foreboding was strong. He should kill him now and take the red hair that would make a good trophy scalp.

Sam fought to keep his own view from wavering. The Indian's smoky bronze face was painted with three long, horizontal yellow stripes on each cheek, three across his forehead, and one down the peak of his nose. A bright red band encircled each eye. The black eyes glittered through the paint with evil intent upon him.

The faintest flicker of some emotion passed over the man's countenance, and he brushed the hammer of the rifle with his thumb. An almost imperceptible shrug moved his shoulders. Two Foxes lifted up the canteen from beside his leg and offered it.

Sam hefted it and judged the gallon container was almost full. He tilted it and let the delicious wet liquid pour down his parched throat. He could have drunk the whole quantity. Instead, he swallowed half a quart and handed it back.

"Thank you," said Sam.

The Indian did not respond. He stood up and moved back from the windy, exposed position on the hill and began to gather tinder-dry kindling from a dead juniper. He piled it just so and struck flint and steel. Soon, a tiny curl of smoke began to rise as he blew gently upon the spark.

Sam stood unmoving and watched the man add larger pieces of fuel to the fire. A flat slab of lava rock some foot across was placed in the edge of the flames. From a saddlebag, the Indian extracted a chunk of meat wrapped in rawhide and began to slice it.

Two Foxes seated himself and placed the strips of flesh on the rock that was rapidly growing hot. Sam interpreted that as a signal his presence was accepted. He dropped down on the opposite side of the fire with a sigh.

The meat sizzled on the hot stone. Small rivulets of juice trickled into the live red embers of the fire and disappeared with little hissing explosions of steam. A tantalizing aroma wafted to Sam, and the sharp teeth of hunger gnawed at the pit of his stomach.

The meat cooked to a brown turn. The Kiowa speared a slice with the point of his knife, waved it in the air a few times to cool it, and began to eat. When that piece was finished, he began a second.

Partway through, he stopped chewing. "You hungry?" he asked.

"Yes. I'm starved. I haven't eaten anything since a little yesterday."

Two Foxes reached into a shirt pocket and fished out two short stubs of jerky. He extended them to Sam.

In surprise, the boy hesitatingly accepted them. He glanced down at the fresh meat on the fire.

"You want some of that?" asked the Indian.

"I believe it might be tastier," answered Sam.

"All right. Help yourself." There was a tone in the man's voice Sam could not decipher.

The boy fingered a piece of the meat from the hot stone. He bit off a large bite. It had a smooth texture. The flavor was strange to him, slightly sweetish yet pleasing.

"What kind of meat?" asked Sam with his mouth full.

"Heart," said the Kiowa.

Sam judged the meat quite fresh. Still, he had stuck close to the Indian's trail all day and knew he had not hunted or made a kill. "What kind of meat?"

"Mexicano."

Startled, Sam looked closely at the Indian. "What do you mean, Mexican?"

"Mexican heart. Man's heart."

"You mean this is human flesh?" Sam felt his gorge rise. He swallowed in revulsion.

"Yes. The heart of my enemy. I have looked for him for many years. Yesterday, I find him. Last night I kill him." The Kiowa's eyes gleamed like black lava marbles.

Sam looked closely at the meat in his hand. This was Joaquin's heart. "He was my enemy too," said Sam, and put the last bite into his mouth, chewed it to a pulp, and swallowed.

The Indian nodded approval at the boy's action but noticed he did not take another piece. The Kiowa finished that which remained by himself.

Two Foxes wiped his hands on his pants and looked at Sam. "Why are you here? Why did you follow me so far?"

"You have guns. I need one to take my sister away from the Mexicans. Will you give me a rifle?"

"No. No rifle." Two Foxes remembered the pretty dancing girl. However, she was not sufficient reason to give away a valuable gun. "I have only one rifle and one pistol. I need both."

"Why did you turn me loose if not to help me?"

"It cost nothing to cut your ties, and it made trouble for the Mexicans. Now you trouble me. Go away."

"Without a gun, I can't kill them. Soon they will have taken my sister into Mexico and I will never be able to find her."

"That means nothing to me. I will not give you a gun." The Kiowa's voice became harsh and he chopped down with the edge of his hand. "No more talk about it. You have already wasted too much of my time."

Sam held his anger in and tongue quiet. In frustration, he turned his back to the Indian and looked toward the faraway river. He saw two riders sitting their horses in the deep shadows at the bottom of the hill.

"Look!" he cried, and pointed.

"Yes, they have been there for a time. I think they are Mexicans from the wagon train."

Sam watched the men who had cunningly tracked him. They would have caught him had they been a little faster.

Only the presence of the Indian kept them from rushing up the hill to slay him.

"They have come a long distance to find you," said the Kiowa.

"They have come to kill me," said Sam. "Loan me your rifle and I'll go and kill them instead. That way, there'll be two less to stop me from rescuing my sister."

"They would probably shoot you first. Or ride off before you got close enough to fire the gun at them."

"Are you afraid of them? Is that why you don't want me to fight them?" asked Sam.

Two Foxes spoke in a hard, flat voice. "There are only two of them. Why should I fear them? Are you afraid?"

"No," said Sam, and knew it was the truth.

The Kiowa picked up his rifle and canteen and climbed to his feet. "I must be going. I have many miles to travel and some men to meet."

He walked down the hill to catch his pony. Sam tagged along behind. He stood, uncertain as to what to do as the Indian tightened the cinch of the saddle and shoved the bit into the unwilling mouth of the horse. The man swung astride and rode off toward the west.

The Mexicans immediately guided their mounts forward. Sam trotted to take up station a few steps to the rear of the Indian. He was going exactly in the wrong direction. However, if he tried to return to the river, the Mexicans with their guns would kill him.

Oh, God! Sarah, I cannot help you. Please forgive me. I will return as soon as I can. A sob constricted his throat. Tears blinded his eyes, and he tripped and almost fell. I will come and find you. I promise, little sister.

Through the dusk of the evening, the Mexicans hounded Sam and the Kiowa's trail. Always they stayed just out of rifle range.

In the last faint light of the day, the Kiowa reached the north end of a tall, black lava mesa. As if knowing precisely where he was going, he angled up a steep slope and out onto a small, grassy bench of about an acre.

Vertical walls of solid lava reared high, rimming the little meadow on all borders except to the west. Facing to the open

side, Sam looked down upon a broad grass and sagebrush
land cut with deeply eroded washes and extending for ten
miles or so. Beyond that, a massive mountain loomed black
against the graying western sky. He could catch no sight of
the men who chased him.

On the opposite side of the meadow, the clear, cool water
of a spring bubbled out from a crack in the lava. The rock
glistened like glass as the water cascaded down over it to the
ground with little splashing noises. It formed a small stream
at the base of the wall and flowed away for a hundred feet or
so before the thirsty sand and soil swallowed it.

Sam hastened past the Indian to kneel and drink deeply
from the spring. He stopped, caught a couple of breaths, and
then drank again.

Two Foxes led his pony up beside Sam, and men and
animal slaked their thirst together.

Sam drank his fill and arose. The Indian also finished and,
towing his mount, went to the edge of the bench and sat
down where the trail came up. Sam followed and hunkered
down beside him.

"I don't see the Mexicans," said Sam, looking among the
rocks and brush at the bottom of the hill. "Do you think they
will try to shoot us tonight?"

Two Foxes did not respond. His dark face was surly. The
white boy's words implied they were partners and the Mexicans were after both of them. That angered the Kiowa. He
would never be a friend to a white man. Always an enemy.

He joined them in raids upon their own kind and then used
his share of the loot to buy the new repeating rifles for his
people. That was the only association he ever wanted.

The last of the daylight leaked away into the sky. The
silver moon rose, and for a brief moment shone full and
perfectly round on the eastern horizon. Almost immediately it
climbed and hid behind the cloud mass that continued to pour
down from the north.

A family of coyotes began to sing off to the west, creating
a cacophony of wavering calls, now singly, now overlapping
and merging together for a few seconds. One a little shriller
rose to stand high above the others. Then all the voices trailed
off in long, sliding tenor cries to silence.

The Indian climbed quietly to his feet and picked up the

reins of his mustang. He crossed the meadow and went down a game trail that was barely a scratch on the nearly vertical flank of the mesa.

At a broken, jagged slab of lava that leaned precariously outward over the valley, the Kiowa turned left onto a narrow shelf. He wound his way through a few shoulder-tall bushes that grew randomly about. Without a word, he unsaddled and tossed his stolen bedroll to the ground. The mustang was tethered on the end of a lariat tied to a bush near the man's blankets.

The north wind moaned cold up the slant of the hill. Sam already felt the chill through his worn cotton shirt, and the day had only just ended. It was going to be a cold and terrible night.

"Here," called the Indian in a low voice.

Sam turned in time to catch the object tossed at him by the man. It was a saddle blanket.

In the lee of a block of lava, Sam found a soft sandy spot. He smoothed it out with his hands, scooping out shallow hollows for hips and shoulders, and dropped down. The blanket, even unfolded, would not cover him completely. However, as he drew himself into as small a knot as possible and wrapped the sweat-dampened covering, rank with the smell of horse, about him, he gave silent thanks to the Indian.

He thought of Sarah. Another day of horrible captivity had passed for her, and he was farther and farther away from helping her. What horrible hurt and fear had she endured?

"I will take revenge for you, Sis," he whispered. "I will find you and kill those men who have kept you prisoner."

He went to sleep with the wind aimlessly rattling the limbs of the brush and the horse making tearing noises as it cropped the grass on the far side of the rock.

During the night, he dreamed of fighting a gun battle with a swarm of Mexicans on a frigid, windy hillside, and a tall Indian stood and watched and would not help.

Sam felt the saddle blanket stripped suddenly away from him. He hastily sat up. The Indian straightened from over him and vanished into the night with the covering.

Nearly frozen, Sam climbed clumsily erect on stiff legs. The wind blew strongly through a black night under heavy clouds. It smelled of rain, maybe snow. A sharp blast buffeted Sam, staggering him.

He caught his balance and listened into the nearby darkness. The horse grunted as the Kiowa jerked the cinch tight on his saddle. Sam hurried in the direction of the sound. He saw the Indian pull himself astride.

The boy called out above the groan of the wind. "Why are we leaving when we can't see yet? Are the Mexicans near?"

The Indian kicked his pony off into the gloom without responding. At the far end of the shelf, he reined the animal toward the abrupt, downward-sloping flank of the mesa.

Sam followed, striving to stay close to the rear of the horse as it descended some invisible path. He fell twice—once hard, ramming to a stop against a rough boulder. Immediately he was up and scurrying after the horse.

They found the bottom and the course straightened. Sam thought they were heading west, as they had the day just past. There was no way to judge, for the clouds hung low, brushing the land with cold, damp fingers and hiding the stars of the heavens.

The Kiowa and his pony were only a darker shade of the black night. Sam chased the shadowy outline through the brush and up and down over the hills. On a downgrade, he almost ran into the horse. The long tail of the brute, stretched out by the wind, switched his face. He caught a handful and, praying the pony would not kick him, let it tow him along. Not once did the Indian look back.

By the time a gray and gloomy day arrived, they had traveled half a score of miles toward the western mountains.

Sam endeavored to locate and record in his memory landmarks that could be used when he returned this way. Off to his right, a thin pinnacle of lava at least a quarter mile tall stabbed up into the clouds. There were two others of lesser prominence south of him. A long flat-topped mesa was three or four miles northwest.

The course crossed a broad, dry wash and began to climb a forested ridge that protruded out to the north from the bulk of the mountain. A mile later, the woods drew back, and the Indian and boy entered a wide, grassy flat.

In the center of the opening, a group of five men squatted around a large fire on the bank of a small live stream. They saw the newcomers the instant they broke free of the woods. All five picked up their rifles and walked forward to intercept Two Foxes and Sam.

One of the men raised his hand and called out loudly, "Two Foxes, it's about time you got your thievin' Indian hide here. We've been waiting since yesterday and we had no whiskey or women."

The Kiowa lifted his hand in return greeting. "Hello, Keesling. Something delayed me."

Keesling spoke again. "What's the war paint for? Did you take yourself some scalps and a slave?" He pointed his hand at the youth.

Two Foxes continued up to the fire and stepped down. He turned his pony loose to graze with the other horses scattered about and spread his palms to the leaping flames.

The white men again surrounded the fire and squatted around its warmth. One of them stirred the pot boiling in the edge of the fire. Sam went up close and found a place near a pile of supplies.

As if no time had elapsed since Keesling's question, the Kiowa looked at Sam's thatch of red and said, "I have been thinking about taking some hair."

"Who's the kid?" asked Keesling.

"I don't know," said Two Foxes.

"What do you mean? He comes in trailing you like a lost sheep."

"I made a mistake and helped him get away from some Mexicans. Now I can't get rid of him."

All the men examined Sam. He returned the measuring stars, shuffled his feet, and edged up nearer to the fire. Now that he had stopped moving, the cold wind was slicing straight through him.

Keesling moved a couple of steps closer to Sam. He spoke roughly. "What's your name, kid?"

"Sam Tollin."

"Why are you with the Kiowa? He doesn't take kindly to white men. He doesn't even like us who ride with him."

"Some Mexicans are trying to kill me. They have my sister prisoner." Sam felt his hope rising as he watched first one white face and then another. He blurted out rapidly, "I need a rifle and a horse to go after them and get her free. Will you give me the things I need? Maybe you'll even go and help me?''

Keesling's eyes sharpened. "Hold up a little. You're getting ahead of yourself. Have you got any money to pay us for our trouble?''

"I don't have any money. A man took it from me in Santa Fe.''

"Well now, you don't expect us to go and get shot at for nothing, do you? Does your folks have anything that we could use?''

"Our place was burned down by some Indians. My dad and mom may be dead.''

"Too bad. Your luck is plumb rotten," said Keesling. He turned to Two Foxes. "Are those Mexicans still trailing you?''

"I expect so. They want the boy dead or a long ways from their wagon train. Either way, I think they are playing for time. Once they have the girl across the border and into Mexico they will be safe.''

"Is the girl pretty enough to bring a goodly sum of money?''

"She is very pretty. Someone will pay a large amount of Mexican pesos for her.''

"Have the Mexicans made any trouble for you?'' asked Keesling.

"No. Just tagged along behind out of rifle range.''

"All right. We'll take care of them if they show up. Where is your partner, Black Elk?''

"I don't know. He will be here when he comes.''

"We're not going to wait any longer. It's turning off damn cold. I suspect it'll snow before the day is over.''

A little, dark sliver of a man, very ugly, stood near the fire. His face was caved in as if struck by some terrible force, and on that horrendous wound the nose was smashed and crumpled, and shoved off to the side. He spoke impatiently through heavily scarred lips.

"Tell us your scheme, Keesling. You've been hinting all day how good it is. Let's hear it and see if any of us want to get in it with you. My face aches like hell from the cold and I want to ride out of these mountains and get down to lower country where it's warmer.''

"All right, Zimmer, just take it easy a short spell," growled

Keesling. He cast a provoked look at the little man. Ever since the horse had kicked him in the face two years before, Zimmer was always grouching. Sometimes that got under a man's hide. However, that was more than compensated for by Zimmer's quickness and deadliness with a six-gun. That skill was sometimes the advantage that had kept the gang from getting shot all to hell.

Zimmer pulled his coat tighter around himself. "Why couldn't we have met in Santa Fe instead of up here in the mountains? After all, it is late October and going on winter."

"I had my reasons for wanting you to come up here. You'll know why in a minute," answered the gang leader. He stepped back away from the fire so he could see the faces of all the men and began to talk.

CHAPTER 6

Keesling pushed his hat to the back of his head, and his gaze roamed to cover the outlaw band. Bartel and Raggan were a pair of longtime partners that had been with him from the first robbery many years ago. They were fair with guns. They could not be beaten in the task of handling cattle or horses.

The Kiowa was the best tracker that had ever worked an old trail. McKone, tall and slope-shouldered, was a mean man who would kill without reason. He went a little crazy in a fight, and it was good to have him on your side.

Zimmer had a small man's touchiness. And the fact that he was now uglier than sin seemed to make him harder to get along with. Still, he made a good *segundo*, second in command.

"In all the years we've been riding together, have I ever got you fellows into trouble that we couldn't get out of?"

"Well, that gunshot I took two years ago didn't make me laugh," responded Zimmer.

"That was your own fault and downright stupid to go back inside to rob the banker after we had already got all the money," retorted Keesling.

A sheepish expression made Zimmer's face even more misshapen than it was normally. "I almost forgot to take his big gold watch. How did I know he had a hideout gun to use on me?"

"Now listen to my plan," said Keesling. "I've been back in Missouri spending my share of the money from those last cattle we rustled. While I was there watching the settlers clear the woods off their new ground, I got me this idea.

"The farmers are flocking into that country by the droves. There's good soil and plenty of rain to make the crops grow

57

every year without irrigating. The only thing that is missing is horses and mules to snake logs to clear the land and to plow the ground. And to do all the other dragging and pulling that has to be done.

"Those farmers are not dumb and prefer mules over horses, for they have more sense when hooked to a load. You almost never hear of a mule running away with a plow or wagon like horses. In a few years those Missouri fellows will get around to cross-breeding and will raise their own mules. But right now they are plenty scarce. A good mule with some size to him is fetching two hundred dollars. Just an average one is worth a hundred and fifty dollars."

"There's hardly any mules around here to steal," said Zimmer.

"Right you are," answered Keesling. "But McKone knows where there are thousands of them. Tell them, McKone, what you saw in California."

McKone tugged at his long black beard and began to talk. "Last winter, after we split up, I drifted out to California. I had heard the living was easy there, with warm winters and pretty women. It was a right smart long ride, but let me tell you, it was worth every step.

"Now about the mules. Mexicans know how to breed damn fine horses. They are just as good at breeding mules. Each one of those big *ranchos* has hundreds of the animals. They use them for everything except riding. One Mexican *caballero* has bred himself up a herd of big gray mules the best you would ever hope to see anywhere."

"So we're going to California and spend the winter enjoying ourselves," said Keesling. "Then in the spring early we'll steal a thousand mules and drive them to Missouri."

"I have heard of the place, California. That is a very long way from Missouri," said Two Foxes.

"Sure, seventeen or eighteen hundred miles," agreed Keesling. "But think of the money we would make. A thousand mules times two hundred dollars would bring two hundred thousand dollars. A fortune for us. And still a large amount of money even after we divide it up amongst us. What do you men say? Will you go with me?"

"We would lose more than half of the mules in a trip from

California to Missouri,'' said Zimmer. ''That's if we could get them away from the Mexicans in the first place.''

''Zimmer is right,'' agreed Bartel. ''Raggan and I have made some long cattle drives from Texas to the railroads in Kansas. We always lost a lot of cattle.''

Raggan nodded agreement. ''We'd lose ten to fifteen percent on every one of those trips, and that was just a pleasant walk compared to what you are talking about.''

Keesling rubbed his whiskered jaw with the knuckles of a hand and evaluated his men. He had ridden some rough miles with every one of them and knew how competent they were in their trade. ''If we're going to lose half of the mules, well then, we'll just steal two thousand of them to start out with. I'm betting this gang we have can do it with some hard work and a little luck.''

''How about water holes?'' asked Bartel. ''That number of animals will need a sizable amount. How far apart are they? I heard there's a lot of desert to get over.''

''Some of them are fifty to sixty miles apart,'' said McKone. ''But they are large enough. Most of them are on the rivers, either the Gila or Rio Grande.''

''We got two things going for us,'' said Bartel. ''We can mark the watering places on the way out, and we'll be coming back in the spring when the water is most plentiful.''

''Like I say, we'll be traveling along a river most of the way,'' said McKone. He squatted down and began to draw a crude map on the ground with a stick. ''Here is the ocean and the shore of California.'' He glanced up at Zimmer. ''You'll like the water, Zimmer. I remember when you got caught in that flood on the Red River last year. We all thought you were done for when your horse drowned. But you swam like a fish and beat the river.''

''I damn near froze to death that time,'' said Zimmer.

''Get on with the map,'' directed Keesling.

''Well, Los Angeles, the town where we could stay, is about here.'' McKone poked the ground. ''Now over here to the southeast is Arizona City, where we can cross the big Colorado River on a ferryboat. Of course, when coming back with the mules, we'll have to swim them and do it somewheres else so we won't be seen. From there we follow along the Gila River Trail until we find El Camino. Then straight north to Santa Fe. Rest a little with the Mexicans, then northeast to St. Joe.'' McKone marked a short curving scratch to indicate the last section of the drive.

"You make it all sound so easy,'' growled Zimmer, "especially that last eight hundred miles to St. Joe. I've been over that trail and it's got some hard places.''

"We'll try to sell some mules all the way along,'' said Keesling. "There will be wagon trains that'll need animals to replace those that they've lost. Probably we can sell a hundred or two at Tucson, and another bunch at Santa Fe. So our job will keep getting easier all the way back. Now, how many of you are game to try it with me?''

Zimmer spoke. "Nobody has mentioned the Apaches. Once we drop down out of these mountains to the south, we'll be in their range. They are tough Indians.''

"McKone made it to California and back and still has all his hair,'' said Keesling.

"He wasn't driving a thousand mules like we'll be doing,'' said Zimmer. "Our dust will be big and sky-high and can be seen for twenty to thirty miles.''

"We've got our own Indian,'' said Keesling. "He'll take care of the Apaches. Ain't that right, Two Foxes?''

The Kiowa was looking morosely into the fire and gave no indication he had heard.

"We'll be traveling thirty to forty miles a day,'' said McKone. "Maybe fifty miles on a right good day. We might just hurry and sneak clear across Apache land without them getting organized enough to attack us.''

"It takes them about two seconds to decide to jump a white man,'' said Bartel. "They sure would want to capture some of those mules.''

Keesling spoke. "We'll take our chances. Now, how many of you are going with me?''

"Me, I'll go for sure,'' said McKone. "I know a certain woman out there I want to see again.''

"I'll go. I like the talk of a warm winter,'' said Zimmer.

"Well, Raggan, we've been on some long cattle drives together. What say you to a mule drive halfway across the country?'' asked Bartel.

"It'll sure be a tough trip,'' said Raggan, "but mules can travel a lot faster than cows. I say, let's go to California.''

Keesling looked at Two Foxes. The gang leader knew the plan to trail such a large herd of mules almost two thousand miles through Indian country and desert was dangerous and more apt to fail than not. With the Kiowa scouting, they just might get the animals all that long distance to Missouri. However, the Indian sat staring somberly at the fire and gave no sign he would ever speak.

"Are you going with us, Two Foxes?" asked Keesling.

The copper-faced man climbed to his feet and twisted about to face unerringly toward his birthplace hundreds of miles distant. In his own land north of the Red River, he felt whole and at peace within himself. A complete being. As he wandered farther away, a strange sensation came upon him and his very hold on life seemed to become weak and tenuous. These white men traveled over tremendous spaces and unnaturally appeared to have little desire to return to their homeland. Another thousand miles meant nothing to them.

The outlaw leader spoke to the silent Indian. "I'll tell you what I'll do if you go with us. There are big supply stores in St. Joe and Kansas City. They will have all kinds of guns and ammunition. I'll go into one of those towns and buy you all the rifles and cartridges your share of the mule money will pay for. We can outfit a pack train and you can head straight south with the guns to the Oklahoma Territory and your people. That won't take you more than seven or eight days. You'll have enough rifles to outfit an army. What say you to that?"

The Indian considered the proposal. Earlier in the fall, he had accompanied many men of his village on a long hunt on the plains of north Texas. Only a few small bands of buffalo had been found. If such a season had come upon the land a few years earlier, the thunder of a million buffalo hooves would have shaken the prairie.

The white hunters and skinners were everywhere on the plains. The stench of rotting carcasses fouled the very wind for hundreds of miles, an endless desolation of bones and skulls. The great buffalo herds were being destroyed, merely for their hides. With their end, the Kiowa people would end.

Next spring a battle must be fought. His people had swift mustangs. But their weapons were hunting bows and old muskets that often exploded, wounding the warriors. Two

Foxes would bring them many repeating rifles and then the Kiowa would join with their ancient enemies, the Comanche, and all the braves together would kill the white hunters, driving them from the plains and back to the East. Then the buffalo cows could give birth to many calves in safety and begin to rebuild the great herds.

"I will go," replied Two Foxes.

In high, good spirits, Keesling laughed and smacked his fist into an open palm. "Come April or thereabouts, we'll all be rich."

"Or maybe dead," observed Zimmer.

Inside his head, the Kiowa thought the ugly white man just might be correct.

"You worry too much, Zimmer," said Keesling. He looked at Sam. "Now, what do we do with the kid?"

All of the outlaws turned their eyes to bear upon the youth. He saw the hard lines of their faces and sensed their hostility.

"How about you, Two Foxes? You brought him here. What should we do with him?"

"I do not care," said the Kiowa.

"Kill him," rapped out McKone, his muddy brown eyes squinting almost shut in hairy sockets. "He heard all our plans. He sure as hell will tell the first lawman or army man he meets what our scheme is."

The shock of the bearded man's declaration shook Sam. McKone spoke as if murder was a very natural solution to his presence. The other men were thoughtfully speculating on the suggestion.

Sam stepped away from the fire and faced the outlaw band. "Now, wait a minute. You got no right . . ."

"Shut up," ordered Keesling sharply. "You've no say in this."

"I say we just leave him here for the Mexicans," said Bartel. "If they want him as bad as it appears, they'll make short work of him. And besides, he doesn't have a horse, so he can't go with us. He doesn't even have a blanket. Look at him. He's shivering from the cold right now."

"He might make it back to Santa Fe and that'd be too bad for us," countered McKone. "I can slip a knife between his ribs slick as a whistle. Then we can come back here and not have to worry about the army or somebody waiting to hang us or throw us all in jail.''

Sam's hair twisted on the nape of his neck as the dangerous talk washed around him. His eyes slipped across the clearing to measure the distance to the nearest woods. Much too far to run with six weapons firing at him. He thought of trying to snatch a pistol from the closest person, McKone. That man looked very strong and quick.

As if interpreting Sam's mind, McKone put his hand on the butt of his weapon. His eyes bore into Sam. ''How does it feel to know you are going to die in a minute?'' he asked, in a low, deadly tone

Sam raised his head to levelly return the stare. Never again would he fear any man. His anger was rising at the threats, and he let it seethe and grow. That helped to settle the uneasy flutter in his stomach.

He had to make his move now before it was too late. He moved away from McKone toward Keesling. His tongue was thick as he spoke to the outlaw leader. ''I'll go with you. I'll take care of the horses and chop all the wood. I'm not much of a cook, but I'll do that too.''

''We can't let him tend the horses,'' said McKone. ''He'll run off the first chance he gets.''

''Not so,'' replied Sam. His father had told him a man's word must be better than a written contract. ''I'll give my word to stay with you until I can prove I'm no danger to you.''

''Kid, you'll never be a danger to me,'' snorted McKone. He pulled a long-bladed knife. ''I'll just kill you now. Then Two Foxes can lift your scalp.''

''Ease off, McKone,'' ordered the gang leader. ''You're always too ready with that blade.''

''You're too goddamn soft,'' snapped McKone. ''If I ran this outfit, this kid would be dead and us on our way to California instead of standing here arguing in the cold.''

Keesling's features became frosty. ''I'm not so soft but what I can't handle a loud-mouthed bastard like you.'' His words were sharp like pieces of metal hitting. His eyes pierced McKone.

Then he deliberately turned to Sam. ''Give me your word on your mother's honor.''

"I swear on my mother's head, I'll stay with you as long as you tell me to," said Sam. He hoped the leader would make it a very brief time.

"Anyone got any complaints about taking the kid with us? Anyone except McKone, that is?" asked Keesling.

Bartel grumbled under his breath and then lapsed into silence. Two Foxes sensed the foreboding of unknown bad things to come with the presence of the white boy. He said nothing.

Zimmer laughed out loud. He understood Keesling's game to challenge McKone, and do it in a manner that would last a long time. A trip to California should be long enough to accomplish that.

McKone shoved his knife back into its sheath with a slap of his hand. His wiry beard trembled with suppressed rage. His hand drifted close to his tied-down six-gun.

Keesling pivoted quickly. "McKone, I can beat you to the draw easy. If your hand moves a fraction closer to your gun, I'm going to shoot you right through that big nose of yours. Now you listen right close to me, for I'm going to say this only once. You keep your knife and gun off the boy. Do you hear me?"

McKone battled with himself, fighting to control his temper that wanted to jerk the six-gun out and begin to shoot. His lower jaw shook with the effort, making the heavy beard dance.

"Do you hear me, McKone?"

"I hear," hissed the man.

Keesling looked at Zimmer. "If McKone shoots me in the back, I want you to kill him. Do it in the worst possible way you can think of."

"It'd be a pleasure," replied the little man. The features of his grotesque face moved as if trying to express some emotion. He liked the idea.

Sam guessed Zimmer was smiling, but it was impossible to identify what the grimace meant. These men were robbers, killers, with no rules except to survive. Treachery of one against the others must always be a constant threat to them. Sam would keep a vigilant watch for his own safety. He would make the journey with them as short as possible, and stay away from McKone.

"Kid, you'll go to California with us," said Keesling.

The leader spoke to Zimmer. "Now you know why I had all of you meet me out here. We are already more than a day's ride toward California."

"I agree this is closer than going south on the El Camino Real and then turning west along the Gila River Trail, but this way is much rougher."

"Maybe so," said Keesling, "but men on horseback with pack animals instead of wagons can travel this route. Save a hundred miles. We are on the east flank of mountains the Mexicans call San Mateo. We'll just mosey south and pass between the Datil Mountains and the Gallinas. Then easy going on the Plains of San Agustin. Up and over the Mogollons and down into the desert country along the Gila River.

"I have been this way before. An army patrol was pushing me hard, but I lost them in the high timbered peaks of the Mogollons. Now we just need to ride fast enough to stay ahead of any snow in this storm. Let's eat and put some miles behind us before it gets dark."

Last in line, Sam filled a tin plate with boiled beans and meat from the pot. He ate with high relish, like a starved wolf pup. Without being told, he gathered up the empty utensils and carried them to the stream for washing.

The outlaw gang saddled and packed with deft, quick motions. Two Foxes finished with his mount and came up to the creek and knelt to wash off his war paint. Sam caught a glimpse of the Indian's face as the man stood up. The features were less ferocious without his paint. However, the black eyes were cold and unfriendly as they slid across Sam for an instant.

Rain began to fall as Sam stowed the pot and metal plates into one of the pouches of the packs. The intensity of the storm increased swiftly, large drops pounding down upon Sam, instantly penetrating his shirt, and pressing cold upon his skin. He hunched his shoulders. In a minute he would be running behind the mounted men. Perhaps that would keep him warm enough to survive.

"Kid, you ride that packhorse with the lightest load," said Keesling. He called out to the men, "Has anyone got a coat or hat he can use?"

"I got an old sheepskin coat and a hat he can borrow if he wants," said Raggan. He dug the articles from a pack and tossed them to Sam.

The youth pulled the warm coat on. The big tears in it meant nothing. The hat was crumpled and too large and came down on the tops of his ears. How great the clothing felt. "Thanks," he told Raggan. "I'll repay you some day."

Busy finding his rain slicker, the man hardly looked at Sam.

"This rain is going to be a gully washer," observed Keesling, tugging on his raincoat. He examined the storm bearing down upon them. "There's some canvas in that right front pack," he told Sam. "Tie a piece over each load of packs and better get a fair-sized piece for yourself."

Sam hurried and covered the supplies as directed. Then he found a section large enough to shelter himself. He clambered upon the top of the packs of one of the horses and wrapped the canvas around himself and up and over his head.

"California here we come," Keesling called to his men. He kicked his mustang into motion.

To Sam, that sounded like a very great distance. He had given his word of honor not to try to run away. Must he keep it to someone that threatened his very life? He would think on that. In this heavy rain, he just might slip off into the trees.

CHAPTER 7

The rain slackened to a drizzle as the outlaw band rode into the storm shadow on the south side of the San Mateo Mountains. The wind slowed and barely stirred the clouds of fog forming in the low coves and valleys. Streams flowed in all the water courses, yellow-brown and noisy in their downward tumble on the steep gradients.

Two Foxes came into sight in the misty haze of the gang's back trail. His cayuse galloped in fast, splashing water and mud. The Kiowa pulled his drippy mount to a sliding halt near Keesling.

"The Mexicans are still coming," said the Indian. "It's time we stopped them."

"Right you are," agreed Keesling. "Zimmer, you know a little Mex lingo, so you go back with Two Foxes. Take a white flag and see if you can get near enough to talk with them. Kill them if you get within gun range. We can use the extra horses."

"Okay," replied Zimmer. "I have an old shirt near enough to white to do the trick."

"The rest of us will push on with the pack animals," said Keesling. He pointed to the south. "We'll hold left of that mesa you can see ahead."

Zimmer nodded, understanding. "I can find you easy." He fished out the cloth and was tying it to the barrel of his rifle as he and Two Foxes rode away.

In less than two hours, Zimmer and the Kiowa overhauled their comrades.

"Those Mexicans were a savvy pair," grunted Zimmer when he had drawn close. "They started back the other direction the minute we got in sight. We gave them a chase for a couple of miles. Didn't do any good. They had good horses and stayed well out in front of us. Too far for any shooting."

"Well hell, if the Mexes want to go to California with us, let them," said Keesling.

"I don't think they plan on doing that. They appeared to be satisfied the kid ain't going to cause them any trouble. The last I saw of them, they were riding east toward the Rio Grande," said Zimmer.

"Good," said Keesling.

The rain began to fall hard and fast as the group of riders rode out of the lee of the San Mateos and into the full brunt of the storm. Sam clung to his uncomfortable perch atop the supply packs as the big water drops, slanting down on a stiff wind, pelted him. The driving rain penetrated the pores in the weave of the canvas and he felt the dampness on his back. The animal that carried him lowered its head and laid its tender ears back to reduce their exposure to the harsh blows.

The mountains fell away behind, vanishing into the storm-filled distance. In the deepening dusk of the evening, the men entered a land of rimrocks and vertical-walled mesas. Juniper mixed with a few scattered ponderosa pine grew thick in the bottoms and lay like a wet, black blanket on the flat top of every rock-ribbed tableland.

They came upon a large sandstone ledge nearly a hundred feet long and half as deep on the side of one of the mesas. Sam was more than glad when Keesling guided the way into the dry zone beneath the outcropping rock. The riders sat their mounts for a minute, enjoying the absence of the pounding rain upon their drenched and chilled bodies.

"This will do for tonight," said Keesling, and stepped down into the dirt. "Kid, take care of the ponies."

Sam dropped the packs and unsaddled the riding horses. He hobbled the weary animals so they could drift about and graze. However, the animals huddled together at one end of the cliff and would not go out into the storm.

Raggan commenced to build a fire from a few small scraps of dry wood found under the ledge.

Keesling looked in Sam's direction and yelled out, "You done with the horses?"

"Yes," replied Sam, glancing at the other members of the gang standing in the back of the cave with their hands in their pockets.

"Then take the ax and go cut some dead pine. Get enough for a fire all evening. Don't bring any wood that's soaked from lying on the ground. Chop down the standing. Now, hop to it."

The boy dug out the ax from a pack. After tying the canvas cover over his shoulders as best he could, he turtled his head down on a short neck and went out into the cold, heavy rain.

The wind fought the branches of the wet trees. In the half-darkness, Sam dodged the whipping limbs that danced like mad things and searched for dead standing pine. He found a clump of bug-killed trees and began to chop. As he bent to his work swinging the ax, water cascaded down his neck, soaking him through in a minute.

One at a time, he dragged in three fair-sized dead pines, limbs and all. No one offered to help as he started to cut the wood and feed it to the fire.

The damp wood smouldered and smoked. The weak flame danced in the wind. The men did not complain, crowding close to dry their sodden clothing. The flame took bigger bites of the wood and blazed higher.

"Damnation, I'm froze to the bone," grumbled Zimmer. He practically stood in the fire, spreading his bony fingers to the flames, and steam boiled up in long, thin tendrils from his damp pants and coat.

"We need hot coffee, kid. Get it started," ordered Keesling. "Stir up some flapjacks and fry some side meat. We'll eat dried fruit to round out the meal."

"I'll help you," Raggan told Sam. "You slice the bacon. We'll cook it first and then the 'jacks in the grease. Taste good that way and nothing'll be wasted."

The two fell busy at their chores. The other men gradually backed away from the fire as the wood dried and the blazes leaped tall and hot.

The heat was most concentrated between the fire and the rear wall of the cave. The men gathered there and began to dry their weapons and discuss how best to drive a large herd of mules two thousand miles.

All except McKone. He sat off by himself and stared

malevolently at Sam. The kid has caused him to be humiliated in front of all the gang. His rage at Keesling for calling his bluff had turned to hate for the boy.

"Here, you don't have to turn the 'jacks with that knife," Raggan said to Sam. "Let me show you how to flip them and catch them in the air after they swap sides once."

Raggan took hold of the skillet handle and with a quick upward lift tossed the half-cooked pancake two feet or more into the air and caught in skillfully, the brown side up. He grinned at Sam.

McKone's control of his hate for Sam broke, and his voice, taut with ridicule, lashed at Raggan. "Right fine little school teacher you are, Raggan. Are you going to tell him a bedtime story too?"

Raggan became motionless as stone. His smile faded. Slowly he placed the frying pan on the coals at the edge of the fire. Still crouched with his buttocks resting on his heels, he turned toward McKone.

"There's no harm in telling the boy a few tricks of how to cook," said Raggan, studying McKone's face to determine how seriously the man meant his words. Raggan did not want trouble, for he knew the larger man could beat him with either fists or gun. The other men had fallen quiet at McKone's sharp statement to Raggan. Bartel looked at his partner and then at McKone.

"He'll turn you in to the first lawman he meets, and your ass will end up in jail," said McKone.

"Well, until he does that, I want him to be a good cook," said Raggan in a quiet tone. "That way we will all have better grub."

"Just slap him around a little bit every time he makes a mistake and he'll learn fast enough," growled McKone.

"No need to be cruel to the boy," said Raggan. "Not his fault he got caught up with us."

"You're a fool," sneered McKone.

Raggan stood up, his face pale and tight.

McKone came erect swiftly, his blood pumping. He wanted to hurt somebody. If not the kid, then Raggan would do.

The two men measured each other across the short five steps that separated them.

In the dead silence, the metal click of a rifle coming to full cock was as loud as the clank of a church bell.

Bartel spoke savagely from McKone's left side. "McKone, my partner Raggan is kind of easygoing. Now, I'm different, and I kinda like a little gunplay now and then. I've got a rifle in my lap that says it's faster than your handgun. Why don't you just turn thisaway and let's you and me have a go at it."

McKone pivoted to look at Bartel. The man sat near Zimmer and held a long gun ready in his hands.

"Make your play," said Bartel, his anger sharp and brittle in his tone.

"Hold up, you two," directed Zimmer. "Neither one of you are so good but what I might get hit if lead starts flying. Now I got the warmest place of the bunch of you, and I don't want to move." His scarred face locked on McKone, and he let the stillness hold for several seconds.

"You're not going to make me move to a cold spot, are you, McKone?" asked Zimmer.

McKone evaluated Zimmer. Several times he had seen the little man draw his six-gun, and though Zimmer sat flat on the ground with his hands lying loosely across his legs, McKone did not believe he could beat the man to the first shot. And only one shot would be needed to kill him, if Zimmer drew.

"No," replied McKone. "I was only joking with Raggan." He turned away from the small gunman that he could break so easily with his hands.

With eyes as hot as the flames that crackled at his back, McKone stared out into the storm as if the cold blackness could cool his burning rage and humiliation.

Zimmer spoke to the man's broad back. "McKone, your big mouth is starting to rile me. I think your string is going to run out one of these days, and someone is going to shut you up, permanent-like."

McKone did not respond, his back ramrod stiff.

"Go ahead, kid, and cook," said Zimmer. "I like my bacon brown and brickle and don't burn the flapjacks."

McKone promised himself to kill the kid for sure. And the others—they would pay very dearly.

*   *   *

Sam slept in all his clothes, curled up in a cold ball. His piece of canvas was spread under him and the extra width draped over his body to break the force of the damp wind.

A few feet away in the darkness, the rain poured down, drumming persistently upon the muddy earth. Now and then a gust of wind drove in beneath the ledge to drop a fine spray of moisture upon everything.

He woke in the drippy, misty no-man's-hour just before the break of dawn. Soundlessly, he climbed from his pallet and went to stand at the edge of the protected zone under the cliff.

The night was black and so dense a man could hold a handful. From the sounds, he judged the rain had slackened, but the wind blew stronger, complaining of the wet and cold. The limbs of some nearby tree rubbed against the sandstone rock with a harsh rasp. He smelled the horses, close there somewhere in the impenetrable gloom.

Sam felt lost and lonely. Sorrow that he could not help his family tore at his heart. He believed with certainty that only he still existed of all his clan to help his sister. Could he stay alive to return from this place called California to rescue her? Or take revenge upon her killers if she was dead?

"Thinking about taking a walk?" asked Keesling from the darkness behind Sam.

"I gave my word not to run off," replied Sam.

"So you did. So you did. Light a fire and make some coffee." What a fool the kid was, thought Keesling. If he had been in the youth's predicament, he would have been long gone with everything he could lay his hands on.

"Are we going to travel in the rain again today?"

"Why not? I'm sure you want to go to California," said the outlaw leader. "Call me and the others when the coffee is hot."

In the uncertain light of the morning dusk, the gang of would-be mule thieves marched out from under the ledge of rock and headed south through the storm.

Sometime near the middle of the day, the six riders traversed a deep, narrow valley. The tall, rugged crest of the Gallinas Mountains on their left, and the even higher peaks of the Datil Mountains soaring on their right, were invisible. The ancient, massive upthrusts of rock were truncated at less than a thousand feet by the thick, dark clouds boiling down from the north.

The wind, carrying a deluge of rain upon its back, was funneled to hurricane force by the steep sides of the pass. The maelstrom slashed and tore at the men. They hunched their shoulders, crouched low over their ponies, and buried their heads in their collars to protect their faces from the onslaught.

Five miles later the mountains retreated on both hands, and the men entered the level land of the Plains of San Agustin. Free of the confining walls of the pass, the wind spread its energy to encompass the whole plain, and its pell-mell speed slackened.

The men hurried fast across the past summer's growth of grass, a strom-beaten tan mat beneath the hooves of the horses. Still, evening caught them in the center of a seemingly endless prairie. Keesling stopped and sat peering south into the rain.

He spoke to Zimmer, sitting his mount beside him. "If we don't find shelter and wood for a fire, it's going to be one hell of a miserable night. I judge it's another five miles across to timber."

"I don't want to hunker out here in the storm all night," responded Zimmer. "The cayuses still have some distance left in them. I say we whip and spur a little hard and we can still make that five miles while we can yet see."

"I hope they don't slip and fall in the mud and break one of their legs or one of ours," said Keesling. "But I think they should be able to hold their feet."

He yelled over his shoulder, "Let's hurry it."

He rolled the sharp rowels of his spurs across the ribs of his mount. The animal broke into a cautious, stiff-legged trot. The other riders hastened to match the pace, tensed to jump clear if their mustangs fell.

The horsemen rode late into the dimness of a pine forest dripping with rain. Everywhere there was the musty, dank odor of rotting pinecones, needles, and wood, made strong in the noses of the men by the dampness. In a dense stand of brown-stemmed ponderosa, the weary men and horses halted. As the men dismounted, the darkness was rapidly closing the trees in around them.

"Make a big lean-to," directed Keesling. "We'll use our slickers and all the canvas to roof it. Also, cut as much pine limbs as you can find for a floor. That'll keep out the wet. Any extra limbs—add them to the roof."

The men worked swiftly. The shelter sprang into form. By the time the full darkness hid all the outside world, they sat on the pine bows in the dry. A fire burned just inside the high edge of the lean-to.

Raggan and Sam worked at preparing the evening meal. Two Foxes silently stoked the fire and the flames leaped. Rain hissed as it fell into the yellow-red blaze. A burning stick fell apart with a snap, and sparks soared up to melt into the wet darkness.

"Keesling, how much farther before we get out of this high country?" asked Zimmer. "I think I'm going to drown."

"In thirty-five or forty miles we'll hit the upper reaches of the Gila. Then it's all downhill until we reach the desert. The bad part is, we got to climb another half mile higher to top the Mogollon Mountains."

"That's not too far if we don't run into snow," said Zimmer.

"There'll be snow by the morning," prophesied Two Foxes, lifting his head and sniffing the wind.

Nobody questioned the Kiowa's words.

CHAPTER 8

When daylight arrived, the snow was falling and two inches of white blanketed the ground. It grew deeper as the men pushed south and their route labored upward. On the crest of the Mogollon Mountains, the drifts were halfway to the horses' bellies.

The riders halted at the crest of the mountain and gazed down upon the faraway desert, visible now and then through breaks in the winddriven snow. The horses stood breathing hard, their hot bodies steaming in the cold air.

"Twenty-five to thirty miles down there and we'll be in the low country," said Keesling, nodding his snow-covered hat toward the desert. "Should be warm there and not snowing."

"With luck, it won't even be raining," said Zimmer.

"This much snow will drive the deer off these high mountaintops," said Raggan. "We should hunt a little and see if we can kill a deer or two."

"They should have drifted down and be herded up right at snow line," said Bartel.

Zimmer reined his horse's head to point down the mountain. "Let's be on our way," he said impatiently.

Five miles later and three thousand feet lower, Keesling spoke to his men. "Quite a lot of fresh deer tracks here. McKone and you, Zimmer, go off to the left. Raggan and Bartel, off to the right. Spread out and go quiet. The kid and me will go straight ahead until about an hour before dark, when we'll stop and make camp. Now bring in some meat."

The men drifted off silently through the snow like phantom hunters.

* * *

Zimmer rode into camp last, just at the close of day. The site was at the base of a tall red-rock pinnacle rearing out at an angle from the side of the mountain. A light rain was drizzling out of the clouds. Its fall was absorbed by the slanting slab of rock to leave a dry area more than ample for the men to spread their blankets and cook.

The little gunman was leading an Indian pony. He walked up to Sam and handed him the reins, a thin length of rawhide tied around the animal's lower jaw and about halfway back inside his mouth.

"Here's something you can ride until I need it. He's a little on the small side, maybe a hand height or so. But then you ain't a heavyweight yourself, so he can pack you easy. From the looks of him, I'd say he is plenty fast. You want to use him?"

"I sure do," exclaimed Sam. "Riding on top of that pack saddle is tough. Thanks, Zimmer."

The young man backed up a few steps and ran an examining eye over the bay mustang. The animal carried a blanket saddle fastened to its back by a wide surcingle. Iron stirrups hung from short leather straps.

The black, intelligent eyes of the horse evaluated Sam with equal intensity. His tail switched once, nervously. Then he stood still as stone. What did these strange men want of him?

"He appears sound, Zimmer. About a six-year-old, I guess," said Sam. "His hooves are wore down and he needs shod. With much traveling, he's going to get sore feet."

"Yeah, he's an Indian cayuse and they don't shoe their mustangs," answered Zimmer. "This buck must have traveled a long trail and there's not much hoof left. You might have to tie some hide over his feet until we can put some iron on him or his hooves grow out. Did anyone get a deer?"

"I got one," spoke up Raggan. "He can have the skin off it."

"Take good care of my new horse, kid. I'll want him back in good condition one of these days," said Zimmer.

"I'll do that," said Sam.

Zimmer spoke to Keesling. "I found something that needed killing more than a deer. I spied this Apache buck coming up the mountain. He got in the sights of my rifle and I just had to shoot him. I thought Apaches died hard. Well, this one died just as quick as any other man shot through the heart."

"Did he have any guns worth keeping?" questioned Keesling.

"No. Just an old smooth-bore musket. I let it lay beside him. That way he'll have a gun in the next world. Ain't that the right way to send off a dead Indian into the Happy Hunting Ground, Two Foxes?"

The Kiowa glanced briefly at Zimmer. He turned away without responding.

Zimmer continued to speak to Keesling. "He had a bow and quiver of arrows, too. It's tied there behind my saddle. Kind of a short bow, but plenty strong. The arrows are straight and have good turkey feathers on them. Figured I could swap it for something I need later on."

"There's plenty of turkeys along the Gila," said McKone. "Also, we can kill deer. There's fish, and I even saw some wild hogs on my other trip. Shot one and damn good eating it was. I suspect some of the settlers or Mexicans that have gone through here lost some pigs and they've gone wild."

"Grub's ready," called Raggan from the fire. "Fried deer liver and steak, a couple of pounds for each of you for the main course."

"God Almighty, ain't this sun wonderful!" exclaimed Zimmer. "It's warm and there's no wind."

"Good chance it'll be like this all the way to California," said McKone. "I bet before we get there you'll be wishin' you had some of that snow from up on the mountain."

Sam looked up from the cactus and brush of the desert to the rims of the Mogollons powdered with white, a highland preparing for winter. Gray clouds cascaded down from the mountain crown, to be devoured by the dry winds of the lowlands and to disappear into nothingness midway along the sloping flank.

The high Mogollons extended west along the northern horizon. South of that and ahead, range after range of short, brown mountains blocked the route to California. On Sam's left, scores of low stony hills, bristly with cactus, stepped off toward the south.

"Rough-looking country," said Zimmer, observing Sam's scouting of the terrain. "I judge Mexico is off there in those hills about fifty or sixty miles."

"McKone, there must be some passes where the Gila cuts through those mountains that we can't make with horses," said Keesling, tracing the course of the river to where it plunged into the highlands.

"Half a dozen at least. But I know where they are. We won't be following every turn of the river. That'd be at least a hundred fifty miles farther to travel. We'll cut across the big bends of the river and try to hold as straight a path as we can. Just go up to the Gila when we need water or to hunt meat. Not much game out there in the rock and cactus." He moved out to the lead and the thieves aimed their mounts for California.

Five days later the Gila River burst free of the constraining walls of the mountain that had hemmed it in for two hundred miles. Its channel meandered across a sand-and-mud flood-plain of more than three miles' width. Sometimes its flow of water divided among three or four small channels. Scores of abandoned oxbows, partially filled with aged water, lay here and there on the flat bottom.

Great expanses of dark green marsh of willow, sedges, and tall rank grass crowded each other in low wet spots. On the edges where the site was slightly drier, large cottonwoods grew. The very periphery of the oasis created by the river was dotted with giant walnut trees.

The autumn sun blazed down from the bowl of a sky bleached to a shimmering gray by the intensity of its rays. The six horsemen rode with bodies drooping and shoulders hunched against the scorching heat.

"Warm enough for you, Zimmer?" chided Keesling.

"It'll do. It'll do," replied Zimmer, mopping at the sweat on his face with a dirty bandana.

Sam followed at the tail end of the outlaw gang. They had traveled swiftly, riding the sunlight of every day into evening dusk. For the first five days, he had bound the Indian mustang's feet with pieces of deer hide. The hooves had grown quickly. Still, Sam carefully watched for any tenderness in the step of the horse as he settled into the routine of the fast, daylong riding.

The young man had found the bay was a willing and hardy mount. Further, he had discovered the mustang had been trained to be controlled by pressure from his rider's legs. Gradually, by trial and error. Sam had worked out most of those signals. Still, now and then, at some movement by him in the saddle, the mustang would instantly obey an unintended command. This morning, Sam had jerked his foot back from imminent collision with a saguaro cactus, and his heel gouging the animal's flank had caused the bay to jump sideways and pivot to dart away at a full run. Sam had almost lost his seat from the amazing swiftness of that reaction.

As the many miles stretched out one after another behind Sam, he fretted constantly. The time when he could go to the aid of Sarah was moving farther and farther into the future. Be brave, little sister, for I will surely come, promised Sam silently.

Holding south of the river, the riders found a route through brush and cactus on the flatland above the river valley. In the middle of the afternoon, the Gila drew close to them in a long, looping meander. They approached the stream and guided their horses out upon a gravelly bank to sight ahead.

The big black boar slept soundly on the cool, damp earth in the shade beneath the riverbank. His nose twitched and moved up and down in his dreaming as if he were rooting for a tasty, buried tidbit. Suddenly his ears flared and he jerked to consciousness. Something large and heavy was shaking the ground above his head. Clods showered down from the dirt roof.

He came to his feet in one swift movement. He snorted loudly in alarm.

The legs of a horse crashed through the weak top of the bank overhang and landed upon him. The boar's snort changed to a shrill squeal and he flung himself into the open sunlight. He had no thought of direction or destination. He only knew safety was elsewhere. His short, muscular legs driving like pistons, his body plowed through the marsh grass of the river bottom.

McKone yanked his rifle from its scabbard and snapped it

to his shoulder. He tracked the running hog in the green vegetation of the marsh. The front sight settled on the animal, and then the rear sight. He fired.

The dark boar did not know what was wrong, only that the sturdy legs that had never failed him, failed now. They became entangled in the tough grass, and he was down. He could not rise. And the world went black forever.

"Fresh ham for supper," gleefully yelled McKone. He cautiously walked his cayuse out into the mud and grass. With a deft toss of his lariat, he snared the boar's snout just above the tusk, tightened the loop there where it would not slide loose, and dragged the body to the dry land.

"We might as well make camp here and butcher him," said Keesling. "But that shot could be heard and bring some Apaches. Two Foxes, find a high spot and keep watch."

The Indian saw a small knoll nearby and rode his horse off toward it for a vantage point to overlook the approaches of the camp.

"I'll cook up the best ham feast you fellows have ever ate," said Raggan. "Sam, there's wild onions there on the bank. Dig a double handful. And over there farther is a currant bush. Get a few of those big, yellow berries off it, too. Then come back and watch how I cook this meat."

Later, after finishing eating, Sam went to wash his hands and face in the edge of the river. His stomach was distended with an impossible quantity of tender, lean ham. Almost too much, and he felt queasy. He found a shady place under a green-barked paloverde tree and lay down, groaning a little at his fullness.

It was strange, he thought, and a little scary, how easily he was settling into the wild life of the outlaws. The pain of the loss of his family was less sharp.

He drifted off into a siesta.

"That Indian girl is kind of pretty," said McKone, nodding at the dark young female on the outside of the group of half a hundred Pima.

"Keep your eyes on the men," rapped Keesling. "There's at least twenty bucks here. We don't want a fight."

"These Pimas ain't fighting Indians—they're farmers, and also traders now since so many people come along the Gila

Trail. Anyway, they have only a couple of guns between them all and we could most likely kill the whole bunch of them if we've the mind to," answered McKone.

"No. I want to leave them behind us friendly. I don't want to have to worry about them trying to ambush us or run off our mules when we come back this way."

The village of the Pima had been spotted from a distance on the second day after the killing of the boar. McKone had told the others of the fruit and vegetables raised by the Indians with water diverted from the Gila. With weapons ready, the gang had ridden close to the settlement to trade for supplies.

Now Sam viewed the men, women, and children who had come out from their homes of brush wicker and adobe to greet the white men. He thought the Pima, with their strong brown bodies and clear black eyes, were handsome people. Some of them smiled, a little nervously, as if not knowing for sure what to expect from the bunch of heavily armed men who had no women with them.

"Trade. We want to trade," said Keesling and pointed to the river, where could be seen ten acres or so of garden and an area of orchard about the same size.

One of the Indian men nodded his understanding. "We trade," he said and led the way to the cultivated land.

Keesling dismounted and pulled out his pouch of paper and metal money. A few pieces of silver should buy all they needed.

"We want two bushels of apples." He indicated the trees and held out his arms in a circle to show the quantity he desired.

The dickering continued, the men sitting on their haunches and the women in a group off a few paces. With gestures, a scant knowledge of Spanish, and a little English, the men struck a bargain. The articles most prized and wanted by the Pima were Zimmer's bow and arrows, once the Indians understood the weapons had belonged to an Apache. They commented with excitement and pleasure among themselves. One of their hated enemies was dead.

The bartering ended with the Indians joining the white men in a feast of delicious watermelons. From holes in the sandy river bottom, the Pima dug out three dozen or more greenrinded melons weighing at least ten pounds each. In the cool, moist earth, they had remained as fresh as when first buried weeks before. With lavish disregard for frugality, the Indians and white men alike gorged in great mouthfuls on the sweet, red flesh of the melons.

Later, with packhorses laden down with apples, dried peaches, cornmeal, squash, and peppers, Keesling and his men rode to the west.

Arizona City, to be renamed Yuma in two years, was three hundred boxlike adobe houses on the caliche bluff above the junction of the clear water of the Gila and the silty Colorado River. The dirt main street terminated at the very edge of the swift current of the mighty Colorado. Keesling and his band had spent only one night in the hot, dusty town, and now in the early morning were preparing to cross the river.

Tied up at the end of the street was a small ferryboat made of heavy wooden planks, crudely built and flat-bottomed. A short wooden ramp extended from the end of the ferry to the bank.

A long Manila-hemp cable stretched about four hundred yards from a stout timber deeply embedded in the top of a low hill on the north shore of the river to a similar installation on the south shore. Three long supporting guy ropes came down from each tall mast to be anchored firmly in the ground.

The ferry was fastened to the thick cable by two sets of pulleys, one on the stern and a second on the bow. The low point of the rope's drooping sag skimmed the water in the center of the river, where it was tugged and pulled at by the current to send a jerky quiver through the flimsy ferry.

"That'll be fifty cents for each man and a dollar for every horse to ride the ferry," called out the operator loudly so all six riders could hear him.

"Seems like a damn high price," said Keesling.

"You want to try swimming?" asked the ferryman testily. "The current is so swift, you'd end up in Mexico before you could get across, if you could swim at all without drowning."

" 'Pears you are right," said Keesling, looking down at the brown flood hurrying past.

"Then pay me and lead your animals on board."

The ferryboat dipped and bobbed as the horses gingerly edged up the wooden ramp. The beasts rolled their eyes and huffed in fright at the unsteady footing. An errant river current swept in beneath the boat's keel and it rolled sickeningly. Bartel's steed squealed and tried to rear. He dragged it down and slapped it roughly across the head with his hat.

Sam's Indian pony, stepping lightly as a dancer, moved to the far side of the ferry. He looked up once into Sam's face as if asking for approval of his courage. The youth reached out and ran the long pointed ears through his hand. Then he looped an arm round the muscular neck and stood watching out over the turbulent, wave-tossed current of the river.

"Crowd your horses up together," directed the ferryman. "How can I make any money if you take up all the room."

"Acts to me like the son-of-a-bitch contraption is ready to capsize," cursed Bartel.

"I've had eight horses on it before and we made it across," responded the operator gruffly. He did not like people finding fault with his craft. "Help me winch up the ramp a couple of feet and we'll be on our way."

The two men cranked a few turns on a dilapidated iron windlass and the gangway rose up like a stiff tongue.

"Now hold on tight to all your animals, for we're going out," called the riverman.

He began to pull the rope through the set of pulleys on the stern of the ferry. Gradually that end of the craft swung to the right. As the angle of the ferry to the river increased, the force of the current on its side could be felt building. Slowly, with the main cable inching through the blocks with a complaining squeal, the boat started to glide sideways out into the deeper, swifter flow.

The operator slacked off some line through the bow pulleys, hiking even more the river's angle of attack on the ferry's side. Grabbing a third skewed toward the far shore, the ferry bravely slid out into the deepest part of the river.

The Colorado had hardly whispered of the power contained in its muddy flow. Now sure that the wooden bauble on its breast was committed to crossing, it pressed all its wet strength upon the full length of the boat. Corklike, the frail boat bounced and bobbed as it was swept swiftly in the direction of the opposite shore.

*   *   *

Northwest of the crossing of the Colorado, the band of men entered a broad expanse of sand hills. The prevailing westerly wind whipped in strongly, stirring the sand and sending it streaming in hundreds of ground currents. The sand sprang along the ground, biting at the ankles of the horses, and piled itself onto the lee sides of long, curving dunes. Some of the dunes, having been blown before the wind for a thousand years, had strayed beyond their birthplace, migrating off to the east to lap against the rock reef of a chain of low hills.

A blistering, hot day was worn completely away to cross the forlorn span of land. McKone led them to water at a weak spring at the base of a rocky mountain.

"How much more of this sand country?" Keesling questioned McKone.

"No more sand. Two days of riding through small, rocky mountains such as this one. Then two days of hills, If we can hold our pace, we should be seeing Mexican *ranchos* on the fifth day. That'd be about forty miles from Los Angeles. It'll be easy going from there on. The roads are well-used."

"Let's hope the horses hold up and don't get lame from all the rock or cactus spines," said Keesling. He waved his arm around at the yucca, agave, and saguaro cactus growing on all sides.

The tall, dry seed stalks of the agave, stabbing up twelve to fifteen feet against the blue sky, reminded Sam of the Indian war lances the Comanche had carried tied to their horses during the attack on his home. He shuddered at the thought that his father and mother might have been impaled by one of those spear weapons. He moved his eyes from the sharp tips of the agave and looked at the giant saguaros towering above all the mounted men like some misshapen and lost desert wanderers.

Sam felt lost himself, and lonely. Out of place in this distant, desolate land. He called out to Keesling in a suffering voice, "Turn me loose and let me go back to my home. I must find out if my parents are dead. And go search for my sister."

"Shut up," growled the gang leader. "You gave your word you would go with us as long as I wanted you to. Now if you want to take back your oath—well, talk to McKone about that.'' He kicked his mount forward through the cactus.

McKone looked at Sam. ''Do you want to talk to me?'' he asked in a deadly, challenging voice.

''I've nothing to say,'' said Sam. It would be worse than futile to ask McKone to release him. That man's temper was short—he might explode and shoot or knife him before Keesling could interfere. If the leader still cared whether or not Sam still should live.

CHAPTER 9

In the morning of the fifth day, the horsemen entered a land of gently rolling hills covered with hardy desert grass. They began to see cattle and small, scattered bands of sheep as the day wore long. In the late afternoon, they passed a fine large *rancho* perched on a rise above the trail. Three small boys playing in the shade of the adobe walls hailed a greeting to them and waved.

Raggan shouted out a return salute to the children. He turned to his comrades. "Looks like a real prosperous ranch. Maybe there *will* be a thousand mules for us to steal in California."

"More than that," said Keesling. "We're going to take two thousand so we'll have a thousand when we get back to Missouri."

"Damnation, do you think we're finally getting close to Los Angeles?" asked Zimmer, leaning forward in the saddle to look ahead.

McKone twisted to face the others. His normally sullen face almost smiled in his own anticipation. "Just over that hill and you can see Los Angeles, and the salt water."

They topped the rise and looked down. On their left some six miles distant, a great blue ocean spread its vastness before them—dominating the scene, shrinking all else to miniature landscapes.

The water was a broad, soft piece of velvet extending north, west, and south as far as the eye could see. A feathery ribbon of white beach hemmed a border to the earth's blue cover.

Sam sat wordless, roving his gaze to the far extremes of

the sea's wet horizon. Finally he turned to examine the land.
Brown hills sloped down to the ocean in long fingers. The
town of Los Angeles was but a splotch of a slightly different
shade of brown, back away from the shore along a small
river. Only one structure could be made out, a large structure
painted a brilliant white and capped with a bright red roof. A
wide belt of green fields and orchards ringed the town.

"California, we are here," said Zimmer. He threw back
his head and cried out loudly and joyously, "Yaahooo!
Yaahooo!"

In an instant the other outlaws joined in, bellowing full-
mouthed pleasure at the end of the long trail.

Sam found himself shouting with the thieves. He cut it off
short and clamped his jaws shut. He had not come to this place
to steal mules in hopes of getting rich. He was here because
he was a prisoner of thieving outlaws.

"Well, McKone, you led us straight to this town called
Los Angeles," said Keesling.

"I never get lost," responded McKone.

"What kind of town is it?" asked Keesling.

"A damn tough town. Los Angeles is as mean a place as
you'll find anywhere. They kill on the average of five men a
week. Have so many fistfights you can't count all of them."

"Sounds like my kind of a town," laughed Zimmer.

"Not much of a good town for Chinamen," said McKone.
"Last year one of them killed a white man and a gang of
town toughs marched down to Chinatown and killed nineteen
yellow faces. Some men wanted to shoot a hundred. They felt
that would be about equal to one white man. From what I
heard, the white man deserved to be killed."

"What size town is it?" asked Zimmer.

"Around six thousand people. Most of that is Mexican.
There's maybe five or six hundred Chinamen and about a
thousand whites. The Mexes and the Chinamen do all the
dirty work. Still, there's some Mexican *caballeros* that have
managed to hold on to their *ranchos* since the Americans took
the country from Mexico. They have money. But one of these
days the Americans will own all the land. The Americans run
everything of any importance now.

"There's about fifty saloons and cantinas, and ten whorehouses. Lots of women in the saloons, too. Women are from

all over the world. They are shipped in by the boatloads to San Francisco, a big town up north of here. Some of them are brought here. Many are downright pretty."

"Fellows, let's ride down and drink a barrel of beer and eat some stove-cooked food," said Keesling. "Then I'll rent a house somewhere on the outskirts of town for us to live in until the weather turns good next spring. Soon as we settle in, we'll go see just how pretty those women really are."

"Don't count me in on the house deal. I know a woman I aim to stay with," said McKone.

"She's probably got another man since last winter," said Keesling.

McKone put his hand on the handle of his skinning knife. "If she does, I'll slice him up good and plant him six feet under," he said.

"I will stay out here," said Two Foxes. "You can bring me some supplies and I'll go up into the hills." He had no desire at all to live with the white men in the white man's town.

"This is only November. It'll be four months or so until we start back with the mules," said Keesling. "That's a long time."

Two Foxes shrugged his shoulders. "That makes no difference. I can meet you here at times and we can talk."

"If you are seen by riders of some of the *ranchos*, you could be in a lot of trouble," warned Keesling. "They might think you are out stealing cattle or horses."

"They will not see me."

"Okay, take one of the packhorses and all the foodstuffs. I'll bring you some more supplies tomorrow after dark. Learn the country real good. We're going to have to rob a bank or something quick to get enough money to live the winter through. We may need a hideout if something goes wrong. You find one."

"I'll do that."

"The rest of us will clean up and buy some new clothes. Hell, no one will know but what we're honest folks."

Laughing, the thieves spurred down toward the town.

The beer was cool, the Mexican food hot. Sam and the five outlaws ate in the shade of a veranda outside the kitchen of a cantina on the public plaza of Los Angeles. It was evening, and to the west on the far rim of the world the sun was a squashed orange ball, floating on the ocean.

Heat radiated from the dusty street and walls of the adobe and stone buildings. It did not seem to bother the old Mexican man that slept beneath a cottonwood in the center of the plaza. Now and then he raised a hand in his sleep to brush away the flies that crawled about on his brown, leathery face.

The whitewashed church on the opposite side of the square from Sam began to sound solemn metal notes from its high belfry bell. The Mexican awoke, stretched himself, and looked around as if wondering what had roused him. His eyes fell upon the dirty, rough-looking *gringos* at the cantina. He quickly glanced away, for *gringos* meant only trouble to him.

Sam examined the town center as he ate. The huge Catholic church occupied one full side of the square. An old but well-maintained hotel with a sign that stated the building was the Lugo House was on the distant side of the plaza. Located on the other two flanks of the plaza were a large general store, a hardware, a second cantina, a saddlery and boot repair, and a few open stalls selling fresh fruits and vegetables.

A broad street named Spring ran off from the square in two directions. Numerous establishments for buying and selling lined the thoroughfare for several blocks in both directions.

A second very large three-story brick hotel with the name of Pico House covered half a block just off the plaza on Main Street. It appeared quite new and expensive. Sam's roving gaze examined the gaslights set atop head-high wooden columns spaced to light the hotel entrance and the boardwalk paralleling the street.

As Sam viewed the street and the few people going about on their private errands, the sun sank lower and long shadows slipped silently across the plaza. In the lessening heat of the day, more people came out-of-doors.

A spanking pair of matched black horses, stepping high and fancy, trotted up Main Street from the direction of the ocean to stop at the Pico House. The driver pulled to a halt and sprang down to fasten the team to a metal ring on one of a series of tie posts.

"There's money in this town," Keesling said and nodded

at the elegantly dressed American that hurried up to the entrance of the hotel.

"You're right," agreed McKone. "A cowboy can spend half a month's pay just staying in the Pico House one night and eating the fancy food."

Keesling chuckled and rubbed his dust-laden beard. "I just got me another good idea. I've thought of a way to get the owners of the mules we plan to steal to round them up for us."

"How's that?" asked McKone.

"I can't tell you now. We got to find some money for me to pull it off. Where's a bathhouse and a barber shop?"

"Two blocks down that way on Alvarez," answered McKone, and pointed. "You can also get your clothes washed at the same time. Me, I'm off to find that woman I had when I was here before. I'll look you men up in a week or so to see what the plans are." He stood up and went down onto the street.

Keesling slid his six-gun out and placed it on the table to point directly at Sam. He spoke in a hard voice. "Kid, what are we going to do with you now that we are in California? Maybe I should take you out to the edge of town after it gets dark and shoot you. Or let McKone do it. He would like that."

Sam stared steadily back at the outlaw leader. He managed to keep his face emotionless, but sweat beaded on the palms of his hands. Either Keesling or McKone was completely capable of doing exactly what he threatened.

Sam studied the other familiar visages. Zimmer watched him intently. The thoughts behind those mutilated features were impossible to know. Bartel gazed off across the plaza as if nothing of importance was happening.

Raggan grinned as Sam's attention rested on him. "You're a long way from home. You might as well make some money on the way back. Now that I've seen how the country lays, I think we have a fair chance of at least getting some mules to a place back East where we can sell them. You're so far from Santa Fe now that no one will ever find out what you do out here. Join up with us, Sam. Help us take the mules."

That same hazardous idea had been slowly foing in Sam's mind. Now with Raggan voicing the thought, it came wholly alive. Like an excited bee, it darted and careened about in Sam's head as he examined it from various angles. He would never give up his quest to find Sarah. However, there was not one person anywhere that would help him. He had neither gun nor horse. Not one thin dime. Worst of all, he could not speak the Mexican language. How could he travel and search without being able to talk to the people?

He was a stranger in this far land of California. Only Zimmer and Raggan had shown him any friendliness at all. It would not be so bad to ride with them and fight the same enemies—to help them steal mules from the big, rich *ranchos*.

But others of the gang were not friendly. Two Foxes and Bartel barely endured Sam. McKone would kill him at the first opportunity. Keesling thought and planned only one thing, to make this job succeed and end up with a large pocketful of money. Sam dared not do anything to hamper that effort.

Sam realized he could agree with Keesling's scheme. He would help drive the mules and get some of the money. In that way, he could buy all those things required to make the long ride into Mexico. He knew of no other way to do it. And maybe Zimmer, who spoke the Mex lingo, would teach Sam what he knew.

No shame for becoming a thief bothered Sam at all. His sister was worth two thousand mules no matter who they belonged to.

"I'm going to help you with those mules," said Sam in a quiet voice. He glanced at Zimmer and Raggan and then back to Keesling. "And I expect to get paid for doing it."

The gang leader's eyes raked the young man, probing to uncover the lie, the trick. "Do tell now. Who in hell said they wanted you to help?"

"You know I can ride good. I've proved I work hard, for I've done more work than any of you on the trip out here. I'm a fair shot, if you'd give me a gun to use."

"Why would you join up with us?" questioned Keesling.

"I've been thinking about this for days now. I've got to have money if I'm ever to find and get my sister free. You fellows can use another hand. I know you can. Probably even one or two more. I think Raggan is right and we can drive mules to Tucson. That's where I would leave you."

"He's turned out to be a right good hand, Keesling," said Raggan.

Zimmer spoke. "I wouldn't mind him coming along as part of the gang."

"How about you, Bartel? What do you think?" asked Keesling.

"I don't care one way or the other."

"All right, kid, you can ride with us and help take the mules to Tucson. For that work, I'll give you a horse and saddle, a pistol and rifle, and enough supplies for a long trip. If you work hard, I'll also pay you one hundred dollars."

"Five hundred dollars if we get five hundred mules there, or a thousand dollars if a thousand mules. And my name is Sam, not kid."

"You drive a hard bargain," said Keesling, and laughed. The smile disappeared. "If you make one move that looks strange to me, I'll shoot you quick."

"I'll earn my pay fair and square," responded Sam.

"You had better," rejoined Keesling.

"Somebody had better tell McKone," said Zimmer. "He's not going to like this. Especially the part about Sam getting a share of the money."

"I'll tell him the first time I see him," said Keesling.

The offshore wind blew at half a gale. It ricocheted off the top of the high cliff created by the cut of the storm waves, missed the beach, and struck the sea. The waves, pushing inexorably forward toward the land, were whipped and distorted by the stiff wind.

Sam lazed in the warm November sun at the sheltered base of the storm cliff. He had been there since midafternoon, resting on the sand with his hat over his eyes. The sound of the ocean fighting the thrust of the wind reached him. A seabird called a sharp yet pleasant cry. From under the brim of his hat, the Indian pony was visible, ambling along the beach, sniffing at the strange salt water, and now and then nibbling at some seaweed washed up on the sand from the ocean depths.

Two weeks had passed since his decision to join the outlaw gang. Time had dragged by slowly. The other band members spent the nights drinking and gambling, then slept the days away. All except Keesling. He had loafed around for a week and then, one morning early, had ridden off with his bedroll tied behind his saddle. Nothing had been heard from him since.

"He'll come back with a good scheme to get us all some money," Zimmer had said. " 'Bout time he showed up, for we're all almost flat broke."

The others had chimed in, complaining of their shortage of *dinero*.

Sam climbed to his feet. The mustang, seeing him stir, came up to nuzzle him.

"Time to stretch our legs, old fellow," Sam told the horse. He removed his boots and shirt and shoved them into a saddlebag.

Barefoot on the cool, damp sand, Sam sped along the narrow beach. Sometimes he splashed through the surf to his knees. He exulted in the pleasant sensation of the cool water on his skin and the movement of his young muscles. He lengthened his stride, increasing the speed.

The mustang tossed his head, nickered in friendly spirits, and galloped with Sam. It tore ahead, then slowed to pace beside him.

The wild wind poured down through breaks in the cliff to buffet man and horse. It caught the long red manes of both their hair, sending them dancing and flicking. Sam breathed deeply of the alien odors on the wind. He laughed in high enjoyment.

Ahead of him, great chunks of brown rock taller than a man had been undercut and collapsed down from the cliff to bar his passage. He slowed and began to wind his way through the barrier blocks. The horse trailed close behind.

Deep within the rocks, he came to the border of a small amphitheater, a flat, wave-eroded zone the size of a large room.

On the shadowy sand in the center of that natural stage, a nude woman danced.

The wind whistled a mellow tone through the jagged rocks. Sea waves clapped a cadence as they broke upon the beach. The water rippled a muted tune as it swirled across the sand and then retreated.

The woman danced to the primitive music created by the

movement and strike of wind and water. She sprang lightly into the air at the crash of the waves and glided in long, graceful steps to the hiss of the silver-frothed water on the grainy sand. And when the ocean was totally silent for a moment, she pantomimed the playing of a long flute in symphony with the wind's music. As she fingered the notes on her imaginary instrument, she pivoted slowly.

She spied Sam and froze there on her tiptoes for an instant. Then her stance changed swiftly. Muscles tensing, she was a rare, exquisite bird ready for flight at the first hint of danger from the intruder.

CHAPTER 10

The woman was small and delicate, yet her naked hips and breasts were womanly rounded. Her skin was light almond. She had blue-black hair and black, rather slanting eyes. A very beautiful face.

For a handful of seconds, with eyes startled wide and rimmed with alarm, she remained in her trance. Her focused sight swept over the young white man and knew he was as surprised as she.

She marveled at the shock of red hair and the big freckles like spots of rust upon his pale skin.

She snatched up maroon silk pants and blouse from the sand and slid into them. With quick, agile steps she sped up a path on the front of the cliff where the rocks had fallen and left a less steep ascent.

At the very top, she halted and cast a curious look backward. The wind caught the loose clothing and pressed it to the doll-like body of the woman. Her hair tossed and tumbled like rapids in a stream of midnight.

A trace of a smile curved her lips as she disappeared from sight behind the rim of the cliff.

Sam remained anchored in awe and wonderment. Had he really seen the lovely apparition? He had to rest his eyes on her again. He raced up the path so recently trod by the unknown woman.

A small buggy pulled by a long-legged trotter was drawing away in the direction of Los Angeles. A black cloth top was up and the driver could not be seen. The vehicle dropped out of sight in a low area and did not reappear.

Sam returned to the rock-enclosed cove. He stood where

the woman had danced in concert with the music of the ocean
shore. With eyes closed, he reran his memory of her performance, savoring the sight of her and the total joy of that
minute or two before she was aware of his presence. He
thought he could feel her essence on the wind trapped within
the rocks. Then it was whisked away and he was completely
alone.

Now he understood the elemental emotions that must have
stirred the Mexican teamsters when Sarah had danced for
them those days long past. A man must be very careful,
reasoned Sam, or he might make costly sacrifices or do
terrible deeds to possess a beautiful woman.

North beyond the rocks, Sam finished a long run. Then he
swam far out in the salty depths of the endless water of the
sea.

The Indian mustang waded after Sam, trailing out into deep
water until only his head extended above the waves. He could
not see the opposite side of this weird river and refused to go
beyond where he could touch bottom. Gladly he splashed to
the safe land when his brave master came stroking back.

In the evening dusk, Sam returned to the ramshackle adobe
house Keesling had rented on the east border of Los Angeles.
He came soundlessly into the flat-roofed structure and stood
in the dim light beside the entrance and let his senses roam
out to test for the presence of others.

The dry, musty smell of old mud and wood lay heavy in
the air. The ancient adobe walls were crumbling and thick
piles of dust were heaped at their base. The dirt floor was
hollowed into pathways two inches or more deep from the
passage of an uncounted number of feet through and between
the portals.

Black splotches of pitch stained the floor in scores of
places. The entire roof was sealed with the tar material.
Beneath the burning California sun, it had melted and dripped
through the pole-and-dirt roof. The bitumen was dug from a
broad pit on the edge of town. Sam had been told that now
and then the workmen found strange, never-before-seen animals trapped and preserved in the goo.

All the windows gaped open. Wooden shutters hung loose,
ready to be drawn shut when the need arose to bar the cold

wind or rain. Flies were ending their daylong search for food, settling with a last buzz of hairy wings to hang upside down from the ceiling joist.

The three-room house was empty. Sam found a chair and sat without sound. The gloom deepened around him.

From the lane leading up to the house came the crunch of gravel. A horse's step, judged Sam. He moved to the window facing that direction. The dark forms of several horsemen were stopped and looking at the house.

Sam slid out a side window and pressed closely to the wall, working his way to a front corner. If these unknown riders made a suspicious or hostile action, he would take off in the darkness and be gone to safety.

Safety. He thought of the meaning of that word. He had not yet committed a crime; still, he was wary and skulking in the dark to identify someone approaching. Did all outlaws live such lives of constant vigilance?

Leather squeaked as one of the men shifted weight. "Anybody here?" called a voice. "Sam, you around? This is Keesling."

"Yes, I'm here," answered Sam.

"Then come out closer where we can see you," directed Keesling.

Sam walked half the distance to the men.

"Kind of coyotey, ain't you?" asked Keesling.

"No more than you."

"Are you alone?"

"Yes."

"Go in and light the oil lamp and boil up some coffee. We got some planning to do. We'll put the feed bag on the horses and come in."

The riders touched their mounts with spurs and trotted past Sam.

He counted seven riders. Two were unknown to him. Two Foxes was not with them. Keesling must have made a circuit through town and picked up his gang. Where did the other pair come from?

Sam squatted down and built a blaze in the ashes of the fireplace. Picking up the coffeepot, he rose and turned in the direction of the water bucket. Two Foxes stood in the center of the room watching him.

In the weak, flickering light of the fireplace, the Indian's eyes were blank, black hollows beneath the heavy bone of his brow. Sam started to speak, but something in Two Foxes' expression said he wanted no talk. Sam walked past to dip water into the coffeepot.

The men stalked in with spurs jangling. Keesling was powdered with heavy dust and began to slap it off in a little brown fog. The two men men hung back near the door.

Keesling waved a hand at them. "Sam, that fellow on the right is Tanner. The other one is Kimbel. They're friends of McKone he met out here last time and he's vouched for them. They're going to join up with us."

The men nodded hello at the introduction. Sam nodded briefly in return. If they were friends of McKone, they might end up being his enemies. And they were tough-looking men. Tanner was broad-chested and thick-boned, with muscles bulging his shirt. He appeared immensely strong. Kimbel, younger by maybe ten years, was shifty-eyed and did not look directly at Sam. His face was pockmarked, like muddy ground trampled by horses.

"Draw up chairs and that bench to the table and let's talk," said Keesling.

He spread a crudely drawn map on the top of the table. "Here's Los Angeles by the ocean. Up here about a hundred miles to the northwest is a town named Cuyama. It was a little good-for-nothing Mexican town until some placer gold was discovered a couple of years ago. Since then the town has grown by three or four hundred people and there's a new bank. Tanner knows the town and says there should be ten to fifteen thousand dollars in it just before payday at the mines. I've scouted the town and been in the bank. On Friday, we're going to walk into it and take all the money. Here's the scheme. Everybody listen damn close."

The gang talked late into the night, plotting their strategy.

The five bandits sat their stolen horses in the wagon road and looked down at the cluster of houses in the center of the shallow valley.

"That's Cuyama," said Keesling. "Main street runs north-south beside a fair-sized live stream. The bank is midway along its length. Two smaller streets parallel the main drag for about a quarter mile. Several short streets cut across all three at right angles. Anyone got last questions about what they're supposed to do before we ride in?''

Bartel glanced at his partner, Raggan. Neither spoke. Zimmer was tracing a scar on his cheek with a fingertip.

"I hope the Indian is ready with the relay of fresh horses," grunted McKone. "I hear tell the sheriff of this town is one hard-riding son of a bitch."

"Two Foxes always does exactly what he says he will," responded Keesling. "He stole us eleven mighty good horses to ride on this little shindig as I asked him to." The outlaw leader's concern was aimed more at McKone and his two friends than at the Indian. The three were plotting something, Keesling felt certain. Well, he had a plan of his own to take care of that.

Sam's muscles were taut in anticipation of the impending danger. Possibly death awaited him down in the valley. His senses had never been more open to the world about him. He heard the slow wind in the old, dry grass beside the road, and it was whispering like a million insects hidden there. A little whirlwind twirled on the roadway, twisting up the ankle-deep dust in a vortex twenty feet tall.

Sam had never seen such lightweight dust. It seemed to have an energy all its own, wanting to sail up into the air and go for a ride on the wind.

A flock of crows fluttered up with a loud clamor from a pocket of brush below the road and drove to the south. One peeled off and landed, to hunker as immobile as a chunk of black lava rock, only its liquid obsidian eyes moving to avidly watch the men.

Sam wondered if the crow knew something the men did not. Would it be feeding on their dead flesh on the morrow?

"All right, if there's no questions, then let's rob the bank," said Keesling. "No shooting. McKone, do you hear me? No shooting!"

A tall plume of dust followed the band into town. The men pulled up at the hitch rail in front of the hardware store on the opposite side of the street from the bank.

Keesling and McKone stepped down and went left along the boardwalk. They hesitated at the center of the block, held a brief conversation, and, as if having decided something, crossed over and entered the two-story stone bank building. Bartel and Raggan had gone right and stopped to examine a saddle in the window of the hardware store. They turned and sauntered across the street to the bank, entering a half minute behind the first two.

Sam slouched against the front of the hardware as if merely waiting for his elders. Keesling had said no one would pay any attention to an unarmed man tending horses. Sam hoped it was so.

He slowly gazed up and down the main way. A man came out of the restaurant a block distant, mounted his horse, and left at a gallop, splashing dust. A young girl walked by. She smiled at Sam.

He tried to return the smile. But his jaws seemed rigid. He bobbed his head at her.

Twisting, he observed the bank. As he did so, a large white blind began to descend in one of the windows on the second floor.

In the center of the shade in bright red letters were the words BANK BEING ROBBED.

Sam's heart leaped and hammered against the cage of his chest. Someone in the bank had managed to signal an alarm. If the town had planned the signal, then they must also be organized to carry out a defense. The outlaw gang was in a trap.

Sam whirled to see if anyone besides himself had seen the awful warning sign. The street was empty. Someone moved behind the windows of the hardware store. A second later a man rushed out and with loud thumps sped along the wooden sidewalk. He disappeared into a stone building with a wooden shingle labeled SHERIFF'S OFFICE.

In a very short time, ten or fifteen guns would be aimed at the front entrance of the bank. If Sam went to warn his comrades, those weapons would be firing at him. However, there was another possibility. No one may yet suspect he was part of the robbery gang. He could mount his horse and quietly ride out of jeopardy.

He realized he could not do that—be a coward. He had agreed to join up with Keesling and his band until Tucson was reached. More than that, Zimmer and Raggan had befriended him at heavy danger to themselves. He could not abandon them. A diversion had to be attempted, or a cover created.

As Sam's mind raced to devise a plan, a man left the sheriff's office and trotted across the street. Little geysers of dust spouted up with each step. A short wind slipped by and grabbed the dust stirred up by the man, billowing it up in a gray-brown cloud.

As Sam watched the cloud coast by, his scurrying thoughts jelled into a strategy. Perhaps there was still a way to save his comrades. Swiftly he yanked the horses loose from the hitch rail and jumped astride.

Gripping the reins of the spare mounts, he wheeled them across the street. Then he turned and galloped them past the door of the bank. Dust boiled from under the pounding hooves. He reversed his course at the corner and rode back through the roiling dust.

Sam saw a man carrying a rifle run into an alley. A second scampered up a ladder to the roof of the hardware store.

Sam passed the front of the bank. The door was closed. Damn it! Why didn't Keesling and the others hurry? It may already to be too late to escape.

Two armed men sprinted up the side street toward Sam as he turned at the far corner to go back. He spurred to a run, spinning a denser fog of dust.

The dirt cloud covered half the street and reached to the top of the ground floor of the bank. Still the red words telling of a bank being robbed flashed their alert for all to see.

Again Sam changed directions and plowed into the swelling cloud. The surge of choking grit almost blinded him. Buildings were only the faintest of indistinct blurs left and right.

A gun crashed and Sam's hat jerked. Some defender had interpreted his plan and was trying to stop him. More shots cracked, slicing through the dirt pall to seek the body of the young outlaw.

A chunk of whizzing lead cut the brim of his hat almost entirely off, and it drooped to flop beside his face. Something hot creased his back. The top of one of his horse's ears disappeared in a bloody explosion of flesh and hair.

One of the trailing horses screamed as lead tore into it. It faltered, then with a great effort ran on for a few steps, trying to keep up with its mates. The brave beast stumbled and fell, wrenching the reins from Sam's hold. It was Zimmer's mount, and Sam let it go with dread. He gripped the remaining leads fiercely.

Sam swung closer to the buildings on the bank side of the street. Through the dense dust haze, he saw the door of the bank burst open and the outlaws stream out. Keesling carried a burlap sack clutched tightly in one hand.

A dozen shots slammed at the robbers as Sam yanked the horses to a halt almost on top of them. Bullets thudded into the wall of the bank, and glass broke and fell with a harsh rattle. Four of the bandits swarmed onto their steeds. Zimmer stabbed a look left and right for his horse.

"Zimmer, ride with me! Your horse is dead," cried Sam through the hammer of guns.

Lithe and quick as a panther, the little man sprang up behind the youth. He encircled Sam's waist with an arm and raked the horse savagely with both spurs. The heavily laden beast tore after the other riders, already lost from sight in the dirt fog.

The gang hurtled from the obscuring dust in a flat-out, dead streaking run. A cascade of shots rained about them. Bartel slumped forward on the neck of his mount.

Keesling veered right into the first cross street at a reckless speed. As McKone's horse turned sideways to the line of fire, a bullet ripped into its lungs. It fell as the corner was turned.

McKone kicked his feet loose from the stirrups and jumped clear of the falling body. He lit running.

A horse was tied to a hitch rail on the side of the street. McKone raced to it, wrenched the reins free, and jumped aboard.

The crash of musketry had stopped. Yet the men did not slow. They sped the length of an alley, charged over the brown stems of an old garden, and broke free of the buildings.

Once out of sight of the town, Keesling slowed the pace to a moderate run. He dropped back to examine each of his men and his mount to see if any were badly wounded and could not keep up.

Bartel was bleeding from the shoulder, but when he met the eyes of the chief, he shook his head that he was all right. None of the rest of the men gave any sign of being hurt. Zimmer and Sam were both lightweight men and the horse they rode was running strongly. It should be able to carry them the twenty miles to the first relay of mounts. Hopefully, ahead of any posse.

Keesling guided up close to Sam and Zimmer and called out above the rumble of hooves. "Spur and whip that horse and keep up."

"We'll be there when you all are," yelled back Zimmer.

Keesling struck his horse with his girth and it leaped into the lead.

Two Foxes sat on a high knob of a rock-strewn hill and watched to the west. Miles of brown desert with rolling hills stretched before him, fading into the heat and haze of great distance. Below him in a brush-choked gully, six haltered horses and one fully equipped with saddle and bridle waited tied to a picket rope.

The Kiowa had been at the lookout since noon. After watering the mustangs at a far spring, he had ridden two hours to reach this rendezvous point. The site had been carefully selected by Keesling and him. The chief, with his keen sense of direction, would have no difficulty in finding the spot again.

The sheriff with a posse would pursue the outlaw gang, the Indian had little doubt. They could be pressing close on Keesling's heels if he had had any bad luck. However, when the lawmen came fogging into this place, they would find their prey already gone on fast horses and the nearest water ten miles away. If they knew where to look for it.

Like a string of black fleas, horsemen streamed over a ridgetop a mile or so distant. Two Foxes climbed to his feet and, shading his eyes with a hand against the slanting afternoon sun, began to count. Four riders, and then, a quarter mile to the rear, a fifth. Without emotion, the Kiowa wondered who had been left behind.

The tiny, hurrying figures dropped down a steep grade and were lost in a gully between the hills. Two Foxes stayed at his station and checked the back trail of his cohorts. No other

CHAPTER 11

Clotted sweat foam flew from the straining neck and flanks of Sam's horse. Its breath was ragged and its gait rough and unstable. Zimmer's cruel spurs had forced the brute to the limit of endurance. Sam knew it was on the verge of collapse.

Keesling shouted and pointed ahead. With relief, Sam saw the remuda of horses and the Indian running to meet them.

The blown and lathered mustangs came to a willing halt. The men swung down. Two Foxes slowed and stopped nearby.

Zimmer walked close to Sam and turned to shout out to the other men. "Listen, you Kiowa horse thief and the rest of you bank-robbing fools, I want you all to know this young fellow saved our hides a little while ago. And mine even more so by sharing his horse with me.

"We come out of the bank and could have got gunned down. But there is Sam riding up and down the street, stirring up dust so thick no one can see us. While he is doing that, fifty to a hundred shots must have been aimed at him. Look how they ventilated his hat."

Zimmer jerked Sam's sombrero off and wiggled his fingers through three holes. He held it up so all could see.

Zimmer tossed the hat back to Sam and danced a light-footed jig around him, his scarred face twisted in a horrible caricature of a smile. He slapped Sam playfully on the shoulder. "There's holes all through his shirt, too. Yet he never got blood drawn on him once.

"The sheriff and his men shot and killed two of our horses, mine and McKone's. They shot the ear off Sam's. He's got a charmed life, I tell you. He's going to be good luck for this

105

gang. Ain't what I say the truth, fellows?'' The gunman cast a quick glance all the way around at the men.

Two Foxes looked from Zimmer to Sam. The Indian's foreboding that the white youth would bring him misfortune was stronger than ever. Somehow this Sam Tollin would do him great harm. Could it be prevented by killing him? It would be easy to do. He would seriously study that idea.

"I'm going to pay part of my debt now,'' said Zimmer. "You can have my new gun.'' From his waist, he began to unbuckle a second belt and holstered six-gun Sam had not noticed in all the excitement. "I took this from the banker. He must fancy himself a *pistolero*, for the sights have been filed off and the holster is cut down some for a quick draw.'' He handed all to Sam. "It's a fine gun, yet it's cheap payment for a man's life. A man I kinda like, by the way.''

Sam strapped the broad leather belt on. Slowly, savoring the feel of the iron in his hand, he slid the six-gun from the well-oiled holster and hefted it. He pointed the pistol at a rock up the bank from him.

"I think I'm going to like it. Thanks, Zimmer.''

"Hell, Sam, it's nothing for what you did.''

McKone disliked Zimmer's bragging of Sam's deed. To put a stop to it, he spoke to Keesling. "How much money did we get?''

"I would guess, without taking time to count it, about eight or nine thousand dollars. Not as much as we wanted, but enough to last if we stretch it,'' replied the outlaw chief. He tossed the bag of paper and gold money to the ground with a thump. "We'll divide it later. Swap your saddles to the fresh horses. Zimmer, appears you'll have to ride bareback.''

"That makes me no never mind to me,'' said Zimmer. "I've done it many miles before.''

Keesling said, "It'll be dark in an hour or so. By morning we want to be fifty miles ahead of any posse. Let's move it.''

While the other gang members changed gear to the rested horses and had a drink of water, Two Foxes herded the jaded mounts off up the valley. He scattered them in deep brush so they would not be easily found by the sheriff.

The sun was a sullen red orb low in the sky as the men thundered up out of the valley. The Kiowa led, holding a straight course south up and down over an endless expanse of hills.

A thick blanket of darkness settled upon the riders. The horses slackened the pace to a walk. The men trailed in line, following the hoof falls and creak of leather of the shadowy horsemen before them.

A bright, white crescent of a moon sailed up over the highland in the far east. It added its light to the sky glow of the stars. The contours of the terrain became more illuminated. Two Foxes increased his speed.

When the moon reached the peak of the black sky, the band stopped in a small cove near the crown of a hill.

"Two Foxes, keep lookout," said Keesling. "We will rest for three hours. Wake us then, or earlier if something goes wrong. Keep the horses close to hand."

"All right," replied the Indian.

Keesling believed they were moderately safe. It was very doubtful the posse could trail them through the blackness. However, he was relieved when the gang was awake again and up and traveling at a good clip.

Late in the night, the wind switched around to the northwest and a cloud reached for the nimbus of the moon. Two Foxes guessed rain would be falling by morning. Still, the weather of this new land was unknown to him. The clouds might burn away with the coming of the sun.

A weak dawn arrived and with it a fine rain began to fall. The men dug out their slickers and tugged them on.

The morning grew brighter and large heavy clouds of mist could be seen drifting down the swales among the hills. An hour later, when Tanner and Kimbel rode out of one of the fog banks and helloed a greeting, it was raining hard.

The two men piloted the course back into the ground cloud and to the temporary camp. Stiff and weary, the men dismounted. They did not talk, silently accepting the food Kimbel dished out for them. They ate, sitting humped up in their raincoats on the ground.

Finally, Keesling spoke to Tanner. "Have you seen anyone?"

"Not one living soul since we got here two days ago. Now with the fog and rain we couldn't see a man if he was within a hundred feet."

"Switch your outfits, everybody, and let's put another

sixty miles between us and that ornery sheriff from Cuyama,"
said Keesling.

The outlaws had saved their own mounts for the final leg
of the escape. The Indian pony nickered a friendly welcome
as Sam slung the saddle that Two Foxes had stolen with the
horses, and Keesling had given the youth to use, into place
and cinched it tight. Sam felt more secure now. With the
familiar and trusted mustang between his legs, no one could
catch him. He guided into last position in the line of riders.

They rode in the falling rain. The hills became higher and
the valleys deeper. The soil turned to slick mud and the
horses struggled to climb the high crests. Sam judged forty
miles would make a long day's ride.

Keesling dragged rein suddenly. Many phantom forms
ghosted off swiftly in the downpour ahead. "What in the hell
was that? A herd of horses?" he asked Two Foxes, who was
near him.

"I think many horses, maybe mules," answered Two Foxes.

"Let's take a better look," said Keesling. He kicked his
mount into a trot in the direction the animals had taken.

A herd of large beasts took shape in the wet haze. They had
come up against the abrupt flank of a hill and halted. They
stood dripping water from their hairy bodies and alertly watched
the men.

"Mules all right," said Keesling. "Plenty big bunch of
them. About two hundred, I would guess."

Raggan pushed to the front. " 'Bout the best mules I've
ever seen," he volunteered. "McKone, do you think this
might be some of those gray mules that Mexican rancher is so
famous for?"

"Could be. He's got some range up this way someplace."

Two Foxes began to uncoil his lariat. "One of our packhorses
fell and broke a leg and I had to kill it. I'll rope one of these
mules and take it along. I can train it to pack this winter
before we are ready to go east."

Keesling studied the ground. The rain struck, with a drumming sound, pounding at the oily mud and running off in
watery rivulets. The upthrown rim of a hoofprint melted away
as he observed it.

"Why don't we just take all of them? A couple of hours of

hard rain like this and our tracks will be beat flat. No one could ever figure out which way the mules went.''

McKone spoke. ''Could be next spring before anyone bothers to check on these mules. The Mexicans just let their animals run free. They take care of themselves during the winter the best they can. Some of them are wilder than wild mustangs.''

Zimmer chimed in. ''This herd would be a fine start toward the number of mules we want.''

''We need a good hiding place,'' said Keesling.

''I think I know where one is,'' said Two Foxes. He pointed southeast. ''Thirty miles or so in that direction there is a valley we could pen them in. Enough grass feed for three or four months and a fair-sized spring. The valley narrows down at the bottom and a short fence could block it off. From time to time, I could look in on them to see how they were doing.''

''Then let's do it,'' said Keesling. ''These mules could be worth maybe up to forty thousand dollars in Missouri. Two Foxes, you guide the direction. The rest of you fan out behind and we'll move them lively. Watch close now and don't lose any in the fog. And don't get lost yourself.''

The men and animals disappeared into the soft, white protective bosom of the rain and rolling fog.

The rain had ceased, the sun had melted the fog, and a high blue sky arched above the laboring men.

The hundred yards of brush-and-stone fence rose to chest height beneath the hands of the outlaw band. It extended from one steep wall of the valley to the opposite side. The task had been moderately easy with the abundant materials, rocks lying about and brush cut on the bottom of the valley.

Keesling backed off a score of paces and surveyed the length of the barrier. ''That's tall enough. It's finished. Two Foxes, are there other places the mules can climb out?''

''There's some steep deer trails up at the other end of the valley. If the mules really wanted to get out, they could. But a few rocks in each will close them. I can do that by myself.''

''Good. I don't think the sheriff and his posse will ever be able to trail us to here. But I've seen some peculiar things happen and I don't want to stick around here much longer.''

"Tanner, and you, Kimbel, go rope one of the mules. Pick a strong one for a pack animal. Two Foxes, let's go over there and talk. There's something special I want you to do while all the rest of us are back in town.''

The mule's ears were laid back flat against his neck and his eyes rolled, showing white. He was fastened between Tanner and Kimbel, each man with a choking noose around the muscular gray neck and the ropes made fast to the pommels of their saddles.

"That's one smart mule," exclaimed Tanner as he led the captured brute through the rocks and up close to the men. "You should have seen him. Once he figured out we were after him, he always kept a bunch of other mules between him and us. But Kimbel there made a lucky throw. That was one surprised mule when that rope sailed over the backs of the others and caught him by the head.''

Kimbel grinned broadly. "That lasso was stretched out so long the loop wasn't much wider than a dinner plate when it settled down over him.''

"Damn big animal," observed Zimmer. "Sam, he'll weigh two hundred pounds more than your mustang does.''

"More like three hundred," said Raggan. "He'll sure be able to pack a mighty load. That is, if Two Foxes can gentle him down enough.''

During the conversation, Kimbel's mount had moved toward the mule to ease the tiring pull of the attached rope. Not liking the mule, the horse turned his front quarters slightly away.

The mule, frantic for any means of escape, sensed the growing slackness on the line that held him. With a powerful surge, he stormed ahead. His thousand pounds of muscle and bone hit the end of the rope and jerked it taut with a snap.

Kimbel's mount went down sideways with a slam upon the ground. The man rolled one time and sprang to his feet. The rope unraveled from around the horn in an instant.

Tanner's lasso held. The frenzied mule, hitting the end of the rope, was pivoted around to face the mounted man.

The gray beast lifted his head, curled back his lips, and

screamed. With head and neck outstretched, he charged the hated man that barred him from freedom.

The savage teeth snapped shut like rocks hitting, missing a full bite of the shoulder but bruising the flesh and ripping off half the shirt. Immediately the dangerous mouth grabbed for the man again.

Tanner dodged to the far side of his mount, and the mule failed to catch him. The man slid from the saddle, his hand plunging into the saddlebag as it passed to snake out a long bullwhip.

The berserk mule whirled to come around the horse after the man. Tanner expertly shook the whip out behind and then lashed it forward. A piece of the mule's lip the size of a man's thumb flew into the air.

The mule squealed at the pain but continued to advance.

Tanner swung viciously. The metal tip, traveling unimaginably fast, reached out a second time to tear out a chunk of the animal's mouth.

The man suddenly seemed to explode with a wild ferocity, hitting again and again. Segments of the head, chest, and ears vanished as if by magic. Blood gushed from every wound.

The animal retreated, rearing and striking out at the horrible thing that cut and hurt so. He tripped on a rock and fell upon his spine.

Desperately he tried to scramble back to his feet, and his legs thrashed the air. But a score of valiant attempts failed, for he was wedged between two boulders.

Tanner glided forward like a lion to the kill. The bullwhip walked a line of wounds down one side of the chest and belly of the mule. Then along the opposite side.

The mule squealed at the excruciating pain. Tanner shrieked his own crazed anger in unison with the animal's cry, and his powerful arm rose and fell.

Sam was furious at the man's cruelty. He did not know he was moving until he stood between Tanner and the trapped animal. He knew only that the senseless beating of the poor, dumb brute must cease.

"Stop! Stop! You're going to kill it," yelled Sam.

Tanner's hate-filled eyes did not leave the mule. He struck past Sam to injure the animal again.

"Tanner, stop, I say," shouted Sam at the top of his voice.

Only the zip of the metal end of the bullwhip past his ear to strike the mule answered.

Sam grabbed his six-gun from its holster and pointed it at Tanner. "Damn it, stop!"

Tanner's fixed attention on the mule did not seem to vary. Yet, the iron tip of the whip hit Sam's gun hand like a hammer blow. The pistol flew from his clutch. And a pain like he had never experience before, a red-hot coal pressed to him, seared the back of his hand.

"You son of a bitch! Pull a gun on me! Why, I'll kill you. I'll whip you to death and then finish off that goddamn mule.

"First, I'll match up that cut in your other ear." A sliver of Sam's ear vanished. "Now goes the end of that nose you've stuck in my business."

Sam leaped back at the warning. He was almost too slow. The metal tip grazed the point of his nose, drawing blood.

Tanner jumped forward, swung to wrap the supple leather whip about the youth's legs, and jerked his feet from under him. "I'll kill you right there before you can get up."

"Tanner!" shouted Zimmer. "You hit Sam once more and I'll shoot you."

Tanner's arm moved and the end of the long bullwhip flicked behind him to lie on the ground, a great snake ready to strike death.

"You'll never see it hit him," warned Zimmer. "I promise you that. Both your eyes will be gone quicker than that." He glided in sideways, facing Tanner, to stand beside Sam.

"He drew on me, Zimmer," Tanner retorted sharply. "You know when someone does that, you got the right to kill him."

"He's a kid. He was only trying to get you to stop whipping the mule. He wouldn't have shot you. It was a bluff."

Kimbel moved up to stand beside his partner. He let his hand hang near his tied-down six-gun.

"Didn't look like he was bluffing to me," said Tanner. "Now like I said, I got the right to do whatever I want with him."

"If it was anybody else in the whole damn world, I'd agree with you. But not Sam. You've paid him aplenty for what he did. Now let him go."

Sam climbed to his feet. Zimmer was trying to save him,

after he had played the stupid fool. His friend might die in his place. Or both of them could be dead in a few seconds.

McKone watched the confrontation between the men. Tanner would never back down, of that he was sure. Kimbel would support whatever Tanner called. Still, it was doubtful the two of them could kill Zimmer. One more gun could do it. McKone slipped forward to stand on Tanner's right, some twenty feet away, and on Zimmer's left. The safest place in the shoot-out that would soon start.

"McKone, are you taking a hand in this little game?" asked Zimmer in a steely voice.

"Tanner is right. He can do what he wants with the boy," said McKone. His implacable hate for Sam and Zimmer boiled in his blood. In his mind, McKone smiled. "You've been running roughshod over me for a long time, Zimmer. Now it ends."

Tanner dropped the handle of the bullwhip and prepared to yank his six-gun.

"I still say you ain't going to beat him anymore," said Zimmer. He calculated the odds and laid his plans. Tanner would have to be disposed of first. He had watched the man move and judged him very quick with his hands.

In more than one fight, Zimmer had observed McKone draw and shoot. He was fast. He would be the second target. Kimbel last.

Could he kill all three of them? Zimmer realized he could very likely be the one to die today. At the irony of dying for a boy he had known for only a few short weeks, his maimed face tried to shape itself into a smile.

Sam looked at his friend, at the twisted, grotesque features. God, he was an ugly bastard. But a brave ugly bastard.

CHAPTER 12

Keesling dragged his six-gun from its holster and fired into the air. He shouted out at the top of his lungs.

"Hear me, you dumb fools. All of you listen hard. I'm going to drive a herd of mules worth a fortune to Missouri. Now, I need every man I've got to get them there. I can't do it with less. I'm going to be downright mad if I lose that fortune because of a fight that should not happen."

The outlaw leader stabbed his gun at the sky and shot a second round to emphasize his words. "Any man still alive after the shoot-out, I'm going to kill him myself. I don't care who it is, he's going to be dead."

A total silence held. The mule groaned, the sound slicing through the quiet with startling loudness. Sam remained completely motionless, afraid any movement might precipitate the battle.

"I'm out of it," spoke McKone hoarsely, his nerve breaking. If Zimmer did not kill him, Keesling would. There was no way to win. He hastily walked away.

"Tanner, McKone appears to be smarter than you," said Keesling. "Call it quits while you are still alive."

The big head of Tanner was thrust forward at Zimmer. His ox eyes were red with his fury at Zimmer for interfering.

'Kimbel spoke sideways at Tanner. "Later, damn it. We'll get them later."

Tanner's chest arched with a deep breath, then quivered as he exhaled. He whirled abruptly away. He yanked himself astride his mount and spurred down the valley bottom. Kimbel picked up the bullwhip, found his horse, and followed at a slower pace.

Sam stooped and retrieved his six-gun. Zimmer spun and glared at him.

"You damn-fool idiot," he cursed Sam. "I should've let him cut you up an inch at a time."

Sam started to speak. Zimmer interrupted. "Shut your mouth. I don't want to hear anything from you."

He stomped off. Sam heard his mumbled last words. "All for a damn worthless mule."

"That little trick cancels out anything I might have owed you for your help at the bank," said Keesling. "If you danger my plan again, well, that'll be the end for you."

Sam felt beaten. He was a clown with a pistol trying to play games with killers. Zimmer had called him—correctly—a fool. It had been a hard lesson.

Behind him the mule made a noise as it struggled to free itself but could not because of the entrapping boulders. Sam turned. He might as well finish what he had begun—save the mule.

He rode the Indian mustang near the mule and dropped the loop of his lasso over the two rear legs. On the horse's second heave, the mule slid clear of the constraining rocks.

The flayed, half-skinned animal required several minutes to climb to his feet. His black eyes rolled with the pain of a million exposed nerve endings. Through its torment, it saw the human coming close. The mule bared its teeth in warning.

Since you can stand, you may live, thought Sam. Too bad you don't know where the water hole is. You must find that soon or all this has been for nothing.

"I'll go find another mule for a pack animal," said Two Foxes.

"All right," agreed Keesling. "The rest of us will ride to Los Angeles."

"Give me my share of the money now," said Two Foxes.

"We might as well split it all up," answered Keesling. He took the sack from his horse, untied the end, and, squatting, began to count it into piles on the ground.

Sam walked to where the men clustered and watched the division of the paper and gold. He noted there were enough lots to mean he was to receive a portion.

"There it is," said Keesling, shaking the last coin out of the bag into his hand. "Two shares to me. One for all the rest

of you except Sam, Tanner, and Kimbel. A half share for
each of them. I'll carry Tanner's and Kimbel's to them."

The Kiowa scooped up his cut. "I'll come to town in a
month or so and tell you how things are going out here."

"Good. See you then. Let's ride, men."

"Okay if I stay out here two or three days?" asked Sam.

"What in the hell for?" questioned Keesling. "It's damn
possible the posse will find this place."

"The mule needs to get to the water hole Two Foxes
mentioned that's up the valley. I'll hide out in the brush so
the sheriff can't find me even if he makes it this far. When
the mule gets to where he can walk, I'll drive him to water
and then come to town."

"He's bad hurt. Best to put him out of his misery."

"No, I believe he will heal up."

"If you get caught with him, you'll get hung for stealing.
That's for sure. But do what you want. We're leaving."

The men rode through the gap left in the fence, walled it
up behind them with rock, and left.

The injured animal stood spraddle-legged with weakness.
His muzzle drooped until it touched the ground. He had no
strength to be driven this day. Sam mounted his horse and,
riding in rocky areas to leave no sign of his passage, made his
way to a dense thicket high on a hillside.

He dismounted and dragged his horse into the center of the
brush. He found a seat and, staring off across the valley,
watched the remainder of the day slowly spend itself. His ear
stopped bleeding but throbbed with pain until late in the night
when he finally sank into sleep.

In the early morning, Sam went down into the valley.
The half mile he could see lay empty. He saw tracks of the
mules, showing they had worked their way up the bottom,
feeding as they went.

He found the injured mule flat on the ground, its long neck
outstretched. It arose stiff and lame at the sound of the man's
approach. Most of the wounds had scabbed over, but a
number still leaked a little blood and pale lymph fluid.

Under the man's prodding, the mule limped a mile before
its strength gave completely out and it stood unable to move.
Sam continued on past it to find the spring.

He returned with two canteens full of water. He poured the contents of one into his hat and walked slowly forward, holding it out. Through pain-glazed eyes, the mule watched the man. The animal pulled its lips back and showed his teeth like a wolf.

Above the odor of the man and his salty sweat on the hat, the mule smelled water. The curl on his lip faded and his parched mouth reached out. He thirstily sucked up the delicious liquid.

Sam gave the mule the water from the second canteen. He fetched two more in the afternoon. These were also greedily consumed. Later, with the shadows long and lengthening to dusk, Sam hazed the mule the last mile to the spring.

The following morning when Sam came down cautiously from his hideout, the mule was gingerly nibbling with its sore mouth at the tender grass growing in the wet marsh below the spring. The gray beast surveyed the man minutely. Then, as if satisfied with his identity, it put its head back down and continued eating.

Sometime near noon the herd of mules filed in, drank, and then drifted out over the lower slopes to graze.

A gnawing sense of alarm surfaced in Sam's mind in the last part of the day. He could not shake the sensation that someone was watching him. The posse could have trailed them here, or Two Foxes could be hidden on a lookout staring down. He casually moved to his mustang and began to brush its hairy coat with a twist of coarse grass. As he worked, he scrutinized the ridge lines from under the brim of his hat. One sign of a posse and he would swing astride and ride for his life.

Nothing moved to give alarm. Darkness settled down. He mounted and climbed the slope on the opposite side of the valley from that he had camped on the night before. He went to sleep with his pistol near his hand.

In the small hours of the morning, Sam came awake abruptly with his nerves jangling. There had been a noise. His ears reached out to check for something that should not be there. His eyes searched for a silhouette against the stars, and he sniffed soundlessly for odors on the slow wind.

The only noise was from the leaves and limbs of the nearby brush rustling under the fingers of the wind. Overhead the thin moon, like a curved silver sail, seemed to be shoving one small cloud across the dark sky.

Something breathed close by. Sam rolled his eyes upward to see above his head. A dark form was outlined on the night sky.

Sam grabbed his pistol and rolled left. Even before he stopped moving, the weapon jumped up to aim at the intruder.

A loud snort erupted and a large animal flinched back, half spinning away.

"You damn mule!" burst out Sam, recognizing the bulk of the brute. He lowered his voice. "What in the dickens are you doing way up here?"

The mule drew close at the gentle tones. Man and beast evaluated each other through the night gloom. Sam stuck out his hand. The mule came still closer.

However, when Sam tried to touch the animal, it backed away, staying just out of reach. Sam stopped his advance and let his hand fall. The mule came forward timidly, one short step at a time. It held its ground as the man lightly stroked the muscular body, the head, the neck, and along the withers. Often Sam's fingers encountered the hard scabs of the wounds made by the metal end of the bullwhip. The mule relaxed; the tautness of his muscles dwindled.

The mustang came in from the darkness. He nudged the man, vying for attention. With a chuckle, Sam obliged the smaller animal by petting the coarse velvet of his neck.

Sam stayed two more days. He lolled about for long, lazy hours on the high shoulders of the hills. The horse and mule hung close around, wandering off to go to the water and then returning to graze in the vicinity of the man. For the first time in many weeks, Sam felt some sense of freedom and ease. If only Sarah was with him so he would know she was safe.

Sam arrived back in Los Angeles at the outlaws' house one week following the bank robbery at Cuyama. The mule was healing thoroughly and quickly, and so was Sam, as young healthy animals are wont to do.

The young man resumed his routine, unobtrusively going about his own business, cooking his own meals, and rarely going downtown. McKone had no association with the gang as far as Sam knew. With money in their pockets, the other members spent more time in the saloons and gambling halls. Raggan informed Sam that Zimmer had had a gunfight and shot his adversary up very badly. Something about little, ugly men did not make good lovers.

Keesling bought expensive business suits, had his long, rough beard trimmed neatly, and moved into the elegant Pico House. Now and then Sam saw the gang leader riding on horseback or in a buggy with prosperous-appearing ranchers. Keesling gave no indication during these encounters that he was acquainted with Sam.

Zimmer did not go to town one evening. He rested on a bench reared back against the outside wall of the house and gazed in the direction of the ocean. He rarely spoke to Sam and this day was no different.

Sam fed the horses hay and a ration of grain in the small corral behind the house. When he came around to the front and saw Zimmer sitting there, he took a seat beside him.

"Zimmer, if you're not still mad at me, how about teaching me how to draw a six-gun fast?"

"Why?" asked Zimmer without turning his eyes from the distant blue sea.

"I'm going to go into Mexico and look for my sister just as soon as we reach Tucson. I got to be good with a gun if I'm going to be able to take her from whoever has her."

"Sam, you'll never find her. Mexico is a big place and the people there won't tell a *gringo* anything. Give it up. Take your share of the mule money, whatever that turns out to be, and start a straight and proper life someplace."

"No. I'm never going to do that until I make a long, hard try for Sarah. Please teach me how to handle a gun good. My father taught me quite a bit about how to aim and shoot, but not how to draw quick. He said I should be older for that."

"You're sure that's what you want?"

"Yes."

Zimmer stood up. "Well, let's see if you have the makings of a gunhand. Probably not. You're going to be a fairly large man. Already you're a half head taller than me, and growing fast. I imagine you're slow and awkward. Howsoever, now and then, a big man is also quick. Stand up and face me. I want to try something.

"Come closer so I can touch you. That's about right. Now give me your pistol."

Zimmer unloaded the weapon and handed it back. "Put it in your holster, loose yet snug."

He extended his right index finger and pressed it to Sam's chest. "Put your hand on the butt and get ready to draw. When you feel me take my finger away, draw as fast as you can and point it straight at the center of me. Don't waste time trying to cock it for now. Look me in the eye. That's right. Get set."

Zimmer's finger released its pressure. Sam snatched at his six-gun.

A hard object jammed Sam in the stomach. He looked down to see Zimmer's loaded gun, the hammer eared all the way back, buried in the front of his shirt. He gaped in shocked surprise.

"I don't believe it. You moved your hand down, pulled the pistol, and brought it back up before I could hardly think."

"You are very, very slow."

"Let's try it again. I know what it is all about now."

"All right. Get set."

The result was little different. Sam barely had his pistol half out of its holster before he felt the barrel of Zimmer's six-gun in his belly.

"Forget about being a fast gun. You don't have it."

"Maybe now. At least show me how it is done correctly."

"The movement is simple. I'll do it extra slow. First catch hold of the butt. Wrap your smaller fingers around it. Start lifting it up. Your finger goes in through the trigger guard. Your thumb begins to cock the hammer while the gun is in about this position. Here the gun is level, just forward, and above the holster—finger on the trigger and gun fully cocked.

"You can shoot from this position, but accuracy will be poor. So shove the gun out toward the target. Aim it better as it moves. Fire here, while there's still a little bend in the elbow. Now you try to do it exactly the same way. Do it slow. Speed will come much later, if ever."

Two hours later and with the dusk shrouding the house, Zimmer finally nodded. "That's getting close to the right way to draw a gun."

"What do I do next?"

"Practice every day for about ten years. Draw the gun while on horseback, sitting down, falling left or right. In the dark, bright sunlight, in the rain. There's no end to practice. But you should give up the idea to be a fast draw. Learn to shoot good by aiming—that's really all an honest man needs."

Zimmer saw the determined cast to the young countenance. Well, let him make his own mistakes. "Ammunition will cost you hundreds of dollars. Even if you get damn good, still somebody will kill you one day."

"I'm going to learn, Zimmer. I've got to. Please understand and help me."

"Only you can develop the skill to be truly fast. Practice your draw ten thousand times, a hundred thousand, a million times. Until calluses grow thick, the gun is a feather in your hand, and the barrel seems to find the target like a magnet to iron."

"I will learn—you'll see."

Zimmer handed the six cartridges back to Sam. He was brave enough to be a fighter. But there was grave doubt his hand would ever be quick. "When you can draw and shoot birds out of the air, then let's talk again. There are many tricks you must know to be a gunfighter."

In the first hour of daylight of the following morning, Zimmer heard Sam ride away. The hoof falls grew faint in the direction of town. The young man did not return that day or the next. Weeks wore away one after another. Zimmer became convinced Sam Tollin had left Los Angeles and would not return.

In the third week of December, cold rain came hurrying in from the sea on blustery winds. The crooked streets turned to mud. The townsfolk retreated into their homes. Shutters and doors were dragged shut to bar the onslaught of the storm. Smoke began to pour from short stone-and-mud chimneys.

The wood peddlers, calling out their selling spiels in loud voices, towed jackasses burdened with tall mounds of wood through the drenched streets. They sold the first loads and went to their woodyards for more. All of that sold out within hours. They smiled, wrapped heavy sheepskin coats snugly about themselves, and struck out for the hills. The winter had been late in coming and now it was time for making *mucho dinero*. Better yet, cold people did not haggle to drive down the price.

From his camp in the high Verdugo Mountains, Sam had seen the building storm at first sunup. He judged it would be a strong, wet one from its appearance. Packing his meager belongings, he struck out for town hoping to beat the rain. He failed in that.

Sam encountered the little army of men and burros when he crossed the forested San Rafael Hills north of Los Angeles. He passed among the woodcutters, busily swinging short-handled axes and often shouting out in the rain for their pack beasts to come forward so the next bundle of wood could be tied upon their bony backs.

Circling around the edge of town, Sam came up through the dripping brush and grass to the house of the outlaws. He dismounted from the bay mustang to slip up and peer between the shutters of one of the windows.

Zimmer sat on the wooden bench behind the table, his back to the wall. Raggan and Bartel rested on straight-backed chairs facing him across the table. They were playing cards. A fire burned in the fireplace. No one else was in sight.

Sam stabled his horse in the flat-roofed shed near the corral and tossed it an armful of hay. He went to the door and shoved it open.

Zimmer sprang away from the table, a six-gun appearing in his hand. A fraction of a second slower, Bartel and Raggan scrambled erect, upsetting their chairs.

"Damn, don't ever come in on us that way again," said Zimmer in a tight voice. With a scowl, he holstered his pistol.

Sam kicked the door shut and leaned his rifle against the wall. The damp odor of adobe and stale smoke hung in the confined air of the house. Water leaked through the asphalt pitch roof in several places, landing with little plopping sounds in puddles of mud on the floor. Somehow it felt good to be back. It was because of the men, Sam knew.

"Did you pull another job or are you still worried about the bank?" he asked.

Zimmer disregarded the question. Sam had lost weight. His clothes hung on him like on a scarecrow. His eyes were bright, as if a fever burned within him. He moved differently from before, more alertly, as if coiled for immediate action.

The gunman said, "We'd gave you up. Thought you had gone back to New Mexico or someplace."

"Nothing like that," said Sam. "Is that grub there?" he asked, stepping near the fireplace to lift the lid from the iron pot swung out from the hot coals. He was ravenous for food, his stomach gaunt.

"Good stew, Sam," said Raggan. "Fresh bread in that pan, but cold by now."

Raggan had also observed the change in Sam. The boy had metamorphosed into a man. The change had begun that day in Cuyama. Now somehow, for some as yet unknown reason, the conversion had been made whole. The tied-down six-gun seemed perfectly proper on the lean hip.

Sam removed his hat, slung part of the water from the drooping, soaked object, and flopped it on the bench where it could dry flat-brimmed. He filled a plate almost to overflowing with chunks of meat, vegetables, and broth and draped a huge slice of bread on top. At the table, seated beside Zimmer, he began to eat.

The food was devoured with high relish. Sam sopped the plate clean and, chewing the last bite, smiled at Raggan. "Great-tasting vittles."

"There's more," said Raggan, pleased.

"That'll do for now."

"Where've you been for the past six weeks?" queried Zimmer.

"Seeing if I could make a six-gun fit my hand."

"Does it?" Zimmer looked intently into the slate blue eyes of the young man.

CHAPTER 13

Sam examined the scarred face of his friend. "It fits, Zimmer." He laid his right hand out on the table and turned it palm up. Heavy calluses rimmed the palm. A thick pad of callus covered the thumb.

"Appears you have been doing some practice," observed Zimmer.

"Just like you told me to. From daylight to dark for forty days."

"If you did all that, that's more than most men do in a lifetime."

"Well, tell us about it," said Raggan, leaning forward with elbows on the tabletop.

For a full minute Sam considered the request. How could he describe all that had happened? Of arising at daybreak and drawing his pistol uncounted thousands of times until his hand cramped and he beat it upon his thigh to loosen the locked muscles. Then starting afresh, pulling the weapon, and the tendons and joints stiffening to rigid claws.

"I bought a new rifle and some ammunition for it, figuring a man needs to be good with it regardless of how accurate he becomes with a handgun. Then I bought fifteen hundred cartridges for the pistol." He centered his gaze on Zimmer. "The mustang you loaned me was so loaded down he could barely walk. I needed a packhorse.

"I rode way up in the Verdugo Mountains about twenty-five miles or better where I wouldn't be bothered. Found a deep, narrow valley where my shooting would not be heard far. Never saw one living soul until I was on my way back to Los Angeles.

124

"You told me how to practice the draw. I did it exactly that way. Hardly shot the handgun at all to start with, just enough to see now and then how close the barrel was to being on the target from pointing by instinct without aiming. For a long time the gun was clumsy in my hand, and the shot was off sometimes as much as a foot at thirty-five paces. I seemed to reach a point where I could not get better."

Sam became silent and the men saw him look backward in his mind to replay old events. At one point his eyes shone as if a tear was half born.

A month had elapsed. The new day was breaking over the far-distant horizon. Sam had finished the previous day with the same level of skill that had existed for more than a week. He felt frustrated, defeated. His draw was moderately quick but far from sufficient to defeat a fast opponent in a gun battle. He waited in the cold morning hours for daylight to arrive and long hours of practice to begin anew.

In the brush at the top of the hill, two brown wrens stirred as light brightened the darkness of night. They rose from a squatting position on their roost. Thin legs straightened, and strong tendons relaxed to unclamp clutching claws from twigs that had held the three-ounce bodies safely all night. Fine feathered wings stretched and sharp eyes examined the set of each feather.

The minute cock cast a flicker of a one-eyed glance at the hen and launched himself from his perch. She was instantly at his side, then ahead of him, pressing down on the cool buoyant air to stay aloft. The first drink of morning was only seconds away.

The birds flew directly at Sam, standing by the spring. The brown wings beat a few fast strokes, then stiffened for a short glide to produce a flight of rises and falls. The aerial aviators drew within a hundred yards of the man, fifty yards, and nearer. They sighted the form that should not have been there by the water. They zoomed up at a steep angle, climbing the soft ladder of air.

Shoot! cried Sam's mind. His hand dipped down and came up with the six-gun. The two shots blended into one rolling explosion.

The small bodies burst into blossoms of feathers to drift downward lazily on the gentle wind. Sam spun left. He triggered the gun at a white pebble on the ground. It vanished in a puff of pulverized rock. The tassel of a cattail growing in the spring was cut neatly off to fall into the water. Before it struck, Sam pivoted far right and placed a projectile of lead into a knot on the stem of a bush.

The plumage of the birds had not yet settled to the earth. Sam's eye picked one single, oscillating feather; and, with full knowledge of the certainty of his skill, he tilted up the barrel of the weapon. The feather vanished.

Sam's blood rushed in exultation of an unexpected triumph. The gun was, as Zimmer had said it must be, one with his hand. More than that, the speed had been enormously quicker than before. Some new link between hand and brain had been forged. As if two red-hot lengths of iron had been pressed together and struck with a hammer to make only one length. When one end moved, so too did the opposite end at that exact same fraction of time. The mind thought; the hand acted instantaneously.

One feather had caught in the dry seed head of a wild rye grass. The delicate down on the end of the feather that had been next to the warm body of the bird was startlingly white. It glowed a little beacon in the dusk of the morning. Sorrow filled Sam for the innocent animals dead under his ruthless hand.

"I'm sorry, Zimmer. What did you say?" asked Sam.

"Go ahead with your story. No, wait. Raggan, Bartel, move aside. Slow now."

"What is it?" questioned Raggan in a perplexed voice. Yet both men rose and went in opposite ways from the table.

"Sam, there is a mouse by the fireplace eating on a piece of bread. See it?" asked Zimmer.

"I see it."

"When it moves, draw and shoot beneath the table."

The animal stopped eating and viewed the now-silent men. It grabbed the bread up in its mouth and started to dart away.

Two six-guns roared. Thunder crashed in the house. The mouse was obliterated. A chunk of adobe wall as big as a wash pan crumbled to dust. More dust rained down from the poles supporting the roof.

"Goddamn. Oh, goddamn," hoarsely shouted Raggan. He held his ears with his hands and rocked back and forth. "I'm deaf. You've ruined my ears."

Zimmer arose and walked across the room. He fished out a

knife and began to gouge the damaged foot-thick wall. In a moment he grunted with satisfaction. On the palm of his hand lay a wad of lead, two bullets welded together.

"You both shot at exactly the same instant," said Bartel in a surprised and marveling voice.

Zimmer's slender fingers closed around the gray lump of metal. He slipped it into a pocket.

"Just being fast and accurate is not enough. You'll be facing a man calculating the best way out of a hundred as to how to put a bullet through you before you can put one through him. Now I'll teach you what I promised. The tricks that a gunhand must know to stay alive."

The storm wore itself out by the end of the third day. The thick cloud drove off to the east, leaving behind a bright blue sky. Sam and Zimmer relaxed in the mild December sun in front of the house.

"Sam, I'd like to oblige you and teach you the Mexican lingo," said Zimmer. "But the little amount I know won't help you much. It's not enough to get you through Mexico and find your sister."

"Then I've got to find somebody else to teach me," said Sam.

"There's a grade school in town. I hear the teacher has a gift of tongue for the foreign languages. She is Chinese and can also talk American and Mexican, and two or three other languages. Maybe if you asked her, she would help you."

"Seems strange the townspeople would let a Chinese woman teach."

"Maybe so, and maybe not. I've heard she may be the smartest woman in this whole town. Not only can she speak several tongues, but can calculate large arithmetic problems in her head."

"Where's the school?"

"I saw it one day when I was riding around. Go downtown, then south along Spring Street. About seven or eight blocks from the plaza, turn west on a dirt street. There's a Mex dry-goods store on the corner where you turn. The school's an old adobe that was built for a stage house and stable but never used. It was reworked to fit the needs of the kids."

"I'll just ride down there now," said Sam. "School should be out in an hour or so and I can catch the teacher before she goes home."

From the raised location of the gang's house on the hill above Los Angeles, Sam looked down into the town. The country courthouse was the tallest building, two stories capped with a steeple and atop that a long, white spire pointing at the sky. Many other large structures lined the wide streets. The brown brick, three-story Pico House with its eighty rooms dominated all others. He wondered what it would be like to live where there were carpeted floors, gaslights, and inside baths, as Keesling had described.

Several business buildings were under construction along the main thoroughfares. Off to the northwest side of town on an elevated bench, the pale sheen of new lumber showed where large new homes were being erected. A giant water-wheel was visible beyond the roofs of town. Some sixty feet in diameter, it dipped its lower rim, to which metal buckets were attached, into the waters of the Los Angeles River, lifting the liquid up from the stream and sending it coursing through canals to the city and outlying areas.

Beyond the town were wide expanses of farmland. Thousands of acres of stubble fields of wheat and barley lay like sheets of gold on the river bottom. Above that, on the sloping hillsides where the frost did not collect so readily, were large green orchards of apples, oranges, and pears. On the choicest south-exposed sites, terraced vineyards of wine grapes clung like dark jade necklaces around the hill.

Sam reined his horse out of the yard and went down the sloping road to the town. The mud was drying. Yet here and there a skim of water remaining in a low spot, reflecting the rays of the sun, shone a bright silver. Scores of people, freed from the idleness forced by the storm, hurried along packed-earth sidewalks or wooden walkways on private errands. Now and then someone crossed the street, searching out a drier footpath, and stepping cautiously.

A big wagon, heaped with capacious wooden barrels and sunk half-spoke deep in the stiff mud, crept slowly past, drawn by six straining oxen. Sam pulled up to let the vehicle pass. A light buggy making only a shallow mark on the ground sped up the street in the opposite direction.

Sam found Spring Street and the business section called Baker Block. In front of a reading room advertising the availability of books and the latest newspapers, he halted and watched the tiny figures of a marionette show perform. Against a black velvet backdrop, two hearty Chinese warriors only a foot tall slashed and stabbed each other with silver gilding swords. A diminutive damsel, dressed in brightly colored silk and obviously the cause of all the strife, stood on the edge of the stage and encouraged the combatants with wide, painted brown eyes.

Sam passed on. A guard with a rifle leaned against the wall of the bank. His suspicious eyes roamed over the crowd. He settled his study for a moment on the lean young man riding the bay horse, and then moved onward.

Los Angeles was a growing, industrious city, thought Sam, but a tough place where a ready gun was needed every day.

The general commercial section was left behind. Saloons, gambling halls, and whorehouses became interspersed with smaller, run-down businesses and dilapidated homes. A man laughed loudly from inside the second floor of one of the buildings. Sam wondered what he had accomplished that pleased him so much.

Sam turned on the cross street Zimmer had described and found the school. Tied in front were seven saddle horses, apparently mounts of some of the students. The low voice of a woman came out of the open door.

Sam stepped down from the leather, tied his horse across the street from the school, and found a warm seat in the sun. He listened to the pleasant tone of the woman, and a child's voice responding now and then.

A bell tinkled school dismissal. Gleeful shouts erupted as twenty or so boys and girls poured into the sunlight. Sam savored their freedom with them as they scattered homeward in many directions. The teacher came outside to the entry stoop and held a short conversation with a small girl, about first-grade size. Then the child, too, skedaddled for home.

Sam arose and crossed the school yard. He removed his hat as he approached the stoop.

"Hello," he called out to the Chinese woman reentering the schoolroom.

She pivoted lightly to the rear. Her loose clothing, black blouse and long black skirt, flared out about her, then collapsed to hang brushing the wooden decking. Bright, intelligent eyes pierced Sam.

Sam stumbled in astonishment on the bottom step as the face of the pretty, nude dancer of the ocean shore came into full view.

The woman smiled guilelessly at Sam's disconcerted expression. "Yes, what may I do for you?" she asked in an innocent tone, as if they were meeting for the first time.

Up close like this, she was more beautiful than Sam remembered, and smaller. Easily she could pass beneath his outstretched arm. She regarded Sam quizzically and waited for his response.

"I have been told you are very good with languages," said Sam. "Would you teach me so I could talk with Mexicans?"

"Perhaps. Why do you want to learn the Spanish language?" She saw the shadow of a somber cloud sweep over the countenance of the freckle-faced young man.

"I must make a long trip into Mexico and take back something very valuable that has been stolen from me. There are many questions I must ask of people there if I'm ever to do that. I have little time to study, maybe two months or less."

"With diligence, much knowledge can be acquired in that length of time."

"I would pay you. Would fifty cents an hour be a fair amount?"

"I will help you. And the price you offer is more than fair. What is your name?"

"Sam Tollin."

"My name is Keging Tai. When would you want to start?"

Sam glanced up at the lowering sun. Slightly more than an hour remained of the day. "If you can spare this evening, how about now? Afterward I will see you safely home."

"Very well. Come inside. However, no weapons are allowed in the school. Please leave your pistol outside."

Sam unbuckled his six-gun and slid it into a saddlebag. He went back up the steps and entered the school behind the dark-garbed woman.

The lessons began. The words came smoothly from her tongue. Sam listened intently, striving to capture every syllable and inflection. Sometimes the sight of her handsomeness or a whiff of her perfume teased him and his senses drifted. He tried to judge her age but could not. Her face held no lines, and her eyes were clear and luminous. Yet there was a maturity about her that spoke of a worldly wisdom.

He was learning, and much faster than he had thought possible. She was preparing a written list of words, phrases, and verbs as they progressed. He would carry it with him for later study.

The light grew too dim to see by. The woman lit an oil lamp and the lessons resumed.

Sam heard the steps at the door of the room. Engrossed in the explanation of a new series of words, he paid no attention until a loud voice called out.

"Hi, little school teacher! I saw your light on. It's mighty late to be grading papers, so I thought I'd just stop in and keep you company."

A big American, wearing a broad-brimmed hat and tight leather pants like those worn by Mexican *vaqueros*, came forward into the rays of the lamp. He seemed to see Sam for the first time sitting in the first row of the desks.

"Hey, kid, get out of here. I want to talk to the pretty woman." He advanced upon Sam.

Sam started to rise. His leg caught for an instant on the top of the desk. The man grabbed him by the shirtfront, jerked him upward, and twisted him about. At the same time, his other hand locked onto the seat of Sam's trousers and he lifted.

"Got you on your tiptoes, don't I?" laughed the man. "Now, out you go." He hustled the youth to the door and, with a powerful heave, slung him from the top of the stoop to the ground. "Go home and let a man enjoy himself."

Sam did not resist the fall. He curled himself, hit on his shoulder on the damp ground, rolled once, and came to his feet. With anger burning in his veins like raw whiskey, Sam spun to face his attacker.

The man, without a backward look, disappeared back inside.

Sam strode to his horse and yanked out his six-gun. Before he reached the steps, the pistol was strapped on his hip.

The woman was bent backward over her desk, the man half on top. She fought against him, one leg drawn up to hold them apart, and at the same time trying to wrench free. He held her easily. Both of her hands were imprisoned in one of his. He fondled her breast and his mouth hunted for hers.

Sam jumped across the dirt floor. His hand clamped hold of the man's hair and jerked his head up. With a savage swing, Sam struck the thin-boned temple of the skull.

The man's strength failed and he wilted. Sam dragged the loose-jointed body off the woman and let it fall to the floor.

"Are you all right?" asked Sam. He lifted Keging gently to her feet.

She rubbed her bruised wrists and shook herself like a kitten that had been mauled by a big dog. "Yes, I think so. Is he dead?"

"Not with his hard head, I wouldn't think so."

"What are we going to do with him?"

"Take him uptown to the sheriff for lockup."

She straightened and her composure returned completely. She made a deprecating stroke with her hand and shook her head. "The law in this town would never imprison a white man for molesting a Chinese woman."

"I can talk with the sheriff, explain what I saw firsthand, and then he will do what is right."

"That would be a waste of time. Most likely it would bring revenge and violence to my people."

Sam believed what she said. Zimmer and other gang members had described the lack of protection for the foreign people of Los Angeles. "Then I'm going to convince him that if he ever comes near you again, I'll kill him."

"You can't kill in cold blood. More than that, how long are you going to be here to protect me? Forever, or just a few weeks?"

"You are correct. I can't simply shoot him. But for now I can get rid of him. Then tomorrow and for several days I will see you safely to and from school. In the meantime, I will look him up and have a serious talk with him. You could be surprised how much he may listen to reason if it is told to him in a certain way."

"I have friends who can walk with me to school during the

day. After dark is the most dangerous time for us, even our men.''

''I feel I'm to blame for your trouble. If you hadn't stayed to teach me, none of this would have happened.''

Sam leaned over and, taking hold of the American's heels, dragged him roughly from the school. He found the fellow's horse and hoisted the limp body to hang over the saddle. A quick turn of the end of the man's lariat secured the hands and feet together beneath the horse's chest. Sam slapped the rump of the mount a stinging swat and it bolted toward Spring Street.

''I will take you home now. Tomorrow I'll look this *hombre* up, and one way or the other he'll not bother you again.''

''Let me blow out the lamp and close the door and I will be ready to go,'' said Keging.

They went along the streets, she guiding the way. The darkness grew deeper. A cold wind began to blow down from the hills.

A drunk came staggering by. She reached out and clutched Sam's hand. He returned the pressure, feeling the firm flesh, like a tiny, warm animal seeking safety in the strength of his hand.

Blocks later, she halted. In the light of the stars, Sam saw the street was lined with small, single-story homes, crowding close together as if for mutual protection. Weak yellow light shone in some of the windows.

''This is where I live,'' said Keging. ''Shall I see you tomorrow after school?''

''Yes. I would like to study every evening you can spare me.''

''That is agreeable to me.''

She slowly, and as if reluctantly, extracted her hand from Sam's hold. Five steps away from him, she could not be seen. A door closed and a bolt was rammed home in its locking socket.

Sam walked back along the night-cloaked streets of Los Angeles to retrieve his horse. That old emotion of distaste when he observed fear on a human face lay heavy upon him.

He ran his callused thumb over the hammer of his six-gun. This was one situation where he could do something about the reason for that fear. Maybe somewhere far away a kind man was helping Sarah to keep safe too.

CHAPTER 14

Zimmer played cards in the gambling alcove off the main barroom of the Gay Lady Saloon. Luck was perched on his shoulder with sharp, unrelenting claws and several hundred dollars in gold and paper money were piled in front of him.

The saloon was crammed with a drove of men packed elbow to elbow at the bar. All the tables were full. Ten women served drinks, moving quickly at times to avoid the hands of the men reaching out to playfully pinch them. A low roar of voices vibrated the walls. Every once in a while the shrill complaint of one of the females punctuated the din as a sly hand found its mark.

Zimmer's restless eyes spied Sam as he pushed apart the swinging doors and came in from the night. Sam had never been in one of the saloons as far as Zimmer knew, and he curiously watched as the young man stepped to the side of the door and began to examine the faces of the jostling throng.

Zimmer recognized the expression on Sam's features. He had seen it before—a man on the prowl, searching for an enemy to challenge.

"Count me out," he said to the other players at the table, and began to stuff his winnings into a pocket.

Sam's eyes roved over the men. In the confined space of the saloon, the loud talk, laughter, and curses of the men merged into a rumbling growl, oddly animal-like, like that of a caveful of bears. Sam observed Zimmer making his way through the throng and nodded a greeting to him.

"What's up?" queried Zimmer, taking a position beside Sam and standing so he could see all the room.

"I'm looking for a man," answered Sam.

"Hell, I can tell that. What for?"

"He hurt a friend of mine and will probably try to do it again."

"Tell me about it."

"This fellow, an American, manhandled the Chinese school teacher in a mean way. Lucky I got to him before he hurt her bad."

"Looks like maybe he had you down in the dirt, too," said Zimmer, pointing a finger at the muddy stains on Sam's clothing.

"Ah, that's nothing. I laid my pistol up 'side his head in pay for that. But that just put him out of action temporary-like. While he was knocked out, I sent off on a horseback ride and I took the teacher home. Now I need to find him again and convince him to leave her alone permanently."

"What do you aim to do if you find him?"

"Have some straight talk and an understanding with him."

Zimmer chuckled. "Any man that'd lay a hand on a woman when she didn't want him to don't have much understanding. How many saloons have you been in?"

"Five so far."

"Only another thirty or so to visit then. Do you mind if I tag along with you? He might have a friend or two that I could keep busy while you tend to your little business with this *hombre.*"

"I'd be pleased if you would. I don't see him here. Let's go on to the next place."

The two men checked all the gambling halls and saloons on Main Street and then entered a dark alley leading to Spring Street. As they neared the far end, a small Chinese man with a long pigtail of plaited hair was dumping trash into a wooden barrel by the side door of a saloon. He drew back against the wall out of their way and warily watched them pass.

When Zimmer and Sam came out onto the gaslit main thoroughfare, three men were in the middle of the block and heading directly toward them.

"That's him," said Sam in a tense, raspy tone. "The one on the inside near the building."

"You sure?"

"Yes, I'm positive. I couldn't forget that face anytime soon."

"I see all of 'em are armed with handguns," said Zimmer. "If the men with him take a stake in this, it could get to a shooting fight. There's three of them and we don't know how fast any of them are. Don't let anything the other two do draw your attention from your man. If it looks like you'll have to kill him, then do it. Don't wait and give him the edge to shoot us up."

Sam stepped fully into the path of the men to block their way. They halted, a streetlight framing their outlines from the rear and their faces in shadow. All of Sam's senses focused upon the man who had hurt Keging.

The saddle horses tied to a nearby hitch rail became immobile. The call of the humans and thud of booted feet upon wooden floors drifting from the buildings faded away in Sam's ear to only a distant, muted drone. He felt the steel in his stomach. He would make this man back away from Keging and in the future do no harm to her.

"Well, I'll be damned," said the man, and pointed at Sam. "*Amigos*, that's the kid I tossed out of the schoolhouse when I wanted to romance that pretty little Chinese teacher." His tone dropped to a growl. "I think you are the one who came up behind me and whacked me with a club or something. Are you the one that did that?"

"I should have busted your head wide open," replied Sam. "And I'm telling you that if you ever go near the teacher again, I'll finish the job."

The man threw back his head and chortled. "Kid, you sure got me scared. But I think you got more nerve than brains." He took a step forward. "That little woman you are so hell-fired determined to protect is a whore. She worked in one of the biggest cathouses in San Francisco about ten years ago. She was brought over from China in a boat with two hundred more girls. She came here to Los Angeles and tried to put on a nice, clean face. But I remembered her from when I worked in San Francisco."

"You're a liar," burst out Sam.

"Why, you're sweet on her," exclaimed the man. He paced a step closer. "Boy, she's more than twice your age and been around places you wouldn't believe."

"She's not what you say," retorted Sam.

"Watch it, Sam," hissed Zimmer.

Sam jerked himself back from the argument. The man had advanced a good thirty feet closer as he had engaged Sam in conversation. His comrades had fanned out into the street. Zimmer was turned to confront them.

Sam was jolted at the ease which he had been distracted. Zimmer's coaching on the many ploys a gunman could use on a foe to throw him off guard came rushing up from his memory. One had just been pulled on him—make your opponent angry and thinking of things other than the gunplay that was surely coming.

This man was Keging's enemy and also his. Never would he let them go peacefully about their private lives. He would repeat his tale of her past again and again, and, whether it was true or not, she would be destroyed.

Sam's hand flashed down and his fingers flipped the six-gun up from its holster. He fired. The shot slammed the center of the man's chest, splintering the heavy bone, and exploded the heart within.

In one smooth, effortless motion, Sam rotated the barrel of his pistol upon the next man to the left. That individual's weapon was clearing the holster. Sam triggered his weapon and saw the man jerk as if a sledgehammer had struck him. He toppled to the ground.

So intent had Sam been upon destroying his enemies, he had not heard the crash of Zimmer's weapon. However, as Sam pivoted farther to bring his gun to bear on the third man, he found him sprawled on his back and looking up at the sky. Zimmer was holstering a smoking pistol.

The echoes of the six-guns died out against the fronts of the buildings lining the streets. Dogs began to bark excitedly. "Get the sheriff. There's been a killing," someone shouted.

Zimmer shook Sam by the arm. "Snap out of it! Don't just stand there. It's over. We got to be moving fast. We don't want to have to try and explain this to the law. Once they see us, they'll remember our faces, especially mine, for no one could ever forget it. I've been in one shoot-out already."

Sam inhaled deeply, trying to throw off the shock of the sudden deaths. "Yes . . . Yes. Let's go. Which way?"

"Back down the alley. Run!"

They sped through the darkness, crossing Main, Spring, and San Pedro streets, and into another alley. Beyond that they turned and, walking swiftly abreast, made a long, circular course through the Mexican section of Los Angeles. At the railroad station, they slowed to a stroll and began to walk back to the town center to recover their horses.

The streets had returned to normal. Where the battle had been fought, the bodies were gone. Sam and Zimmer mounted and, passing through the thoroughfares, began to climb the hill where their house stood.

The two men did not speak. Vigilantly they examined the eerie black silhouettes the moon created with the brush and trees and hollows of the land. They reached the house, entered, and shut the door against the cool gloom of the winter night.

"You take a seat while I boil up some strong coffee," said Zimmer.

The house was cold and extraordinarily full of musty smell. Sam breathed of the odor and wondered why it was so strong this night. He looked at his hands lying on the top of the table. There was not one sign of a tremble. Yet he had just killed two men.

His gaze roamed the room. He saw the wall that he and Zimmer had shot partly away. Was he truly as quick as the gunman?

The small body of Zimmer was crouched low over the fireplace hearth as he blew on a tiny live coal under a pile of kindling. This man had committed murder, had killed a man he did not know, merely because he was Sam's friend. For the first time, Sam realized fully the importance for survival of having an unquestioning comrade in an unpredictable, violent world.

Zimmer hung the coffeepot on the metal hook and swung it to hang over the growing fire. He set a tin cup in front of Sam and one for himself. "Won't be long now," he said as he sat down across the table from Sam. "The wood's dry and will burn hot."

"Thanks for your help tonight," said Sam.

"Nothing to it. Maybe you could have beaten all three of them without my gun."

"Hardly likely. Don't it bother you that we shot three men?"

"Not much. I calculate they needed killing from what you

said. At least that one you pointed out did, and the others decided to back his hand. They're dead because they made a bad judgment. Anyway, they all had guns and sure as hell were ready to plug us.''

"Do you think there's any chance the sheriff can track us here?"

"Not much. I hear he's a good enough sheriff. But things are mostly out of control here. He'll look to see who got killed. Then act busy like he was trying to really find the culprits who did it. But once he puts on that show, he'll just go off and mind his own business and try not to get shot himself before the next payday.''

"I sure hope you are right. I'd hate to get hung before I find Sarah.''

"I'd hate to get strung up anytime,'' grinned Zimmer. He propped his chair against the wall and watched the orange flames lick around the black, sooty bottom of the coffeepot. He did not mention to the youth that his handling of the six-gun had been about the fastest he had ever seen. It was best a man always remain a little doubtful of how skilled he really was, and then he would keep trying to improve.

Zimmer chuckled silently to himself. McKone and Tanner were going to be surprised *hombres* if they ever tried to come up against Sam in gunplay.

Sam's lessons continued with Keging. He did not mention the shoot-out with the Americans. Nor did Keging, though she knew most of the facts about the gunfight. Her people were a tightly knit group and for their very survival had developed a thorough network to pass information on the important happenings of the town. She had been informed within a quarter hour of the death of the man who had attacked her.

The weather remained relatively mild into January. Keging and Sam laid a plan to move the language session to the beach for a day. "After all, why can you not practice there by the beautiful ocean as well as in the schoolhouse?" Keging had asked. Sam had laughed and agreed.

As the time of the day drew closer to meet with the teacher, Sam spoke to Zimmer. "Would you like to go with

Keging and me to the seashore? I'm sure she would not mind.
And she always has a delicious bit of food.''

To Sam's surprise and pleasure, the little man stood up and
reached for his hat. ''Nothing better to do. I've been aiming
to ride down there sooner or later anyway.''

They guided their horses along the busy streets, listening to
the call of the people, the cracks of bullwhips upon the hides
of laggard draft animals, and the grind and groan of wheel
hubs on axles. In the good weather, construction had recom-
menced, and hammers rang on nails and saws rasped as
lumber was cut to size for fitting.

A thin pall of fine dust hung between the rows of buildings. The folks seemed to pay it no attention. Sam noticed
one woman scoop up the tail of her dress to keep it out of the
dirt as she crossed the street.

A Mexican in a heavily embroidered jacket and trousers
trotted by on a spirited horse. A Scotsman, ruddy-faced and
freckled, threw a friendly hand greeting at Sam. The young
man returned it. Two small Chinese girls saw the exchange
between the two strangely colored men and giggled to each
other.

A frail scarecrow of a Mexican beggar sat beneath the roof
overhang of a cobbler shop. He coughed raggedly and spat on
the sidewalk. He saw two riders, a young man and an ugly
one, were going to pass near, so he picked up his metal cup
and held it out toward them, shaking a copper coin to rattle it
and draw their eyes. They paid him no heed.

Keging spied the horsemen approaching along the street
and stepped up in her small buggy. The men removed their
sombreros as they came close.

''Keging,'' said Sam, ''I want you to meet Zimmer. I
don't know his first name, for he has never told me what it is.
Perhaps he will tell you.''

She smiled very charmingly at the scar-faced man. ''You
are a friend of Sam's. I have heard of you and am very glad
to know you.''

Sam wondered about her words, for he had never mentioned Zimmer in any of his discussions.

''Hello, Miss Keging,'' said Zimmer, and bowed his head
at her. ''Sam has invited me to go along with you two this
afternoon. I hope that is all right with you.''

"It would be my pleasure if you did," Keging responded. She glanced around as if endeavoring to see who was watching them. "Shall we go?"

With a snap of her buggy whip that deliberately missed the pacer and only popped the air, she led the way west down the street. The men urged their horses forward to take positions, one on each side of the buggy, where they could talk with the woman.

On the shore beside the blue ocean, the hours went pleasantly. Zimmer joined in the Spanish lessons. He was much more knowledgeable about the language than he had led Sam to believe.

In the evening, Sam grew restless and, noticing the interested looks Zimmer was casting at Keging, decided to give his friend some time alone with the pretty woman. "I've had enough studying for today," said Sam, and without giving them a chance to say anything, strode off along the sandy shore.

He was gone nearly two hours. When he came back, the temperature was dropping and a gray bank of clouds was speeding in over the ocean. An ocean that had turned almost black. A rising wind began to strike the sea. Whitecaps formed and scurried for the beach.

"When the storm comes in from the north in the winter as this one is, it turns very cold," volunteered Keging, gathering up her books and a basket that had contained food. "It will be dark in a short time and we should go."

"Zimmer, will you see Keging safely home?" asked Sam. "I want to stay here a little longer. I'm not ready to hole up until another storm blows itself past."

"Be glad to. Are you ready to go, Keging?"

"Yes. Do you want to ride in the buggy with me? We can put up the top if it starts raining before we get to town."

They sped off, Zimmer's horse trailing faithfully behind. Sam stepped astride the bay and rode to the northeast along the beach.

The storm strengthened. The clouds scudded upon the land. The temperature fell thirty degrees in as many minutes. Rain began to pour down from the black bottoms of the clouds.

Sam made his way around a massive headland jutting far out into the thrashing sea. The brunt of the wind and rain lashed at his face, and water ran in rivulets from his slicker. He tilted his head to protect his eyes.

The tumult of the storm somehow matched the turmoil in Sam's mind. He knew the reason for his unrest. In some distant, unknown place, Sarah was a captive. A cruel person could be inflicting great pain upon her. Yet he lingered in this land of California. At intervals, he even had felt a certain pleasantness in these last days. God! He felt guilty. Keesling must soon steal the mules, or Sam would be forced to abandon the gang and, penniless or not, hurry into Mexico.

The ill-tempered wind frothed the waves with thick silver crowns. Twilight began to settle upon the wet sand. Still he traveled north, braving the storm. He finally stopped, climbed down, and stood for a long time watching the waves grow to mountainous combers. He breathed deeply, smelling the wind, and his tongue tasted it, tangy and heavy with salt.

The winter night wrapped Sam in its cold darkness. The wind became biting as the temperature continued to plummet. The blast shrieked south.

Sam stretched out his hand to catch the bridle reins to mount. They were stiff, frozen and encased in a sheath of ice. He shook them, and ice broke away to fall with a tinkle upon the ground, also freezing.

The iron-shod hooves of the bay crackled and crunched the rimed grass as it made its route toward Los Angeles. As Sam entered the town, the storm front passed him, and the clouds began to break up. On the far dark eastern rim of the horizon on top of the Sierra Madre, a moon rose, round and frozen and wintery wan.

The beggar still sat beneath the overhang of the cobbler shop. His head was lowered, looking at the metal cup between his feet. Sam halted and stepped down. He said in Spanish, "Here, old man, is a dollar. Go buy yourself some supper and rent a bed."

There was no movement from the bowed figure. Sam walked nearer and leaned down, holding out the silver dollar.

"Wake up," said Sam. He dropped the coin into the cup with a metal clatter.

Still there was no stir. Hesitantly, he touched the cheek of the man. It was ice-cold and rigid with death. Sam backed up a step. He pulled his eyes off the motionless form and looked up at the black sky and the stars like shards of ice strewn over it. Even in California, a man, if he should have the misfortune to become weak, could die merely from the cold.

Sam mounted with a strong yank of his arms. Without being told, the bay went off along the street and up the long hill to its stall.

The wind was singing an endless dirge as Sam shut it out with the door. He stripped off his damp clothes, sank wearily down on his cot, and pulled the blankets around himself.

A sliver of wind came in through a crack in the mud wall to cut at his already chilled feet. The wind droned coldly all night.

CHAPTER 15

Every day throughout January, Sam endlessly walked the hills and ocean shore surrounding Los Angeles. He was troubled about the delay in leaving, and the only way he could sleep was to exhaust himself. The language lessons went on; however, they grew shorter as his fitfulness increased.

On the first day of February, he noticed a tinge of green on the south-facing sides of the low hills. The weather had warmed significantly, with a balmy wind coasting in from the south for several days. Now the hardy grass, woken from its winter dormancy, stretched thin, green fingers to bask in the golden sunlight. This California was a strange place where grass grew in the wintertime.

After dark that night, Keesling came to the house. He had gotten word to all his men and gradually they drifted in and found places to sit. Two Foxes arrived last and, leaving the door ajar, stood close to the opening. A breeze found the door and swirled inside to flicker the flame of the coal-oil lamp and make the shadows of the men dance like misshapen demons upon the brown dirt walls.

"You all look like you're wintering well and getting fat," said the outlaw leader. "All except Sam—he doesn't have a spare ounce on him anywhere. I bet your asses are tender and your horses couldn't run a mile." He shook his head in reproach.

"We'll be leaving in two weeks," he said, his eyes roving to see how his men would take the notice.

Zimmer grinned in good humor. "About time, too. Sam has wore all the hilltops off walking 'round here waiting for you to name the day."

"There'll be plenty of feed for the mules," said McKone. "The grass should be half a foot tall in two weeks' time."

"Seems like you are ready to move out," said Keesling. "Well, that's good. I have arranged for several ranchers to round up mules for me. Each will have the pick of their herds in pastures just waiting for us to take. More than two thousand of them." He laughed. "The owners think I'm going to buy the animals to drive to Tucson to supply wagon trains on the El Camino Real."

"Well, they're party right," said Raggan.

"All except the paying part," said Bartel.

"Here's what I want you all to do," said Keesling. "Take your gear and horses and go up in that little mountain range the Mexicans call Verdugos. That's about thirty miles from here and plumb deserted this time of year. Two Foxes has a camp all located for you. Also, he has stolen a dozen or so horses and they are stashed there. I want every man to ride thirty to forty miles a day from now until we leave. Drag along an extra mount or two so all of them get toughened up. You'll need hard asses and strong horses if you're going to ride off and leave behind those men who will surely come after us."

"How's the plan going to work?" asked Tanner.

"Very simple," replied Keesling. "We hit one herd right after another, starting northwest of town, and then keep driving southeast and finally east toward Arizona City. We'll run the legs off the mules. If we're lucky, we may have a day's head start on any posse chasing us."

"A lot of animals will be lost in the brush and gulches," said Tanner.

"There sure will be," agreed Keesling. "And the sooner we lose the ones that are hard to drive, the better off we'll be. About the third or fourth day, we should have the mules trained to go where we want and as fast as we want."

"Still, men on good horses can catch up, us having to work a drove of mules," said Tanner.

"I've got a plan to take care of any posse when they get too close," answered Keesling. He turned to face Tanner squarely. "Not thinking about backing out now, are you? It's too late for that."

Tanner slid his eyes away and looked at the floor. The

gang leader recognized the expression—not one of fear, rather a calculated decision by Tanner not to challenge him now. The man was plotting something. He would have to be killed sooner or later.

Keesling spoke to Zimmer. "You run things up at the camp until I get there. Nobody comes back to Los Angeles once they leave tonight. Not for any reason." Keesling faced the roomful of men and raised his voice. "And don't tell your women what we got planned. I know a lot of people in this town, and I'll find out right off if one whisper gets out. I'll come gunning fast as hell for that man that talks.

"Now, does anybody have objections to Zimmer being the boss? If so, make your say now."

No one spoke. McKone, Tanner, and Kimbel studiously examined the dirt floor.

"All right then, that's the way it is," said Keesling. "I've been working with Two Foxes and he has everything we need to make a long trip. Those of you staying somewhere else besides here, go get your gear and come back here. Two Foxes will guide you to camp tonight."

Keesling relaxed and chuckled good-naturedly. "Play this close to your vest and you'll all be rich in a few weeks."

McKone and his two cohorts filed out. A moment later their horses could be heard leaving at a trot.

"Those are the ones to watch," said Keesling.

"Two Foxes and I'll keep a sharp eye on them," said Zimmer.

"Kill them quick if anything looks crooked," directed Keesling. He glanced at Sam. "Are you still with us?"

"All the way to Tucson. You have my word on that. Then I head south into Mexico."

"Fair enough. Let's hope we can sell a couple of hundred mules in Tucson so you'll have some money coming." With a jangle from a big pair of Mexican spurs he had taken to wearing, Keesling left the house.

"Let's saddle and pack," said Zimmer. "I want to be ready to ride out soon as the rest gets back."

Forty minutes later, McKone called from the blackness outside the house. "All three of us are here. Let's hit the trail."

Zimmer blew out the lamp, and he and the others went out

cautiously. They mounted and the Kiowa led off. The remaining men fell into line, indistinct forms in the deep darkness.

The outlaw gang reached camp in the small hours of the morning. They separated, and after some stumbling about in the gloom bedrolls were spread out. A few grunts sounded as comfortable positions were sought. Then the camp became quiet.

"Saddle up and let's ride," called Zimmer in a loud voice.

"What the hell is going on," cursed Tanner, raising himself up from his blanket. "I just got to sleep."

"We're going to our permanent camp," said Zimmer.

"This ain't it?" asked Tanner.

"Nope. It's several miles more up there in that rough country," responded Zimmer. He chucked a thumb to the east, where the steep, snow-covered peaks of the Verdugos were outlined against an orange morning sky.

"Keesling doesn't trust us, appears to me," growled McKone.

"Now, why wouldn't he trust you, McKone?" asked Zimmer. "You're straight as a tight string."

The Kiowa loped in from the direction of Los Angeles. "No one back there on our trail," he said to Zimmer. He continued through camp and up a rocky gully.

Zimmer mounted and followed Two Foxes. The remainder hastened to saddle and catch up. The horses huffed, and iron-shod hooves rang upon the stones as the animals climbed steeply upward.

When the sun was a full hand width higher, the outlaws arrived at a hidden cove, a couple of hundred yards wide, on the south side of a brush- and tree-covered hill. A dozen horses were staked out on long lariats. Every blade of grass within reach of the mustangs had been grubbed to the ground. They nickered hungrily at the sight of the men.

Raggan began to rummage through one of four packsaddles bulging with provisions and camp equipment. "It's almost dinnertime, but I missed breakfast and that's what I'm about to cook. Anybody that wants something different can cook it himself."

"The horses need tending to," said Zimmer to the other men. "Go help Two Foxes take them to water and move their stakes to new grass. You heard what Keesling said about toughing up the horses. So divide them up among you. Plan to start riding this afternoon. Ride a long ways, but only to the east away from town.''

The men moved toward the horses. As Sam passed, Zimmer signaled for him to wait.

Zimmer spoke in a low voice. "Those three are too damn quiet and too easy to get along with. They have something planned. Whatever it is, it won't be good for us. You guard my back and I'll guard yours.''

"I wouldn't bet against the idea they're up to something,'' agreed Sam. "And I'll watch them. They'd shoot us quick and smile all the time they were doing it.''

"Soon as they calculate a way to make a profit out of it, they will act,'' said Zimmer. "Maybe they're close to figuring that out. Go on about your chores now.''

Sam selected a horse, a roan with long legs and deep chest, from the bunch of stolen animals. The Kiowa had a good eye for what to steal. Any one of the horses would pass muster for a long, fast ride. Sam promised himself both his mounts would be in racehorse condition before the time came to steal the mules.

Keesling came ghosting in silently with the morning dusk of the tenth day. He wore his old clothes, his gun tied down snugly, and his pack was light.

"You look like you rode all night,'' said Zimmer.

"Most of it. I stopped for a couple of hours near midnight. But we've little time to waste on sleep,'' responded Keesling.

"You're a few days earlier than the two weeks you mentioned,'' said Zimmer.

"When you are going to pull a job, don't ever do what people expect of you.''

"Did you throw away all those fancy town clothes?''

"I left them in that fancy hotel room. They'll think I'll be coming back in a day or so. Instead we'll be a hundred miles away and riding fast with the mules.''

"All you gather around,'' called Keesling, raising his voice. "I'll tell you how this is going to work.''

The outlaws clustered around the gang leader. He raised his arm to point to the west.

"Down there thirty miles is Los Angeles. This late in the winter, all the grass is ate out for fifteen to twenty miles in all directions from there. If you had your eyes open, you saw that as you rode up here. So the livestock of all the ranches are a long ways from their headquarters.

"I've arranged for several ranchers to gather their best mules for my inspection this coming Tuesday. They'll be bunched in pastures I've been showed while riding and dickering with the ranchers. Now, this is a Sunday and no one should be guarding those mules. So we take the mules today and drive into the night. On Monday we push like mad all day long. With luck we should have a full day's jump on everybody.

"That herd of mules we stole last fall is the closest to us, so we pick them up first. Now, piss on the fire and saddle your broncos. We've got two thousand mules to steal by nightfall."

The herd of gray mules lazed in the warm sun on the bench above the spring. A big mule lying on the fringe of the herd raised his head and sniffed at the wind gliding past. For one breath, he had smelled the odor of man. He turned in the direction of the breeze. His nostrils quivered and sucked at the air. There was the scent again, but faint and diluted by distance. His intelligent eyes rose to search the hilltop to the south.

A group of mounted men and riderless horses on lead ropes left the trees on the ridge and came down the slope, sliding and rattling rocks on the nearly vertical incline. The human scent built. Among the musty men's smells, the mule detected one that excited and pleased him. He left the herd and trotted a hundred yards out in the direction of the riders crossing the valley bottom.

Two Foxes spoke to Sam. "He acts like he still remembers you. Do you think you could catch him?"

"Maybe. I don't know," answered Sam. "Why?"

"What are you thinking, Two Foxes?" asked Keesling.

"I have tried to drive half-broken horses dozens of times. They always go better and faster if there is a point man with several animals out in the lead a little ways. The others tend to follow when pushed from behind. These mules should behave the same way."

"Same thing with cows," joined in Raggan. "Cows will actually get to following just a man on horseback after some days on the trail."

"Good idea," said Keesling. "Sam, put a rope on that critter and lead off down the valley."

"Sure thing. I might as well take along my extra horse. That way there'll be more animals for the mules to see and follow." Sam wanted his second mount to be close to his hand if he should have to ride for his life from an avenging posse.

"All right," agreed Keesling. "I'll stay out in front of you a quarter mile or thereabouts and guide the way to the next herd. Two Foxes, you bring up the rear guard and warn us if anyone comes up behind. Raggan, you handle the remuda of extra mounts and pack animals. Bartel, you ride right flank, McKone left, and Tanner and Kimbel work drag. Zimmer, you help wherever you're needed most. Keep an eye all the way 'round, especially behind us. If we run into anybody, let me do the talking. I'll tell them I've bought the herd, and they might just believe me since they may have seen me with the rancher at one time or another.

"Start the herd at a walk and gradually increase the pace to a trot. Don't go any faster or you'll get their blood hot and they'll stampede on us.

"Sam, move out now. I'll go throw down the fence to make an opening for you."

Sam went toward the mule.

A few horse lengths distant, he stepped down and went forward with his lasso. The mule tossed his head and came another half score steps closer, angling to the side to stay in the wind carrying Sam's odor.

Sam took off his hat and, hoping the animal would remember when he had been given water from it, held it out. The gray beast moved inquisitively up and smelled of the hat. His gold-flecked brown eyes never left the young man's face.

"You do recall your old water carrier," said Sam. He noted that all the wounds had healed, the scabs were gone, and only hairless patches of scar marked the spots.

Sam stroked and smoothed the flat, hard cheeks of the

mule, all the time talking in a low voice. He draped the end of the lasso over the animal's neck and reached under to catch the opposite end to complete the loop.

As the noose began to narrow, the mule whirled, jerked free, and bolted a third of the distance back to the herd.

Picking up the contagion of the alarm, the remaining mules began to snort and mill nervously. Some of the younger ones pranced about on stiff legs. A few of the older, wiser mules edged out to the border of the group, where their escape would not be impeded.

Sam knew if some broke away, all would follow in a wild stampede. He retreated back to his horses, coiling the rope as he went. He mounted and, removing his hat, waved it slowly in an arc over his head. He guided his mounts toward the lower end of the valley.

The mule regarded the man drawing away. He nickered and Sam waved his hat twice in response. The mule nickered again. Sam waved the hat in a circular motion and pulled to a halt.

The gray mule came at a trot. He watched for any false movement, any trick to put that hated rope around his neck.

Sam placed his hat on his head. He squeezed slightly with his legs and the Indian cayuse picked up a trot. The mule quickened his stride and drew alongside, his nose even with Sam's body.

Behind Sam, the yip and cry of the outlaws hazing the remaining mules filled the valley and floated to the hilltops. This was going to be one noisy operation, concluded Sam.

"Open the fence," Sam called to Keesling, already busily throwing rock and brush aside to create a passageway.

With one last muscle-straining lift and toss of a massive boulder, Keesling finished making the gap in the fence. He scrambled astride his mount and dashed ahead. The mules poured through the break in a long, gray line.

On the big flat sloping down from Echo Mountain, Keesling sat his horse and studied the six miles of stone fence walling in a pasture. The range belonged to Luis Charris. The old *caballero* had told Keesling of the seventy winters that had been consumed in the erection of the fence. Neither Luis nor his father before him had ever allowed his *vaqueros* to loaf.

At the slightest slacking of tasks in the off months, the men were set to hauling rocks and mounding them in a long, solid livestock barrier.

Keesling regarded the herd of four hundred mules inside the enclosure. This was the fifth and last bunch to be stolen. It was a good way to end, for Charris had gathered first-rate animals. He was going to be one mad son of a bitch when he found them gone.

Keesling judged this *hombre*, of all those to be robbed, was the toughest and smartest. He had over thirty hard-riding *pistoleros* afraid of nothing. If they ran down one of the gang of thieves, that poor bastard would be hung quickly by the neck in a choking noose.

Keesling had seen men hung. Not a pretty sight. He pushed the remembrance aside and dismounted.

Earlier the outlaw leader had spoken to Sam, giving him directions on how to find this pasture, and had ridden on ahead. Now Keesling hurried to tear down the fence.

Two tons of stone later, he had dismantled twenty-five feet of fence at a corner. With the converging walls funneling the mules, he should be able to drive them from the pasture by himself.

Cricling widely, he rode to the rear of the herd and began to crowd the mules out onto the open range.

Less than a quarter mile distant, Sam and the hundreds of mules he led came up out of a swale and into full view. The just-freed animals hesitated only a minute, then rushed off in haste to join the herd trotting past.

In the gray hour of the evening with the last rays of the sun glancing skyward from the barren crown of the Santa Ana Mountains, Sam stopped and looked backward. The tremendous drove of mules was spread over more than half a mile of country, and the thousands of hooves rumbled like muted thunder. In the dusk light, the hills were alive, moving, undulating, and coming toward him.

Keesling rode near the halted. "Beautiful sight, ain't it?" he said.

"Looks like a whole big piece of California is coming along with us," said Sam. "I've never seen so many mules in one place before."

"And all of them are ours if we can drive them fast enough to keep ahead of the posse. Let's be moving. I'll ride point with you. We'll keep the San Gabriels and the North Star on our left hand. After a couple hours we'll stop and rest."

"What about a posse chasing us?"

"If they get past Two Foxes and Zimmer, we could be dead men come morning. But for tonight, any posse will have to stop and wait for light."

Sam shivered as a wind blew down from the snow-chilled San Gabriels. He pulled his sheepskin coat from its tie behind the saddle and tugged it on. There was still winter just over there a few miles. And most likely a small army of angry men only a few miles behind.

CHAPTER 16

The mules walked in the dust as if they themselves were particles of dust. Churned up by the thoughts of stomping hooves, the dirt cloud moved with the animals, hanging over them in a thick haze that dimmed the sun to a pale, one-candle moon.

The gang of thieves had passed the Santa Ana Mountains and pushed hastily southeast over steep hills for two days. Sam still rode point on the herd. He trailed Keesling, who was scouting ahead to locate a navigable route, one that would not lead into a dead-end valley or an impassable rimrock that the mules could not climb.

As the miles wore away, Sam watched a small, new mountain range grow up out of the horizon. Above the green, lower bulk of the mountain, three sharp peaks capped with a sparkling, white snow crown speared the sapphire blue sky.

Zimmer loped his horse through the sparse, saddle-tall brush on the left flank of the herd and came toward Sam. He took station beside the lithe young rider, noting the striking change that had taken place in him since that rainy day he had followed the Kiowa into camp like a gangly, long-legged wolf pup, leery of every man.

Sam was growing rapidly. He was still lanky, yet, like those of a young wolf close to reaching full growth, his movements were becoming ever more swift and sure. The most striking change was in the cast of his eyes, the way he looked at strangers as if measuring the strength and skill of each. He showed absolutely no fear. He had already proven himself a very dangerous *hombre* in a gunfight.

He was very young to have killed a man, and to have done it with such quickness. A gunman could be born easily that way.

"Damn big hound dog you got following you there," said Zimmer, and flicked a thumb at the gray mule pacing on the far side of Sam.

Sam's freckled face split into a wide grin. "You're right. Almost big as a mule."

"What in the hell is he good for?"

"Haven't found out yet. Soon as I get a chance, I think I'll try to train him to pack."

"From what I've seen of him, he sure hates a rope. For you he just might behave. But anyways, I hope you do have time to try him out."

"How far behind do you think the posse is?" asked Sam, knowing fully what was on Zimmer's mind.

"Hard to know. But I bet they've found the mules gone by now and are riding like hell to overtake us."

"It'll be dark in three hours or so," said Sam, checking the height of the sun sinking on his right. "Let's hope they don't catch us before then." He pointed ahead. "Keesling said we'd camp at the base of those mountains, the San Jacintos he called them."

"Warm as it is, that snow on top of them should be melting and plenty of water running down to the low country for the mules."

"How many mules do you think we have lost?"

"I tried to guess at that as I circled 'round them. I'd say about four hundred."

"At that rate we won't have any left by the time we get to the Colorado River," said Sam.

"It's to be expected we'd lose a lot in the first days. The trail has gone over some damn rough land and mostly covered with high brush. The animals just naturally split off from the herd and are left behind. They'll get used to traveling and soon the country will be more open. Then everything will go smoother."

"I hope so," said Sam. He stood up in the stirrups and peered intently to the front. "I don't see Keesling. I wish he would wear something white so I could better make him out way out there in the brush."

"There could be a reason soon why he won't want to be seen. When the posse gets close."

"I see him now," said Sam. "He's angling more to the east and less to the south. Must be planning to camp at the very bottom of the mountains."

"In a couple of more days we'll be on the trail we've ridden before. Then there'll be more chance we can find water and stay out of ambushes. It's time I go find Two Foxes and ride out to the rear and see if the posse is close," Zimmer reined away.

In the valley at the south end of the San Jacintos, the new grass was velvet beneath the feet of the tired mules and horses. A stream of cold, snowmelt water tumbled down a steep, rocky channel, struck the gentle incline of the valley, and meandered away. The animals drank deeply and hurried to graze the sweet young grass.

The men wearily gathered near Raggan and the small cooking fire he had built among some large boulders where it could not be seen for any distance. They nervously glanced into the dusk to the northwest along the route they had just passed over.

Zimmer and Two Foxes came in at a gallop, barely beating full darkness. "Nothing back there within at least ten miles," Zimmer reported to Keesling.

For a long moment, the outlaw leader stared in the direction that danger should most likely come from. "Do you suppose by some good luck they didn't discover the mules missing until the second day?"

"Maybe," said the Kiowa. "Two hour's driving tomorrow and we will be in the Borrego Desert. Then three more to reach Borrego Spring."

A look passed between the Indian and Keesling. The white man nodded ever so slightly.

Sam saw the silent transfer of understanding and wondered what was to happen at Borrego Spring.

Two Foxes finished eating and strode off into the night.

"Keep your eyes open," Zimmer called after him. "I don't want to wake up with a rope around my neck."

Keesling assigned the men to their night riding duties to hold the mules in the valley. Some saddled horses that had not been ridden that day and went toward the herd. Others rolled into their blankets.

Sam had the midnight-to-dawn watch. Removing only his boots, and with his weapons ready to his hand, he wrapped his blankets about himself. The last sound he heard was the hiss of steam on red-hot embers as Raggan doused the fire with a pan of water.

A low, grating noise sounded in the darkness as someone stepped on a gravelly zone near Sam. He was instantly awake, his hand snaking out for his six-gun.

Zimmer's friendly voice spoke. "Get up, Sam, and let old Zimmer catch some shut-eye and dream a little."

Sam relaxed. He spotted the little man's vague shadow standing very still. "Do you really dream, Zimmer?"

A murmured whisper came floating back to Sam on the black air of the night. "I had me a dream 'bout a pretty Chinese woman not too long ago. It was very pleasant." Zimmer vanished into the gloom to seek his bed.

Sam untied his spare horse from its picket and saddled. He took his bedroll and the bay mustang with him as he went to start his patrol of the herd.

Keesling found Sam while it was hardly light. "Take your place on point and lead off. Go down the valley. Hold to the low country and you'll be going right. Move fast, for we're going to run the mules most of the morning. I've got a feeling the posse will catch us today. If they do before we are ready, we've lost everything. I'll be in the rear with Two Foxes. Now, move it!"

The gray mule separated from the half-night and trotted after Sam. The balance of the herd began to stir under the press of the men and soon was rumbling along the sloping valley bottom.

Sunlight fell into the valley, thrusting the cold shadows back, melting them, and killing their traces in the rocks. In the full light of morning, Sam broke free of the tall canyon walls and led the mules out onto the barren, sun-drenched Borrego Desert.

The sun climbed its fiery arc. Miles passed under the

clattering hooves of the animals. Ever descending, the noisy cavalcade reached Borrego Spring shortly before noon.

The spring gushed up from the bottom of a shallow, cobbly wash and ran off to the east in a stream of little pools and riffles. Four hundred feet from the spring, a second, smaller one surfaced beneath some large rocks on the slanting side of the gully and poured down to join the water of the first. Together they forged a damp path for another hundred yards before the thirsty sand and gravel consumed the entire flow.

Sam allowed his mounts to drink and then crossed the wash to climb the far bank. Keesling rode up and hardly had time to water his animal before the thirsting mule herd thundered in and the depression was filled with crowding, shoving beasts, each striving to be the first to reach water.

Several more of the gang members came in and, stinging the mules with the ends of lariats, worked a path down to the spring. They filled canteens where the water came up clean and allowed their mounts to drink. Quickly they scrambled back up to the top of the gully and circled the milling herd to come and sit saddles near Sam and Keesling.

"Not enough room for all to drink at one time," said Zimmer. "Going to be many animals hurt."

"Need half an hour for all to drink," said Keesling. "I doubt there'll be that much time, for I see Two Foxes coming at a hard run."

All the group watched the Kiowa racing in from the west.

"Two Foxes don't run his cayuse like that unless there is some damn important reason," said Zimmer.

"Keesling, you'd better run out your plan to stop the posse," growled Tanner. "There's no place for us to escape in this open land. If you've made a mistake, we have lost the herd and a hell of a lot of time has been wasted."

"If their horses are better than ours we might be the main attraction at a hanging party," said McKone.

Keesling ignored the comments. He moved his eyes from the upper spring to the lower one as if mentally measuring the distance.

Some of the mules quenched their thirst and climbed the bank to drift slowly to the east. Others immediately took their places at the stream and began to drink.

Keesling spoke to Tanner and McKone. "To give you two

fellows something to do instead of worrying—go over there and help Raggan get the remuda of horses through the mules and into the water. Clear a track for him down at the lower end. Hurry it up." He swung his hand in a sharp, commanding gesture. His nerves were stretched tight and the two men sensed it. They wheeled away without a word.

The Kiowa pulled to a sliding halt in the center of the group of men. His face was without expression, but a film of sweat shone on his copper forehead. He looked at the gang leader.

"They are maybe three miles back and coming fast. Thirty-five men or more, I'd guess. Looks like a small army."

"Half an hour earlier and they'd have won," said Keesling. "Now we have a good chance to pull this off. What do you think?"

Two Foxes hastily looked along the wash. "Everything is just as we remembered it," he answered.

"Who do you want to help you?" asked Keesling.

"Him," said the Indian, and pointed at Sam.

Sam blinked in surprise. "Me to do what?"

"Why do you want Sam?" questioned Keesling.

"He'll do what I say," responded Two Foxes. And he might, just by chance, get himself killed, thought the Kiowa. His premonition that the white youth was bad fortune to him had not diminished at all over the weeks.

"What is it you want me to do?" Sam asked again.

"Stay here and help run off the posse's horses," said Keesling.

"How can we do that? There's no place to pull an ambush on them."

Keesling called to his men and stabbed a hand at the west side of the draw. "Get over there and get ready to run the mules east. We'll let as many drink as we have time to. Watch for my signal." He looked at Sam. "Do exactly as Two Foxes tells you. Give me your spare horse, and run that pet mule off with the others."

The men spurred to the far side of the herd. The Kiowa leaned on the pommel of his saddle and sighted in the direction of the posse. Sam stepped down, gathered up a handful of rocks, and began to pepper the mule's gray hide.

In disbelieving astonishment, the animal trotted off. Once

out of range of the thrown missiles, he stopped and looked back uncertainly to watch Sam.

Keesling yelled shrilly. The men picked up the call and moved upon the mules. The ones not yet finished drinking stubbornly refused to move until the ends of the lariats stung their rumps. Then they reluctantly trailed up from the water and out onto the flat desert.

The new dust rose high and yellow. Sam judged it could be seen easily by the posse for miles.

Two Foxes spoke to him. "We'll ride over to those boulders at the lower spring."

"They are not tall enough to cover us."

"If we throw our horses, they will be. Come on."

The Kiowa stopped at the patch of rocks and turned to check the angle of the water that lay nearest the approach of the pursuers. Satisfied with his location, he grabbed the bridle of his mount, and at his order the well-trained beast lay down.

The bay mustang responded obediently to Sam's command and also dropped to the ground.

"Tie his feet. If he starts to move when they come, fall on his head and hold him," directed Two Foxes.

"He'll stay put without being tied."

"Tie him," ordered the Indian sharply. "You'll have to rise up to shoot and he'll think you are getting set to leave and he'll jump up, too. They will see him and shoot the hell out of us."

"All right," said Sam. "But I don't want to kill anybody."

"I don't want you to. We are going to kill as many of their horses as we can and try to stampede the rest. Without horses, they can't follow. Is your rifle loaded?"

"Yes."

"Then tie your horse and get ready to shoot."

"Suppose they don't stop," said Sam as he secured the legs of the bay with a knot that could be jerked loose with one pull.

"They will stop because the next water is forty miles away."

Sam took a seat very near the horse, for the clump of rocks was hardly large enough to conceal them all. He could see over the rocks and up to the head of the wet area, and on to the west for a mile or so. Nothing moved on the eroded desert waste.

He lay back and looked up at the hard blue of the sky. God, how he regretted being in this place. Soon he would be firing upon honest men merely trying to take back what was rightfully their property.

He glanced at Two Foxes. The man's eyes were strained, riveted on one spot. He grunted. Sam swiveled his eyes in the same direction. A column of dust was coming precisely along their trail.

The body of men slowed at a long rifle shot from the springs. They came in warily, holding their weapons ready and fanning out so each had a clear line of fire.

Sam peered through a narrow crevice between two boulders and counted the mixture of American and Mexican riders. Thirty-eight fighting men on good horses and heavily armed. Every one would be an excellent marksman. Soon they would be shooting at him. Sam commanded his pounding heart to behave, and it slowed.

One tall Mexican inspected for a very long time the rocks where Sam and Two Foxes lay hidden. He said something to a man near him and both reined toward the boulders.

Two Foxes cursed in a whisper. "That damn mule has got us killed."

Sam hastily looked up the bank. The gray mule was standing above them, looking down, his ears thrust exactly at their hiding place.

The two posse members came half the distance to the rocks. Sam thought he could feel their eyes, penetrating the rock to touch him.

Not liking the nearness of the strangers, the mule suddenly spun about and galloped off in the path of the herd. The men stopped their advance, surveyed the boulder patch for another minute, and then rejoined the comrades.

Several of the men's mounts tried to go down the bank to drink. The men held them back with a hard bit and talked among themselves, gesturing to the east. Sam thought the dust cloud of the herd must be very visible.

One man let his steed go to water. The others followed.

The horses lined up bordering the small stream and began to suck hurriedly to slake their thirst. The men holstered their weapons and dismounted to dig into the spring to find clean water at the source.

"Shoot the horses closest to the men," whispered Two Foxes. "Kill them if you can, but shoot each one only once. The second they have run out of range, jump on your horse and follow me. Are you ready?"

"Ready," said Sam.

"Then shoot."

Both men rose to their knees and lifted their rifles.

Sam fired at a big sorrel horse and it crashed down with a shrill squeal. At the second shot, a dun, badly wounded, tried to escape up the bank. It fell partway up, quivering and thrashing in death throes. The Indian had also felled two.

Every horse still standing bolted in headlong, panicked flight up and out of the gully. Sam and Two Foxes fired their guns again and again, striking an animal every round.

The long, shattering roll of rifle shots ended. Eleven horses were dead or dying. The remaining beasts stampeded to the northwest. One ran on three legs, the fourth broken and flopping crazily.

Some members of the posse flung themselves in pursuit of their mounts but stopped after a few paces, realizing the futility of the effort to catch them. The tall Mexican yanked his six-gun and began to fire at the men in the distant boulders.

Sam remained frozen, staring at the killing ground, hearing the moans and screams of the dying horses, and smelling the stench of the burned gunpowder. What a horrible waste of beautiful horses.

One of the Mexican's bullets struck a rock, fragmented, and stung Sam's bay with rock chips and splinters of lead. The mustang lunged about and tried to rise.

Sam ripped the rope loose from the bay's legs and the horse sprang erect. Sam leaped into the saddle before the animal was fully up. He was slower than the Kiowa, who was already whipping up the bank.

The bay tore up the incline. Sam thumped him with the barrel of his rifle and screamed into his ear. He heard more explosions of handguns. Then came the sharp crack of a rifle, and a bullet slammed the ground beside him, to ricochet and wail wildly into the sky. Someone had found a long gun on one of the dead horses.

Sam and the Kiowa crested the bank; then were beyond it, dropping out of sight. Two Foxes guided abruptly left. Three hundred yards along he turned left again and an instant later was back in sight of the posse and scurrying up out of the draw.

The group of men saw the intent of the two riders to cut them off from their running mounts. They aimed a fusilade of long-range shots at the horsemen rushing past.

Sam heard a pair of rifles working now. A bullet zipped by with a deadly buzz. But the range was opening rapidly. He heard no more close ones.

During the next twenty minutes, Sam and Two Foxes rounded up all the horses except the one with a broken leg and another that seemed to have gone completely mad. Two Foxes killed them both with rifle shots.

The posse yelled curses at the two riders as they herded the drove of captured horses to the east. Sam glanced at the men, now out of rifle range and throwing empty threats. They had a hard walk back to Los Angeles. Worse, they had much ridicule to endure when they returned. How could it be explained that two thieves took the mounts from thirty-eight honest fighting men.

Sam evaluated the twenty-five horses galloping ahead. They were outstanding, every one without exception. Some individual mounts would be worth more than a thousand dollars. In addition, all had saddles and bridles, bedrolls, and rifles in scabbards. A fortune in total.

He felt sad at the death of those that he had helped kill. He spoke to Two Foxes. "Too bad we had to shoot some."

The Kiowa did not answer. His visage was bleak. The white youth had received not one scratch. The Indian's foreboding of danger to come was stronger than ever. He was not sure anything could be done to prevent it.

CHAPTER 17

"Damn bad luck," cursed Keesling. "I was afraid of this. The hot weather must go all the way up to the headwaters of the river, and the snow is melting fast. The spring runoff has started already."

The sun had gone full circle three times since the posse had been turned back. The outlaw band with the herd of stolen mules had forged through the foothills of the long chain of chocolate-colored mountains, crossed the dune country of the sand hills, and reached the valley of the Colorado River.

Keesling, Zimmer, and Sam stood on the bank of the river. It spread before them in flood, a tide of rushing brown water more than an eighth of a mile wide.

"That's going to be one hell of a swim," said Zimmer.

"Most of that distance is floodplain bench," observed Keesling. "By the looks of how much the brush is still sticking out, I'd say the water is about waist-deep. The horses could still wade that."

Zimmer nodded agreement. "Yes, but the current in the main channel is most certain several times deeper than that. A lot swifter, too. I see brush and some fair-sized pieces of trees being washed downstream. I'd say she's still raising."

"Yep. She's up an inch since we've been standing here jawboning. It could be weeks before it comes back down. If we're going to make it across, it has to be now."

"The mules are getting close," said Sam.

Neither man looked. Keesling paced nervously along the bank a few steps, and then spun to come back. "How fast do you judge the current is?"

"Five or six miles an hour," said Zimmer.

"Same thing I figure. Anyone swimming it for that width will be carried downstream quite a distance. Still, the other bank is gentle and can be climbed for the next half mile or maybe a little less. Beyond that they'd be in between those steep cuts and would be washed a long ways without being able to get out."

"They'd probably drown," said Zimmer, taking a long look downstream. "The current would be swifter in there and some mighty rough water and tall waves to knock a body around."

Keesling looked at Sam with a challenging eye. "Are you game to try and lead a crossing with your mule? We should keep the herd moving straight into the water. Once they start milling here on the bank, we'll never get them to take to the river."

Sam put his hand into the water and swished it about. The river noise filled his ears like some monster on the verge of breaking free. He felt a little quiver of doubt in a corner of his mind. "It's awful cold, straight off snow. A man couldn't stand it for very long."

"Here's some matches in this bottle. Start a fire soon as you reach the other side. Make it a big one, for there's going to be a lot of frozen men in a little while." Keesling handed Sam the glass container.

Keesling saw the reluctance in the youth. "They're used to following you, Sam. Mount up and take them across."

The front of the herd was within a hundred yards when Sam cast loose his spare mount and guided the bay into the swirling torrent. Keesling and Zimmer trotted opposite ways a short distance and then halted to funnel the animals between them.

Sam crossed the water on the floodplain. The gray mule waded easily beside him. Twice it walked through deep water that the horse had to swim.

As each step brought them closer to the main channel, the velocity of the current increased. The bay gradually angled into the flow to maintain his footing.

Sam checked ahead. The boiling tide raced swiftly past. It made him dizzy to watch. A floating mass of brush struck and lodged against the side of the horse. Sam kicked at it until it washed clear.

The bay took another step and the bottom fell away. The horse went under headfirst. Sam's breath caught as he plunged beneath the frigid water. He held his seat as the bay fought to resurface.

They came up heading downstream at a rapid speed. With a hard rein, Sam managed to turn the bay across the current. However, his weight was forcing the struggling mustang deeply into the water, with only the top of his head showing.

Sam kicked free of the stirrups. He would work his way back, catch the tail of the horse, and let himself be towed.

A giant cottonwood, a century old and weighing ten water-soaked tons, ponderously swapped ends in an eddy at a bend in the river. The tree had been undercut from its high bank above the river and carried off by the flood. Hammered by thousands of blows during its two hundred miles of travel in the turbulent, rocky river channel, the tree had all its bark stripped, limbs beaten to short stubs, and the tough, knotty roots worn to less than a yard in length.

The tree trunk rolled, drowning one half of its roots and surfacing the other portion. It stabilized with the massive bulk aligned with the flood, an enormous battering ram charging downriver.

Neither Sam nor the horse saw the behemoth cottonwood bearing down upon them. It struck the mustang a savage blow on the ribs, just missing Sam's leg but dumping him into the river. The roots caught in the leather of the saddle, became entangled there, and shoved the horse with the flood.

The equilibrium of the tree was destroyed by the weight of the horse. The tons of wood began to rotate. The momentum built; then swiftly the log rolled toward a new balance point.

The beast entrapped on the root end of the tree fought to stay on top of the water. His feet churned and his neck arched upward, nose stretching to remain in the life-giving air.

A thick, gnarled root, spinning with the roll of the trunk, came down upon the neck of the mustang. The beast was driven beneath the water.

Sam surfaced, spitting out the foul-tasting water that had slopped into his mouth. He saw the bay horse go under—and not rise again.

He looked for the shore. It was an impossible distance away across the swirling, frothy maelstrom. He tried to swim.

His boots seemed to weigh tons, drawing him down. He treaded water and spun himself around, searching for something to keep him afloat.

The gray mule was on his right, downstream and swimming powerfully. With cold, stiff arms, Sam stroked an intercepting course. He reached the mule's side. He grabbed at the long, wet mane, caught a handful of the coarse hair, and muscled himself up to lay along the broad back.

"Swim, you big bastard," whispered Sam. He shivered. His teeth chattered until he was afraid they would shatter. He was freezing to death. A foolish thought about the mule came to his numb mind. If you get me safely to shore, I can tell Zimmer what you are good for.

The mule battled the roaring river. His lungs pumped like the bellows of a gigantic forge. The round hooves made for running on hard earth could find little hold upon the water.

Finally the mule's feet found the bottom. He lurched from the cold, muddy waters of the Colorado.

Sam slid to the ground. His legs betrayed him and he fell to his knees. He climbed back up and stumbled to a head-tall mound of driftwood that had been deposited by some past and even higher flood. He fumbled a match from the bottle with fingers that could not feel. Careful not to get the head of the match wet from his dripping clothing, he lit a fire in the edge of the pile of wood.

The desert-dry wood caught easily, flaring up in a bright flame. Sam leaned into the wonderful warmth. He breathed the heated air.

The shivering subsided and he turned to look across the river to see how the other men and animals were faring in the crossing. The first mules had swum the main channel and were splashing for the bank. A group of about eighty animals had splintered off and were angling downstream. They were going to be trapped in the steep-sided gorge of the river.

Dead animals every one. Just like the bay that Zimmer had told Sam to take good care of. He felt a moment of sorrow for the loss of the faithful little mustang. He shoved that emotion aside and scanned the river for Zimmer.

The man was upstream of the herd. Keesling was on the opposite side. Both appeared in good positions to make a safe passage. Bartel and Raggan, flanking the main body of the herd, also seemed to be making a proper crossing. Sam could not see the remaining four men. They should be somewhere to the rear of the last mules, which were just now entering the water.

Keesling and Zimmer made the riverbank and came hurriedly to stand by the fire. The mules by the score waded out of the water and began to scatter out over the land. Raggan and Bartel rode up and dismounted. They shoved in close to the flames.

More mules by the hundreds finished the long, cold swim. Then the last mule, with Two Foxes and McKone and his two cohorts close behind, scrambled up the bank to safety.

Keesling lifted his shaggy black head and shouted with relief and triumph. Then he faced his men. "The worst is over. The posse is gone and the Colorado is crossed. All the distance that's left to drive will be easier. I can feel the dollars in my pocket already.

"We'll rest a few hours and get warm and eat. Spread your bedrolls and hang up your clothes to dry in the sun. Raggan, check the packs and see how many supplies have been ruined by the water. While we're this close to Arizona City, we'll restock.

"Bad luck, Sam, you losing the Indian pony," said Keesling. "Right good mount. Take your pick of the horses you and Two Foxes rustled from the posse."

Sam looked at Zimmer. "I'm sorry. There wasn't anything I could do."

"Forget it, Sam. I saw what happened. Glad you made it over."

Sam brought the drove of one hundred and fifty mules into the green glade between the two small hills. He circled the animals until they lowered their heads and started to graze the quick-growing desert grass and forbs. Satisfied they would stay in the little basin until the following morning, he lifted his mount into a rocking gallop west toward the camp at the river crossing.

The outlaw band had remained by the river, resting for half a day. During that time, many of the mules had wandered away, grazing over the lowland and up into the hills beyond.

In the afternoon, Keesling had sent the men riding with orders to round up the stray mules and place them in locations where they could be collected as the drive resumed its eastward march on the morrow. Raggan had struck out southwest for Arizona City with two packhorses.

The sun was a large orange ball on the evening horizon when Sam came into camp. Raggan had returned from Arizona City and was busy at a cooking fire. He glanced up at the sound of the hoof falls.

"Hi, Sam. Grub'll be ready in about twenty minutes. Coffee's ready now. I bought considerable fresh cartridges for our rifles and six-guns. Over there in that smaller pack. Best you change all yours, 'cause they went into the water and may not fire. Keep them, though, and use them for practice when it don't mean anything whether they go off."

"Good idea. Thanks."

Sam unsaddled and replaced his ammunition. He went to squat by the fire and pour a cup of coffee.

"Some fellas riding double coming from Arizona City," he said to Raggan. "One looks like Tanner. Who do you make the second one to be?"

"Kind of a small fellow, mostly hidden behind Tanner. Can't be Zimmer. He'd just take Tanner's horse and make him walk." Raggan laughed at his own joke. "Also, another rider coming from over there to the northeast. Appears to be Kimbel."

Kimbel arrived first. He dumped coffee in a tin cup and flopped by the fire. His pockmarked face was as glum as usual and he said not a word.

Tanner came up, pulled his mount to a halt, and began to chuckle. "A sorry bunch of *hombres* you all are. But I've got something that'll spark you up. Look here."

He swung down and immediately reached and lifted a young Mexican woman from her seat behind the saddle. She wore a long, blue skirt and blouse to match. She held herself stiff within his grasp. A metal rattle sounded from a thin-linked iron chain coiled around her neck.

"Now, ain't she a beauty?" asked Tanner, and began to unwind the chain.

"Where in hell did you find her?" asked Kimbel.

"Didn't find her. Bought her in Arizona City." Tanner

finished unwrapping the chain. One end remained looped around her neck, fastened there by a small lock. He retained hold of the loose end of the some fifteen feet of chain.

"While I was out chasing some of those mules, I got to thinking. It's going to be a long trip to Missouri and, being a man who likes his lovin' regular-like, I just rode in to town and to a place I know there. Well, this little filly was the prettiest girl they had.

"Seems she sold herself to work at this hotel in Tucson for two years for a thousand dollars and gave the money to her family." Tanner dug a piece of paper from a pocket and waved it in the air. "Here's her contract. Her dad's X mark is on it, and so is her signed name.

"Howsoever, she soon found out the hotel wasn't a regular one, so she ups and runs away. They bring her back, but she slips off again. So they put this chain around her neck to make her stay put. Still, she raises so much hell they sell her contract to a house in Arizona City, figuring if she was that much further from home she'd behave herself and earn back the money that'd been paid her. Well, she still proved stubborn and the owner of the place was downright mad.

"When I hear all of this, I just up and plainly made an offer for her. Bought her for three hundred dollars American."

"That's cheap enough," said Kimbel.

"No human being is suppose to be chained unless they are a criminal," said Raggan.

"A person don't take money and then run off without paying it back," retorted Tanner.

"She was tricked," countered Raggan. "Keesling won't let you take her with us. Anyway, you wasn't suppose to go to Arizona City."

"Keesling will let me keep her. I'm selling shares in her. For fifty dollars each, every man in the gang can have a piece of her." Tanner swiveled toward Sam. "Have you ever had a woman, boy?" he asked mockingly.

Sam ignored the man's taunt. He watched the woman—no, younger than that, hardly more than a girl. Probably about his age. Her sloe-eyed gaze touched his for a moment and then rose to look over his head at the sky.

Before Sam could respond, Tanner yelled at the girl. "Turn around and show these fellows how pretty you are." He jerked roughly on the chain. She staggered and her hands flew sideways, fluttering like the dark wings of a stricken bird.

She pivoted slowly, her skin like dusky silk and her hair sleek and black as the pelt of a sea otter. She kept her gaze on the sky as if what was happening on the riverbank of the flooding Colorado was in another world.

Sam came to his feet. His anger burned cold and bright. He felt his compassion for her ready to override his good sense. His hand brushed the butt of his six-gun.

Raggan whisperd from his side, "If you shoot Tanner and Kimbel, you'll have to fight Keesling. He's already told all of us there must be no gunplay."

Tanner stepped to the girl. He stroked her cheek with his coarse fingertips. She flinched as if burned, but stood her ground, eyes locked on the faraway sky.

Sam saw her concentration on something distant. She seemed to be counting. He almost believed she was counting the stars coming to life along the dark gray eastern horizon.

"I'll take a share for sure," said Kimbel. He pulled out a roll of paper money and began to count.

"Raggan, how about you?" asked Tanner.

"I want no part of this deal," answered Raggan shortly.

"How about you, kid?"

"Turn her loose, Tanner, and let her go home," said Sam. He shifted position slightly to better face the man.

"Nothing doing. I paid for her fair and square."

"Let Keesling take care of this," said Raggan, and took Sam by the arm.

Sam wrestled with himself. He swept the girl with his eyes. If she would look at him—give some kind of sign she wanted his help—he would draw upon Tanner. Kimbel, too, if he took sides.

She gave no indication she was aware of the offer of aid.

Sam pulled away from Raggan's grip and strode hurriedly toward the river. He heard Tanner laugh behind him.

Sam stood on the river's edge, calming his anger and listening to the hundred noises the flooding river made. He let his mind plunge into the torrent that rolled rocks along its bed, skipped sand grains in long arching hops near the bottom, carried silt in every drop, and floated wood and froth upon its bosom. He remained there listening to the river as it fought and argued with everything that resisted its might and would not be swept downstream.

Sam's mind was as full of turmoil as was the flowing Colorado. Memories of Sarah came crowding back. How fair had been her skin, and golden her hair. And her laugh so beautiful, a true delight. He missed her sisterly pranks most of all. God! Where was she?

Were uncaring men abusing her as Tanner was the Mexican girl? He could not yet help his sister. He could assist the girl so close, just a hundred feet away. However, he did not want to fight Keesling. He hoped the gang leader would show up soon.

Sam looked toward the fire. Tanner was offering the dark young woman some food. She refused, shaking her head.

The night became fully dark and Sam knew Keesling would not return this day. He circled the fire in the gloom and went to his blankets. He saw the girl sitting by Tanner's feet as he passed. Raggan was not in sight.

The fire burned down and the conversation between Tanner and Kimbel ceased. Their footsteps scuffed the ground as they walked to their beds.

Sam lay staring up at the black night's vast sky. Was he seeing the very stars the girl had counted? A whimper rushed from the darkness. Sam lurched upright. He heard the sounds of a sharp slap and the girl's cry, searing in its torment. Another slap was followed by a sobbing echo in the dark night. Then that was abruptly cut off.

Sam shuddered. He felt as if he was an intruder listening to private agony. Swiftly he sprang up and grabbed his blankets to run into the darkness.

Sam awoke at daylight. He had slept poorly.

Raggan was cooking pancakes over a fire. He glanced at Sam and saw him check the loads in his six-gun and replace it in its holster.

Kimbel sat up and stretched. He strapped on his pistol and began to bundle up his blankets.

Tanner arose from his bed. With his holstered pistol in his hand and the girl still chained and trailing behind, he came to the fire.

Irresistibly drawn Sam looked at the girl. She stared at the place where the sky met the horizon, as seemed to be her wont. Both of her cheeks were bruised.

The wolf rose in Sam's heart at the sight of the chain and the bruises. He should have freed her the past evening. He had been a fool, but not anymore.

He spoke quickly to the girl in Spanish. *"¿Quiere Usted ir su casa?"*

Suddenly, questioningly, her dark brown eyes dropped from their skyward slant to see him. *"¡Sí! ¡Oh, sí!"* she exclaimed.

"What did you ask her?" growled Tanner.

"I asked her if she wanted to go home," said Sam. He set himself for a fast draw.

"Listen, kid, she's mine. She does only what I want her to do."

"Give her a horse and turn her loose, Tanner."

"No. And besides, Kimbel has a share of her now. He wouldn't like that."

"Are you taking a stand in this, Kimbel?" asked Sam, watching both men.

"I sure am. She stays here." He faced Sam squarely.

CHAPTER 18

Raggan called out, "Keesling is coming over the ridge. You all had better let him settle this."

The bandit leader dismounted. His eyes flicked over the men, sharp and inquiring. "What the hell is going on here? Who's the girl?"

"I bought her in Arizona City," said Tanner truculently. "Kimbel's bought a share in her and I aim to sell more of her to any of the others that want some."

"What's your stake in all this?" Keesling asked Sam, seeing the hot anger in the youth.

"I say she should be let go. Given a horse and sent home," answered Sam in a tight voice.

"Tanner, we've got no time to be slowed up by a girl," said Keesling.

"She rides good as most men and can keep up fine," responded Tanner.

Keesling pondered the situation. If the girl remained, she would cause fights. Of that he was certain. Yet it was doubtful that Tanner would release her without a fight. He did not want to kill the man.

The gang leader sensed a minute shift in Sam, preparing for gunplay. The damn kid was going to force the issue. However, this time he was correct in his action. Best to send the girl on her way.

Keesling readied himself to pull his six-gun. "Tanner, take that blasted chain off her neck and send her back to Arizona City."

Tanner's ox eyes squinted almost shut as he studied Keesling. Then he grinned and glanced at Kimbel. "He's

174

the boss. We'll do what he says. Which horse should we give her?''

"Well, let me think on that," said Kimbel. "Let's go pick an easy rider." The men walked off slowly toward the remuda.

Keesling watched the two men as they ambled away. He was surprised at the ease with which they had given in to his demand. He watched them for a minute and then turned to Raggan. "Take Bartel a horse. His has broke an ankle up there about five miles to the north at the base of that big hill.

"Sam, go up the river and help Zimmer bring in a big bunch of mules he found."

Raggan hurried past Tanner and Kimbel. They had halted and Tanner was fumbling with the lock and chain on the girl's neck.

Raggan loped away towing a second horse. Keesling seated himself by the fire and reached for a pancake from the stack of them Raggan had prepared.

Sam took a deep breath and let his nerves loosen. It was good that the girl was to be set free. He felt the hunger now, unfed since noon the day before. He picked up one of the pancakes and, munching on it, walked toward his picketed horse.

The girl stood very quietly. It was taking the man an extra long time to fit the key and open the lock. He toyed a bit longer; then his hands drew away with the chain still remaining around her neck.

She heard Tanner murmur to Kimbel. "Let's kill both of them. You shoot the kid."

Her heart lurched at the words. *¡Madre de Dios!* If they should do that, she would be a slave forever. Her possible saviors both had their backs turned and would be easy targets.

She screamed piercingly at the top of her voice.

At the shrill cry of alarm, Sam spun around. Tanner and Kimbel were drawing their pistols. Keesling was in an awkward squat by the fire. He was rising hastily and almost exactly in Sam's line of fire.

Sam's hand flashed for his six-gun. He would have to shoot past Keesling, miss the girl, and hit a target much too far away.

Tanner's draw was faster than Kimbel's. Sam put the point

of his aim on the center of Tanner's chest and fired. He saw the man recoil at the stinging slam of the bullet.

The lead projectile struck the thick chest bone and was deflected, skittering off along a rib and tearing flesh and tendons. Tanner stopped his flinch and brought the barrel of his pistol to point directly at Keesling.

The outlaw leader jumped to his feet and reached for his gun. Even as he did so, he saw the sure death coming from Tanner's leveled pistol.

Sam shot a second time. The bullet found the weakness between two ribs of Tanner's chest, rammed through breaking bones, and plowed into the lungs. It crashed onward into the spinal column, nearly severing the pathway of corded nerves. The heavy body fell, and bucked and rolled and twitched like a berserk marionette.

Keesling completed his draw as Tanner collapsed. He shifted his intended point of attack and fired into the center of Kimbel.

Keesling held his smoking gun and looked at the dead man. He was still alive because Sam had been lucky and killed Tanner at an impossibly long range. But had it been luck? Bartel had told him of Sam's skill. Until this moment, Keesling had not believed it.

The Mexican girl hurried to Sam. There was a strange brilliance in her eyes. She reached up with both hands and cupped his face. Her fingers caressed the hard planes of his cheeks.

"*Mucho hombre*," much man, she said.

Never had Sam been touched like that before. He felt impelled to reach out and touch her in return. He clasped a gentle hold on the cool flesh of her arms.

She smiled at him, and the beauty of the smile compelled him to smile in return.

Sam knew an amazing change had occurred. The boy was burned out of him by the battle and the touch of the woman.

Keesling watched the two young people. He owed them his life, for surely Tanner and Kimbel would have killed him.

"Take her to Arizona City and buy her a place on the next freight wagon or stagecoach going to her home," said Keesling. "Search those two"—he waved a hand at the dead outlaws—"and use their money."

"*Gracias, señor. ¡Gracias!* I want to go to Tucson. I have family there. Where do you go?"

"To Tucson," said Keesling.

"*Bueno*. Then I go with you. I can ride good. I will work very hard."

Sam considered what the girl proposed. He drew close to Keesling. "It might be best if she did go with us. She doesn't know the mules are stolen—still, we wouldn't want her telling what she saw."

"I think you are correct. I've seen Mexican women that can ride good as a man. You bury those two and fix her up with a horse. I'll go help Zimmer."

Keesling strode toward his horse.

Mariana rode swiftly, crossing behind Sam to pass to the opposite side of the herd. The tall-legged horse ran effortlesly, carrying the small rider with the streaming long black hair as if she were nothing. She smiled a quick, white-toothed smile at the man who had killed her enemy. Sam returned the friendly greeting.

He had selected for the girl and himself the two best mounts from the extra horses in the remuda. Zimmer had insisted she replace her dress with his spare trousers to protect her bare flesh from the rub of the saddle during the long ride to come. She accepted, bestowing upon him a most beautiful smile.

Sam threw a second look to the rear. Mariana had already been engulfed by the dust. He marveled at her endurance. The drive had started fast and continued that way all day. Never once during the weary miles of journeying had she rested. For hours she had ridden the dusty drag position. With Tanner and Kimbel gone, McKone often needed assistance to keep the herd moving.

In the tail end of the evening, outlaws and mules forded the Gila River where it brushed the northernmost sweep of the Mohawk Mountains. The rock foundation of the mountain extended beneath the water of the river, and the crossing was made easily on a stony bottom.

The gang drove the mules into a basin between two rocky prongs of the mountain and bedded them there. Camp was swiftly set up and Mariana hurried about helping Raggan cook the evening meal.

She tended to get in his way, but he too was conquered by her winning smile and said not a word to discourage her.

McKone did not like the girl. He believed she had caused the death of Tanner and Kimbel. He had planned, with the help of those two men, and at the correct time, to kill the other gang members and take the mule herd. That scheme was nothing now. He hid his feelings toward the girl, for Sam watched him carefully.

Under a warm sun the next day the herd traversed the flat desertland of the San Cristobal Valley. The angular, cactus-covered Aguilar Mountains were passed on their right near high noon, and the Sentinel Plain lay spread before them.

"Godforsaken country," said Keesling, sweeping the sand-and-rock desert with its widely scattered patches of brush and cactus. "There'll be no water out there. Head a little north or east so we can pick up the Gila before dark."

"Right," agreed Sam, shading his eyes to scan ahead. "I'll go left of those mountains you can see out there about twenty miles. Seems I can remember that white hill lying just off the end of the mountain from our trip coming west."

"Those are the Sauceda Mountains, or so the Pimas told us. Their village is on the banks of the river just the far side of the mountain. We're only a little ways off our old course."

"Then Mexico would be off over there someplace," said Sam, and motioned with his hand to the south. His heart felt better. Soon now he would begin his search for Sarah.

"Yes, maybe forty miles or so. Appears a storm is building down there." Keesling inspected scores of clouds puffing up in white mounds.

In the heat of the afternoon, the front of the storm had reached the Sauceda Mountains and was brewing giant thunderheads over the high rock-spined crests. Thunder grumbled within the towering cumulus clouds, and gray curtains of rain hung beneath the black bottoms.

Mariana galloped to the head of the herd and angled up to Sam. "May I ride with you?" she asked. "I'm afraid of thunder and lightning."

"Sure you can. I'm glad for your company."

"Are you scared of storms?"

"No. In fact, I kind of like them. They make you feel more alive." He watched her face as she nervously eyed the clouds, swollen and heavy with rain.

At a primitive level, Mariana sensed the signs and omens of the imminent attack of the storm. She drew even closer to Sam.

The thunderheads grew swiftly, towering upward forty thousand feet and hiding half the mountain. The storm moved down from the mountains into the desert.

Lightning flashed among the clouds and set whole patches of sky afire. Splinters of lightning shot down to the earth and skipped over the rugged land. Thunder pounded Mariana's and Sam's ears.

The first faint puffs of a cold wind stirred the air. Quickly it strengthened and charged upon the herd of mules with a roll of dust and shrieking a wild song.

It buffeted the two riders and pulled at their clothes. Sam yanked his hat down more firmly. Above their heads, the sky was an ocean of swift wind, churning and boiling the dark gray clouds.

Sam yelled into the keening banshee scream of the wind and pointed ahead at a jumble of boulders. Mariana could hear nothing over the maniacal roar of the storm, but she understood his meaning.

They drove their mounts forward and took shelter in the cluster of rocks. The frightened mules, their eyes white and rolling, milled and stomped, uncertain what they should do.

Lightning slammed the earth close by. A boulder exploded fragments of rocks like shrapnel from a cannonball, and the smell of sulphur filled the air. The mules stampeded.

From the seething clouds, a twisting funnel snaked down to suck and tear at the desert. The mouth of the tornado, moving faster than a horse could run, struck here and there like the broken pendulum of a gigantic clock. Brush tore loose, and dirt and sand by the ton rose up, and all went spinning upward in the vortex.

Not satisfied with the destruction being wrought, the cloud birthed a second monstrous tornado. It dropped down upon the mule herd. The maw of the funnel fastened on two animals and lifted them from the ground.

Up, up they were pulled, twenty feet, sixty feet. Sam saw the mules' bodies strain against the mighty wind as they whirled around. Their mouths were open in a terrible cry that could not be heard.

Then, tired of the game, the tornado tossed the mules aside, and they fell to crash horribly upon the ground. The tornado whipped away, bowling over a hundred animals and splitting the herd as though with the stroke of a sword.

Both tornados drew upward into the turbulent belly of the cloud. The wind howled onward, trying to blow itself off the earth. Thunder reverberated, ripping the sky open, and rain cascaded down in torrents.

The panicked mules rushed up the slant of the white hill and vanished from sight on the far side.

Sam and Mariana jerked slickers from behind their saddles and struggled into them. They huddled together with the horses drawn in close to partially break the force of the wind. The rain fell cold upon them. Mariana caught Sam's hand and held it tightly.

The storm shoved past Mariana and Sam. It rumbled and growled its way north, crossing the Gila and climbing up into the Maricopa Mountains. Its lightning bolts, diminished by distance, became tiny, winking fireflies.

The wind slowed on the desert. Updrafts resumed. Buzzards rose up from their roosting perches and again took control of the sky, so recently relinquished by the thunderheads. Tracing wide, swinging circles, the scavengers soared high for an aerial view.

Soon they began to drop toward the earth. They had located the dead things the storm had provided for them to feed upon.

The gang of thieves spread themselves in a line two miles long and swept to the east. Some of the stampeded mules began to collect in front of them. The riders moved up and over the slope of the white hill. They halted abruptly as they came to the edge of a high, vertical cliff. At the bottom of that long fall lay a mound of crushed and mangled mules. A multitude of vultures, flogging their mates with hard, stiff wings to win space at the corpses, gorged themselves upon the flesh.

The featherless heads on the long red necks of the vultures craned around to examine the humans above them. Disturbed at the nearness of the riders, the buzzards took wing, a living black pall rising up to block out most of the sun.

"Damn bad luck. At least seventy mules run off the cliff and got killed," said Zimmer.

"More of them than that. What an awful waste," Sam said.

"No use to sit here and moan about it," said Keesling. "Let's catch the rest of the mules." He kicked his mount along the lip of the ledge and back into the desert.

The others followed.

Keesling and Sam stopped their mustangs on the bluff above the Gila River. Leaning on the horns of their saddles, they gazed down upon the Pima village with its dome-shaped wickerwork structures resting in a curve of the river some three quarters of a mile distant.

The large orchards and gardens could be plainly seen. Also visible was the main irrigation ditch from the river to a point where it divided into several smaller branches. All the ditches were dry, for there was still a danger of frost and the gardens had not yet been planted.

"Nice place for a town," said Keesling.

"Yes, it is," responded Sam. "How do you suppose they know when to plant their crops? They don't have a calendar."

"I've heard Indians, wherever they live, have figured out that when the sun gets to a certain height in the sky at noon, it's the season to plant."

"That time should be soon."

"Yep, probably in only a few days. Let's move on."

The mule herd came up behind the men and broke over the hilltop. Within three or four minutes, a group of fifteen mounted men came hurrying out from the Indian village.

"They must have lookouts posted," said Keesling. "It didn't take them long to see us."

"I hope they are as friendly as the last time we were here," said Sam.

Keesling twisted in his saddle and motioned with his hat for Zimmer and Two Foxes to come up to the point of the herd.

"Best we meet them out there away from the mules. If there's going to be gunplay, I don't want a stampede."

The four outlaws veered off from the course of the herd and rode to intercept the Indians.

"Black Elk is with them," said Two Foxes.

"I wondered whatever happened to your partner," said Keesling. "He acts like he's right at home with the Pimas."

Sam scrutinized the approaching horsemen. He had heard talk of the second Kiowa gang member. Sam thought he had him identified, an Indian dressed in a fashion similar to Two Foxes, with a six-gun strapped around his waist.

The Indians slowed and came on at a walk. Black Elk raised his hand in salute. He was a thin man, with a thin face, and no longer young.

Sam examined the black horse the Kiowa rode. Somehow it appeared familiar.

"Where the hell have you been all winter, Black Elk?" the gang leader asked.

"I followed your sign to here, to this Pima country. They told me you bought much food from them and then traveled west to some land called California. I thought about that place. I did not know it. When I saw all the pretty women here, I decided I did not want to go to this California. It has been an enjoyable winter here."

"I bet it has," Keesling said.

"Two Foxes, how was this California?" Black Elk asked in his native tongue. He reined his cayuse to face his fellow Kiowa. The left side of the horse came within Sam's vision.

Sam's blood chilled as he saw the brand on Black Elk's mount. A SLANT T was plainly marked on the brute's left hip. That was his father's brand, T standing for Tollin.

Sam spoke to Black Elk. "Damn fine horse you're riding." Sam strove to keep his voice calm. "Where did you get him?"

Both Kiowa glanced at the white youth. Two Foxes felt a sudden caution. Sam never made idle talk, so what was the purpose of the question? Two Foxes surveyed the black horse of his partner. It was an animal unknown to him.

Black Elk was proud of his fine cayuse. He had taken it fairly in combat from a strong fighter. "I got it in the Santa Fe country," he answered.

"Who was the owner?" asked Sam in a deadly quiet voice.

"He is dead, so it does not matter what his name was."

"And the woman with him?"

"She is dead, too." Black Elk realized the white boy should not have known about the woman. Unless he had been there at the attack. Was he the one who had sped from the cabin? If so, why had not Two Foxes killed him? It made no difference why he was still alive. Black Elk would remedy that mistake now.

"You murdering bastard, I'm going to kill you," Sam shouted. Even as he cried out, his mind was racing. The Kiowa were partners. If Black Elk had been at the fight at the cabin, then Two Foxes must have also been part of it.

Black Elk plunged his hand for his six-gun.

Two Foxes' foreboding about the danger Sam was to him crystallized into full knowledge that it was true. Sam had to be destroyed. Two Foxes would assist his Kiowa comrade to do it.

Sam drew his pistol with a swift blur of his hand. He triggered it at Black Elk. The man was bringing his weapon to bear on Sam as the bullet tore into him, going straight to his heart.

Black Elk tried to catch his balance, failed, and toppled from the saddle.

Sam did not wait for the man to fall. He began the long swing, more than ninety degrees, to reach his second enemy. Sam's eyes spun the arc faster than his hand, and he saw he was too late. Two Foxes had drawn swiftly and his pistol was aimed directly at Sam.

Two Foxes squeezed the trigger. In perfect clarity, Sam saw the finger move. He waited for the explosion and braced for the strike of the bullet.

Neither happened. The gun misfired. An unbelieving expression swept over the countenance of Two Foxes. His thumb jumped to the hammer to recock it for another attempt to shoot.

Sam shot him through the center of his chest.

Two Foxes dropped his pistol from unfeeling fingers. He fell from the saddle, struck his head upon a sharp, angular rock, and rolled to his back. His face was badly injured, and clear liquid leaked from a collapsed right eyeball. His teeth showed like those of an animal caught in a deadfall that was breaking its back.

His one good eye fastened upon Sam. In a whispery, ghostly voice, he spoke. "I always knew you could never be killed by me. That is why I never tried to do it before."

The Kiowa's last eye died.

CHAPTER 19

The Pima whirled their mustangs and whipped them back toward their village. They wanted nothing to do with these white men that killed Indians, even those that rode with them.

Zimmer stepped down from his horse and picked up Two Foxes' six-gun. He ejected the faulty cartridge and caught it in his hand. "The hammer hit the firing cap. The dent is plain. But it didn't go off. Damn, what luck you got, Sam."

Sam dismounted and looked at the dead men. He should have felt good after killing these two. He felt terrible. He walked away.

The black horse recognized Sam. It nickered and came after him to nuzzle and smell of his hands and clothing.

Sam patted the sleek, black body. With his fingers, he traced the SLANT T brand burned into the hide of the animal. No longer was there the slightest hope his parents were still alive. This one horse was all that was left of his family's ranch and all the plans and dreams.

He turned and looked to the southeast where Tucson lay. Only Sarah remained. Yes! She must still be alive!

The band of thieves halted at the south base of the dome-shaped Sacaton Mountains. The mules, hungry from being only half fed for days, began immediately to bite at the tender tips of the paloverde and the green ephedra, and crop the scanty clumps of grama grass growing among the cholla cactus and the giant saguaros.

Keesling called his gang near him. He pointed out over a broad, flat plain at a tall, dark chain of mountains on the far-distant horizon.

"Tucson is about fifty miles due south—lays at the bottom of those mountains, the Santa Catalinas. She's a town of about three thousand people. A mean town—worse than Los Angeles, I'd judge.

"We'll cut Zimmer out two hundred head or so and he can take them there and sell them. Tucson is a booming place and has lots of freight outfits and should be needing mules."

He said to Zimmer, "The town will be easy to find. Just go half a day's travel out into the center of the flat country and pick up the channel of the Santa Cruz River. It'll probably be dry. Follow it up the grade to the right side of the mountains.

"The river starts in Mexico and is a fair-sized stream running all year. It flows north, cutting through Tucson, and still has plenty of water. They irrigate several thousand acres of land from it. But then as it comes on it gets smaller and smaller. Finally it plumb peters away to nothing out there in those sand flats."

"There's no problem," Zimmer said. "I can find the town. I've been wanting to visit it for years now."

"I'll get you some bill-of-sales." Keesling went to his saddlebags and extracted several sheets of paper from a waterproof pouch.

Keesling handed the paper to Zimmer. He spoke in a low tone so that Mariana, sitting her horse nearby, could not hear. "I had a man with the hand of a true artist draw up bill-of-sales. They look very legal and you should not be questioned."

"Sounds fine by me," said Zimmer. He turned to Sam and Mariana and, raising his voice, called out, "Are you two ready to go to Tucson?"

"I already feel as if I'm home," said Mariana.

"Let's go," Sam said impatiently. He sighted ahead, examining the rock- and cactus-strewn land, warming under the winter sun. Finally his search was truly commencing. He would push hard, for he had delayed far too long.

"We'll drive the rest of the herd on toward Santa Fe," Keesling said. "Our course will be east to the Rio Grande and then north along the river. You should be able to catch us before we get to Santa Fe."

"We're short of riders, so I'll see if I can hire a couple and bring them with me," Zimmer said.

"Let's get the mules cut out," said Sam. He touched the spurs to the black horse that had once belonged to his father and rode into the herd.

Sam and Mariana rode opposite orbits around the herd in the bottom of the valley of the Santa Cruz River. The brown adobe buildings of Tucson cluttered the flatland beside the stream a quarter mile to the southeast. Tall mountains reared high on all the horizons. Pine-cloaked and sharp, they stabbed upward into the hard blue sky.

On the edge of town, Zimmer sat his horse and spoke to a man leaning against a rick of cedar posts. "Fifty cents a day for each head seems mighty costly to me," said Zimmer. He sighted out over a pasture of seven or eight acres, fenced with brush and rocks and divided into two approximately equal parts. One of the divisions was full of bawling longhorn cattle.

"Worth every penny," countered the man. "Business is good and getting better. Folks by the dozens are coming up from Texas. They're even coming all the way from Georgia and Tennessee and other places back East. Appears they don't like it at home since they lost the war. This town is going to boom."

"Then mules might have buyers. What's good, strong mules worth?"

The man shaded his eyes and looked toward the herd. "Depending on just how good they are, they could fetch two hundred dollars." He slid a sly glance up at the ugly little man on the horse. "You're going to need a right and proper piece of paper to show you own them."

Zimmer ignored the implication of the man's words. Probably much of the livestock coming into this area would have questionable ownership. That was often the way growth occurred in boomtowns. He would bet his last dime that every mule would be sold without a question asked about the nature of his papers.

"You had better get a good price," the man said. "Costs are high. Drinking brandy costs forty dollars a gallon, coffee is four dollars a pound, and a bar of soap is fifty cents."

"With those prices, a freighter could afford to pay a lot for a mule to pull his wagons. How many freight outfits in town?"

"Six or seven. Only two amount to much. They're big and got several wagon trains coming and going all the time. They go west to Yuma, north to Santa Fe, and to dozens of towns in Mexico. One of them goes all the way to Mexico City. If you want to sell your mules, see the Mexican Vallejo of Vallejo Freight Company, or Cartland of the New American Freight Company."

"Thanks for the talk," Zimmer said. "I'll bring my mules in. You feed them good."

"I'll do that. Got more than three hundred tons of grass hay in stacks down on my meadow by the river."

Zimmer rode a short distance toward the herd and up on a small rise. He began to wave his hat above his head. Almost immediately Sam signaled back. Soon the dust began to rise and the mules came at a trot.

The mules were penned in the pasture and Zimmer, Sam, and Mariana moved in the direction of town.

"How long will you be in Tucson?" Mariana asked Sam. Her large eyes observed Sam intently and there was a wistful tone in her voice.

"Almost no time. I'm going to leave soon as I buy a few things to round out my outfit."

"Then this is goodbye." She urged her mount up close to Sam and put her hand out.

Sam returned the gentle pressure of the small, firm hand. She was a very nice person to be near. "Maybe I can come back this way one day."

"I would like that," Mariana said. She smiled at Zimmer. "*Adios*, Señor Zimmer. I will leave your horse at the livery on Ochoa Street."

"He is your horse. Sam and I have already agreed on that."

"*Muchas gracias*. Now I am doubly in your debt. Remember, you have a friend in this town. No, more than that, for all my family will say they are in your debt." She whirled her mount and loped it northeast around the border of the town.

"Let's go find a buyer for the mules," said Zimmer.

"I'm way past ready," responded Sam.

They rode along the rutted, dusty thoroughfare lined with drab, single-story adobe buildings, baked and cracked. Sam reined the black horse around a pile of broken barrels and other trash lying in the street. Two coyote dogs lurking in the alley inspected the two horsemen as they passed. They licked their chops and went back to eating on a dead burro lying on the ground near them. A filthy town, thought Sam.

A group of armed men, a mixture of Mexicans and Americans, loafed on benches in front of a large saloon. Sam judged them not honest working men. More easily, they could be bandits, killers, or thieves. Just like Zimmer and him. Not a good thought.

As the riders continued, the businesses and homes became newer and larger, and some had whitewashed walls. Sam's gaze swiveled here and there, trying to see everything. From horseback, he could see into the private patios of the homes. In those hidden little worlds, everything was clean and neat. Brown earthen bake ovens, like domed beehives, occupied almost every yard. Some gardens were in the process of being spaded up in preparation for the spring planting.

He observed especially carefully the people in those intimate walled patios. Just maybe, against nearly impossible odds, Sarah might be in Tucson. However, all he saw was dark faces and black hair, not one blonde head among them.

Two blocks ahead, the shallow canyon of the street was broken by a wide vacant lot. In the center of the lot was the workshop of a smithy. At least twenty big wagons were drawn up around it.

The clang of a heavy hammer beating on iron rang out from the smithy. At the sound, Sam spoke to Zimmer. "I would guess somebody is setting rims on wagon wheels. Must be getting ready for a trip. They might need mules."

"That sign there on that wagon says Vallejo Freight Co. I was told he's one of the biggest. Let's ride down there."

Two men, an American dressed in a townsman's suit and a Mexican *vaquero*, came out of a building in the block beyond the blacksmith. They strode purposefully up the street. Both were armed with pistols on their belts.

The American shouted out at a Mexican man entering the blacksmith shop. "Vallejo, wait. I want to talk to you."

The man called Vallejo turned his head to look, then pivoted completely around to face the men.

The American again yelled something at the lone Mexican.

Sam heard the menacing tone but could not make out the words. Some men on the thoroughfare halted to cast curious glances at the commotion. Others came out of nearby buildings to investigate.

Hammering stopped at the forge, and the blacksmith hurried to join the group of gathering men. A woman and a little boy passing by hesitated a moment to listen. Then, grabbing the child by the hand, the woman hastened away.

"Looks like a ruckus brewing. I want to take a look," said Zimmer.

They traversed the block and pushed up to sight over the heads of the men on foot. A small, bony Mexican stood in an opening ringed by the crowd. He shoved his wide-brimmed sombrero from his head to hang by a strap around his neck. There were streaks of gray in his hair. Casually he hooked his thumbs in the waistband of his leather pants. A long-barreled six-gun hung close to his fingertips.

"Slocum, make your talk fast," said Vallejo. "I got more important things to do than listen to you."

"Vallejo, I say you dealt crooked cards last night," Slocum said. "I want my losses back—six hundred and forty dollars. My friend Cavasos also wants his pay that he earned honestly by hard work for you coming up from Mexico."

"I do not cheat. You lost because you are a lousy gambler. And Cavasos, I paid you three hundred dollars soon as we arrived in Tucson. You know that very well."

"You have not paid me, Vallejo," said Cavasos.

"Both of you are liars," said Vallejo scornfully. "I know why you say those things. Cartland of the New American Freight has sent you to make these claims against me. He knows I will not pay and then you two will try to shoot me. He cannot compete fairly with me in the hauling business. With me dead, he thinks all the routes will be his. Well, I will not be easy to kill." He let his hands fall near his tied-down pistol.

"Cartland knows nothing about this," said Slocum. "Cavasos and me, we aim to have our money even if we have to take it off your dead body."

Sam listened intently. Somewhere he had heard Slocum's voice before. Not recently, of that he was sure. Yet it had not been too far in the past. He pulled his horse away and circled to come up almost behind the Mexican, Vallejo. He sighted across the opening at the American.

Sam had seen the man only in half-light weeks before. Still, recognition surged swiftly as he noted the shape of the head, the short mustache, the dark suit and flat-crowned hat. It was the man who had stolen his money in Santa Fe.

Sam did not know whether to laugh or curse in the pleasure and the fury of his discovery. This man had caused his sister to be carried away as a prisoner. And Sam himself to be almost killed. Sam felt the certainty of his coming revenge, as elemental as water flowing downhill; he was going to shoot this tricky, thieving bastard within the next minute.

He sprang down and strode forward. With an iron hold he kept his emotions bottled. Nothing must slow the speed of his hand.

The crowd, sensing a gunfight ready to begin, started to retreat and scatter out of the range of possible stray bullets.

Sam shoved men out of his path and came to a stop by the side of Vallejo. The Mexican flinched, startled at the sudden appearance of the tall figure so close. He quickly scanned the freckled face of the *gringo* youth, trying to read there his intention. A pair of ice blue eyes, as emotionless as spheres cut from the blue sky, looked back at him.

Then the two orbs whipped across the street to watch every move of Slocum and Cavasos. Vallejo hastily returned his stare to his enemies.

"What do you want here?" Vallejo asked from the end of his mouth. "These men will be shooting at me in a moment."

Sam answered, "You say they are liars. Well, I know the American is a thief and liar. Are you fast with a pistol?"

"Not fast. But I hit what I aim at."

"Then shoot the Mexican. The other man is mine."

Sam raised his voice to speak. "Slocum, you robbed me in Santa Fe a short time back, and tricked me into thinking you were going to send soldiers to help my father and mother against the Comanche. You are not fit to live. I aim to send you to hell."

Slocum's face twisted in anger. "An old Mexican and a kid will never send Slocum anywhere."

Sam remembered what Zimmer had told him. If there is to

be a fight, then start it. Sam drew and fired upon the hate-filled face.

Then he fired instantly again, driving a ragged, bloody hole completely through Slocum's chest. The man cried out once, a guttural cry of death.

A gun crashed beside Sam as Vallejo shot his six-gun. The bullet went true to the heart of Cavasos. He fell backward into the dirt.

Sam pivoted to sweep a fierce glance over the throng of men, threatening them with the hot barrel of his six-gun. He was in a completely unknown town. Any man might take up the fight. He saw Zimmer also checking men standing on the street and in the doorways.

Walking up to Slocum, Sam kicked the toe of his boot under the loose-jointed body and rolled it over on its back. He searched the man and rose. In his hand he held a pouch of gold. It was the very same pouch that had been stolen from him, but there was now more gold in it. That made absolutely no difference at this moment.

Sam lifted the heavy bag of coins above his head. "Slocum robbed me of this gold," he called to the crowd. "I claim it. If there is anyone that says no, then let him come tell me now."

Sam rotated slowly, holding his pistol and waiting. No man moved.

He fished out one of the gold coins and tossed it on Slocum's chest. "That's for the undertaker and gravedigger."

Vallejo walked toward Sam. He sensed the young man's readiness to do battle—more than that, the eagerness to kill at the slightest hint of danger. Vallejo said, "Come with me to my office and we will talk. If that man on the horse is your friend, ask him to come too."

Sam gestured to Zimmer, who nodded his understanding. However, he came slowly, guardedly watching to the rear. They entered a large adobe building on the side of the street opposite the smithy.

Vallejo took a seat behind a scarred wooden table. Silently he evaluated the two *gringos*. This was the very first time a *norteamericano* had ever helped him, even by accident. It was strange to be beholden to one of them.

"I have never seen you *hombres* before. However, that is

not strange. During the past year hundreds of people have come to stay in Tucson or are merely passing through on the way to other places." Vallejo looked at Sam. "What is your name?"

"Sam Tollin." He wondered what Vallejo would think if he found out he was talking to two thieves. "This is Zimmer," Sam said.

"Well, Sam Tollin, my name is Juan Vallejo. You have saved my old body from getting shot full of holes. I thank you for that. Zimmer, I saw you were his friend and were ready to protect his back. It is good to have friends in a town such as Tucson, for there are many *banditos* here. They have been run out of Texas, Chihuahua, Sonora, and a dozen other territories and come flocking here because this is a lawless place. But enough of that. How may I repay you for saving my life?"

"You owe me nothing for that," said Sam. "I shot that man to settle a private score. We do have two hundred mules to sell. Can you tell us who might want them and what would be a fair price?"

"Good fortune is with you," answered Vallejo. "There is much need for mules. I have a *rancho* out in the valley and raise my own. However, many others buy theirs. They generally get them from Juan Carillo. He is the largest trader of horses and mules in all Arizona. He has an office and corrals on Ochoa Street. That's five blocks south of here and then over to the left. See him. I am sure he will buy all your animals."

"What should a good, strong mule bring in price?" asked Zimmer. "Those not broken to harness yet."

"If they have not been trained to work, about a hundred and fifty dollars. Come, I will show you to Carillo's place of business."

"You two go ahead," said Sam. "I'm going to drift around town and see what I can find."

"Very well," said Vallejo, and left with Zimmer.

Sam walked unhurriedly, his attention alert for an American woman. He saw not one. There were a fair number of American men, every one armed.

The evening wore on as Sam trod the dirt streets. Shadows

grew long and he observed businessmen locking the doors of their establishments and going off along the avenues.

Coquettish *mujeres*, faces powdered pale lavender and smoking *seegaritos*, came outdoors to laze lightly along the street. One of the languid ladies of the evening, the lilac laces of her bosom loose and a little teasing smile upon her lips, slowed and stopped in Sam's way.

Sam understood the invitation. He stepped around her and went on, for time was pressing him. When his search for Sarah ended, there were many things he must explore.

CHAPTER 20

Long after dark, Sam returned to the office of the Vallejo Freight Company. A heavy wooden door was closed, barring entry. However, light shone in a window behind a thick curtain.

"¿*Quién es?*" who is it, a voice asked at Sam's knock.

"Sam Tollin."

The door swung wide. Vallejo stood to the side of the opening, a pistol in his hand. When he saw Sam was alone, he smiled broadly.

"Come in, *mi amigo*," Vallejo said.

"Did you find anything?" asked Zimmer from where he sat counting a large stack of gold coins at a table.

"No, and I walked nearly every street in this town."

"I don't think you will," said Zimmer.

Vallejo spoke. "Your friend Zimmer has told me of what you search. There is only one *norteamericano* woman in all Tucson. She is about thirty years of age, with brown hair. She is married to a *gringo* man who last year opened a hardware store on Congress Street. I have hauled merchandise to him from Missouri."

"I did not expect to find Sarah in Tucson, but I had to look. But how can you be certain my sister is not here?"

"I have many relatives in this town. My family has lived here for a hundred years. Our women would know if a blond girl had been brought to Tucson. I think the women actually know more of what is happening than the men who are officials here. I would bet all my wagons on that."

"Maybe she is being held prisoner on one of the *ranchos* in the mountains."

"We would know even that, for all the people within two hundred miles trade here. Still, I shall ask some questions. Tell me of the man that took your sister."

"His name is Bastamente. He was boss of five freight wagons going south from Santa Fe along the Rio Grande. Said they belonged to a man in Chihuahua. This was last fall, in October."

"I know of this man," said Vallejo. "I have met him on the El Camino Real. He is a scoundrel. The very type that would do what you say. Yet he is wise enough to take the girl deep into Mexico where she would never be seen by a *gringo*. You have a very difficult task ahead."

"I will find her," Sam said in a hoarse voice. "And I will kill whoever has her or I will die myself."

"To die is never a solution. You must plan well and win. All men have weaknesses. Discover what that weakness is in your foe and then attack.

"I will find out what I can about your sister. Tomorrow we will talk again.

"I have invited Zimmer to stay here tonight. You are also more than welcome if you so desire. There are beds in the adjoining room. Lock the outside door so you can rest in safety. You now have strong enemies in Tucson."

Vallejo touched the brim of his hat in *adiós*. With swift steps he went through the lighted doorway and into the darkness.

"Sam, I've struck a bargain with the mule trader, Carillo," said Zimmer. "Being as how I'm in a hurry, I've made a deal to sell all the mules to him. Got a good price, too a hundred and forty-five dollars each for one hundred and seventy animals and a hundred and twenty dollars each for thirty that had sore feet from stone bruises or are lame from cactus thorns."

"It's not fair to sell him stolen mules."

"That Carillo is one savvy *hombre*. When he saw those mules were gaunt from a long, fast drive and carrying five different brands on their hides, well, he knew they weren't come by honest. Not even when I showed him the bill-of-sales. He almost walked off right then, but his greed got the better of him. He dropped his offering price and started to dicker with me. I'd say he's bought stole animals before. Tomorrow he's going to head out for Mexico to sell them there.

"You have worked hard, Sam, and deserve good pay. Carillo gave me three thousand dollars in gold and a bank draft for the rest. You take the gold. Then you can leave whenever you like. I will cash the bank draft in the morning."

"I don't want any of the money from the mules. I don't feel right about stealing them. I should never have spent any of the money from the bank robbery either."

Zimmer studied Sam in surprise. "You'll need every bit of this gold where you're going."

"I've got the gold from Slocum. That and my dad's horse and my guns are all I'm taking."

"Well, at least take that gray mule."

"Not even him. Nothing."

Zimmer looked into Sam's eyes for a moment. Without a word, he put the gold coins into a leather bag and tossed it onto the table with a thud and jangle. "That's the smartest thing you've done since you met us. Stick to those ways and you'll come out a better man."

"Zimmer, why don't you stop riding with Keesling and go with me after Sarah?"

"I'd like that. But that's your way. Me, I aim to finish the drive to Missouri. Then before summer comes like the fires of hell on the desert, I'm going back to California. There's a pretty Chinese woman there who once looked at my face and did not see a monster." Zimmer rubbed his disfigured countenance, and his eyes had a faraway expression. "Sam, she actually touched my face. You know what she said? She said, 'There's a handsome man beneath those scars.' "

Sam said, "I know there's a friend beneath those scars I will never forget." He would have liked to have the tough, fearless man ride with him into Mexico. However, Zimmer was correct. From here their paths went in different directions.

Vallejo aroused Sam and Zimmer at daylight and they went along the street to a cafe. While they sat and waited for the food, Vallejo observed Zimmer looking across the street at the bank.

"Be very much on guard as you travel, for there are many *banditos* in Tucson," said Vallejo. "Some of them may have seen you bring your mules here, and when you go to the bank, they will know you have sold them. Somewhere on the road they will be waiting to rob you."

"Good advice. I'll see that no one gets ahead of me and sets an ambush," Zimmer answered. He grinned crookedly. "But, if they do, they might get a surprise."

Vallejo turned to Sam. "I have questioned the women of my house and they assure me there is no blond *gringo* woman in this part of the Arizona Territory."

"Then I must go search for her in Mexico. What route would Bastamente take to Chihuahua from Santa Fe? I want to follow the same road and ask the people if they have seen her."

"The El Camino Real is used by all the wagon trains. Most of the population of the country are in the towns located near the road where the wagons can bring supplies. For that reason, I am going east to El Camino Real at El Paso. There I will join with ten of my wagons coming from Santa Fe. Then together we will go south to Chihuahua, Torreon, and last to Ciudad de México."

Vallejo contemplated some thought silently for a minute. "I would like to assist you to find your sister. Why do you not ride with me? I need another guard. Also, I can ask the necessary questions of my friends along the way. They will give me truthful answers when most likely they would give you no answers at all."

"Damn, Sam, can you beat that offer?" exclaimed Zimmer.

"No, I can't," said Sam. "Vallejo, you are more than generous. I accept with much thanks, for I know I will need considerable help."

"*Excelente*. Then it is agreed. I will pay you fifty dollars a month."

"I do not want any pay."

"You are a rich man?" asked Vallejo.

"I have only a little gold and a horse."

"Then I pay. We leave in two hours. Meet me at the blacksmith shop."

The string of twelve heavy freight wagons, each drawn by three teams of stalwart mules, passed below the towering southern flank of the Rincon Mountain in the late afternoon. Two *vaqueros* armed with pistols and large-caliber rifles rode guard in the rear. Sam and Vallejo scouted ahead, one of them always within hailing distance of the lead wagon to call out a warning if needed.

A four-foot white flag with a red cross extending from corner to corner fluttered from a tall staff on the lead and last wagon. Sam had been curious when Vallejo hoisted the pennants. The wagon master had noted the question on his young friend's face.

"That is Vallejo's standard. The Indians know that it means Vallejo pays a tribute for passage across their land. Bandits recognize it to mean a fight to the death if they should attack my wagons. Honest men see the sign of a trader who would never cheat them.

"The men of my family have hauled goods over this road for ninety-two years. Always they have shown the banner, my father before me and his father before him. Now I have flown it for thirty years. It is good to have honor to live by."

Sam saddened at the last remark. He had no honor. He was a bank robber and mule thief. He had killed beautiful horses that belonged to others. To save his life he would have killed the men that owned them. He reined the black horse away from Vallejo and rode out ahead on the wagon road.

The ancient *camino* led past the Dragoon Mountains and then onward, passing range after range of north-south trending desert mountains and intervening valleys. Once for several miles, the wagon train made its course over a great playa, a flatland of soil gray-white from the mixture of silt and salt crystals concentrated there in some ancient time from the evaporation of a great inland sea.

A small band of three Apache intercepted the wagon train, and Vallejo gave each of them a gallon of sweet molasses and a blanket. Two soldiers carrying dispatches for the army post at Tucson halted briefly to exchange words about conditions on the trail and then galloped west.

On the thirteenth day the wagon train came down into the valley of the Rio Grande. Vallejo guided the course beside the swampy river bottom for an hour, until the south end of Comanche Peak was reached. There they forded the river on a rocky shoal and entered El Paso.

Vallejo's wagons from Santa Fe were waiting, drawn up in a line along the main street of El Paso. The newly arrived wagons from Tucson were parked beside the others, and the mules were turned into a nearby corral with the first teams and fed.

The wagon master spent the remainder of the day and a portion of the next in delivering cargo ordered by business-men and restocking for the trip into Mexico. As he went about his tasks, he asked about Bastamente. In the afternoon of the second day, he received a bit of information.

"I saw Bastamente last fall," said the wheelwright. "He stopped for an hour or so while I put some new spokes in a wheel for him. He seemed to be in a very big hurry to go into Mexico."

"*Muchas gracias*," said Vallejo. He glanced at Sam and they moved off together. "Perhaps we will meet him on the trail coming north on his spring trip."

"I would like that," Sam said. "How soon can we leave?"

"I must collect some money owed me. That will take about an hour. Go help the teamsters bring the mules from the corrals and harness them. Tell all the drivers to stay with the wagons."

"Right." Sam strode away with long, quick steps.

The trek continued on El Camino Real, a road worn and deeply rutted by countless wagon wheels, the hard hooves of animals, and the footsteps of men. Every day travelers were encountered coming north—men on horseback traveling swiftly, drovers herding cattle or sheep, and wagon trains of varying sizes. Bastamente was not among the men.

Vallejo made his subtle inquiries of those people met and of his relatives in the scattered villages beside the *camino*. Had anybody heard mention or seen a young blond *norteameri-icano* woman? All answers were the same, and each was no.

Sam held his impatience in check. At every opportunity he practiced his Spanish with the teamsters and others. And to raise his skill with a six-gun to the highest level, he practiced often in the bottom of obscuring gullies or in the dark of night where others could not see him.

On the last day of March, Vallejo's wagons entered Chi-huahua and proceeded a mile across the city to his company's local headquarters, a giant warehouse adjoining a large stone corral. A man came out of the cavernous building at their approach and hastened to greet Vallejo.

The man resembled Vallejo to a remarkable degree and Sam judged the two were closely related.

"This is my brother, Carlos," Vallejo said. "Carlos, meet Sam Tollin."

Sam acknowledged the introduction, feeling the strong hand grip of the other.

"Carlos, whatever Sam wants, please provide it. Without his help, your older brother would now be dead."

"One Vallejo's debt is all Vallejos' debt," said Carlos. "Come inside where it is cool and take wine with me. The men know what is to be done with the mules and freight and do not need our help."

On stuffed leather chairs in the shadowy office of the warehouse, the three men talked and sipped at their drinks. Carlos was leaning forward and listening as Juan described Sam's quest. After his brother finished talking, Carlos sat reflectively rubbing the point of his chin.

He arose and went out a rear door into the main part of the warehouse. Sam heard him calling to someone. Shortly he returned with a young man.

Carlos spoke in Spanish to the fellow. "Rocio, tell these men of the *señorita norteamericana* in Torreon." Carlos turned to Sam. "Rocio only speaks his native language. I will translate what he says for you."

"Thanks," Sam said. He thought he could probably catch what would be said. However, he did not want to misunderstand something that could be very important.

Rocio commenced to talk. "Two months ago I went with Señor Vallejo's wagons to Torreon. While I waited there for the wagon master to trade our wares, I took my rifle and went for a deer hunt up in the hills close by."

Carlos interpreted and added, "He was poaching on a private *rancho*."

Rocio resumed speaking. "I slipped quietly among the brush and trees. After a while I heard voices of women. The cover was good, so I went very close to see. On a road I had not expected to be there, was a horse and buggy and two saddle horses. The people, four of them, were all standing on the ground. A man worked to repair one of the harness straps of the horse that pulled the buggy. A second man stood and watched. He had a rifle in his hands as if he were guarding something.

"There were two women. A woman of our people, very large and I would believe very strong. The other woman, more a girl, was very fair and had long yellow hair. She was very beautiful.

"I went closer to be sure I truly saw this lovely girl. I accidentally made a noise. The big woman saw me and yelled and pointed at my hiding place.

"I ran, for to be caught on this land would mean my death. The man with the rifle shot many times into the brush. Some came very near. But I ran fast. I am like the rabbit. I run into deep brush, fall down, and cover myself with leaves. I hear them riding and searching. I do not move. When it is dark, I come back to Torreon and hide in one of Señor Vallejo's wagons until we leave."

"Sarah! It must be Sarah!" exclaimed Sam. "This is great news."

"Not so good," said Carlos. "Rocio was on the property of Ramos Paz. He is the richest and most powerful man in all the state of Durango. He has gold mines, *ranchos*, and many friends in high places. He could muster a hundred *pistoleros* in an hour to do his bidding. He is a master duelist. It has been said that at least fifty men have met their death at his hands.

"He lives most elegantly. Items from many parts of the world are shipped to his hacienda for his enjoyment. The price means nothing to him, for he simply digs more gold when he needs money."

"Where is his hacienda?" Sam asked.

"On the highland east of Torreon," responded Carlos. "It is a walled fortress—more than a mere hacienda."

Sam climbed to his feet and began to pace back and forth. Finally he knew Sarah was alive and where she was. "I must leave at once," Sam said to Juan.

"If this woman is indeed your sister, then you have a most formidable enemy," answered Juan. "But I understand you must go and find out."

Sam jerked his hat off and faced Rocio. "Could that girl be my sister? Did she look anything like me?" he asked in Spanish.

Rocio examined Sam's features. "She could be. She has only a few freckles across the nose. She is pretty, while you are not. But, yes, most certainly she could be your relative.''

Sam jammed the hat back on his head. ''Juan Vallejo, and you, Carlos, thank you for your help. I must leave now. How far to Torreon City?''

''Five days' fast riding straight south on the main, traveled road, El Camino Real,'' answered Carlos.

Juan spoke. ''Carlos, give Sam the swiftest *caballo* we have. The very best. With two mounts, he can reach Torreon in four days.''

Sam left Chihuahua at a ground-devouring pace. He towed a deep-chested, gray gelding behind.

''With those two horses, he will make a quick trip,'' said Carlos, watching the trail of dust.

''He hurries to his death,'' said Juan sorrowfully.

CHAPTER 21

The sun was yet hidden, the morning cool.

Sam arose and rolled his blankets in the faint, gray light that promised the sun's soon arrival from its nighttime hiding place below the horizon. He prepared no food.

It was the black horse's turn to be ridden. Sam mounted, and his two willing steeds hastened from the camp and along the road beside the wooded bottom of the Rio Nazas. If his judgment was correct, the town of Torreon should lie just a mile or two away.

In an opening in the trees ahead, Sam saw two men. As he came nearer, four more riders and a buggy carrying two men came into sight and stopped beside the first arrivals.

The men tied all the horses to trees. Then they began to go about some apparently known routine. All congregated on the edge of the clearing where a man in black spoke a few words. Three men remained standing there, while the other five walked to the center of the opening.

Two of those in the meadow threw off long cloaks to stand all in white. They were lean men, and moved lithely. Each of the two held out a hand and was given an unsheathed sword by the man nearest him. The men with the empty scabbards walked back to the border of the clearing, leaving the swordsmen examining their double-edged weapons and the man in black silently watching them.

Sam stopped his mount by the men gathered on the perimeter of the clearing. One of them held a leather satchel. That individual glanced up in surprise as Sam swung down close to him. He almost said something, but thought better of the idea and looked back at the men with the swords.

The man in black, as if he were some kind of an official, called the two armed men to him. Sam heard him speak in Spanish. "Is there any argument I can make that will persuade you to forgo this duel?"

The duelist farthest from Sam and on the east side of the meadow was the older. He was richly dressed in silk and wore a short, black beard. Sam estimated him to be in his late thirties. "No." He answered first, speaking quickly as if in a hurry.

The second man was young, in his early twenties. He was very handsome, with clean, finely chiseled features. "No," he said, his voice strained.

"Then take your places," the man in black said.

Sam heard the man with the satchel whispering in a mournful voice, "Fool! Fool! It is no contest. He is a master duelist."

"Let the contest begin," cried out the dueling judge, and he clapped his hands with a loud, piercing sound.

The men in white came together with a sharp ring of steel upon steel. Each struck with his two-edged sword—here, there, and every time to be met with a parry by his opponent and instantly followed by a return counterthrust.

The swords moved so quickly through the dawn's weak light they were invisible. Only the harsh ring of metal proved the deadly weapons existed.

A smile began to play about the lips of the master duelist. Sam watched the smile grow as the man's sword sliced and stabbed ever nearer to the body of the second combatant before it could be fended off. Then suddenly the smile vanished.

Swift beyond comprehension, the master duelist moved forward. His sword was even swifter. It darted out to pierce the neck of his handsome adversary—to grate off the bones of the spinal column.

The young man's eyes flared wide in immense surprise. The whites showed brightly all around the dark pupils. His mouth popped open and he screamed soundlessly.

The master duelist in a lightning movement cut sideways to sever the jugular vein. A great gout of blood gushed out to cascade down over the white shirtfront of the dying man in a crimson tide.

Sam heard a moan from the man with the satchel as he

rushed toward the man kicking and squirming in the grass. The two seconds hurried after him.

With a snow white handkerchief, the master duelist calmly wiped his blade and handed it to his compatriot. He glanced at his fallen adversary and then surveyed the orange blush coloring the eastern sky. "Sunrise is almost here. Shall we continue?" he said to the man in black.

The dueling judge nodded. He looked at one of the men who had stood so very quietly near Sam during the contest. "Are you ready, Diego?"

With an abrupt, stiff swing of his arm, Diego cast off his robe to let it fall to the ground. He was dressed all in white. His face was weathered and fierce-looking. He appeared very confident.

He and his second marched to the center of the clearing near the judge.

"Present them their weapons," said the judge.

The seconds handed their principals holstered pistols. Each accepted the weapon and strapped it around his waist. They drew the six-guns and handed them to the judge.

The judge asked, "Is there any argument I can make to persuade you to forgo this duel?"

Both men answered in the negative.

"Shall one cartridge suffice?" asked the judge.

Again both men responded no. The judge flipped open the cylinders of the guns and examined the loads. "They are satisfactory," he said and returned the handguns to the duelist.

Each man holstered his weapon.

"The contest will begin at the first stroke of the church bell. Take your places."

The survivor of the first duel stepped out first, going fifteen paces east, the direction the city lay. His opponent went the opposite direction a similar distance. They turned and looked at the judge.

The man in black nodded his approval and retreated to stand by the seconds and Sam. Leaving the corpse of the dead duelist, the doctor also went to the edge of the clearing for safety. The combatants locked their sights upon each other.

"This is murder," said Diego's second. "He has killed more than thirty men from that very position."

No one responded. A deep hush fell upon the meadow and the surrounding woods.

The duelists were as motionless as the boles of the trees. The master duelist's head was slightly turned to the side as he listened. The other man faced straight ahead.

The light continued to brighten. A raucous call of an awakening bird ravaged the silence of the morning. A horse stamped a foot.

The peal of a church bell rushed over the land. The duelist to the east drew, the six-gun appearing in his hand as if by magic.

Even to Sam's quick eye, the movement was almost unseen. More than that, the draw appeared to have begun before the sound of the bell was heard.

The pistol of the master duelist spouted red.

The opposing duelist had barely touched his weapon as he died. He half turned to the left toward the other dead man and then toppled, his face plowing into the grass of the meadow.

For a handful of seconds all the men remained motionless. Then the man who had been Diego's second began to sob.

The *médico* broke from his trance and ran to kneel at Diego's still form. After a short moment, he removed his hand from the body. He shook his head. "It is done. He is dead."

The master duelist retrieved his cloak. As he flung it about his shoulders, his gaze flicked over the thin redheaded *gringo* youth standing with the other men. What was one such as he doing so deeply in Mexico? He shrugged the question aside and stepped astride his horse. He and his second left to the east, toward Torreon.

The judge walked slowly to the buggy and climbed up in it to sit down. In the first rays of the sun, Sam saw the face of the man, crinkled and gullied with age. A sad look of disapproval lay heavy upon the furrowed countenance.

The two seconds came carrying the body of the man slain by the sword and placed it on the floorboards of the buggy. They turned to go after the second man.

"What was the reason for the duels?" Sam asked the judge.

"The first man claimed his wife had been abused. The second believed he had been cheated in a horse race. But the

cause of the duels is not important. We Mexicans have
inherited a monstrous legacy, this act of dueling, from the
days of the French rulers. We have gone beyond them—now
we always fight to the death. No mere wound will suffice to
atone for an insult to our honor.''

The last body was gently laid beside the first. The seconds
mounted their horses.

'That was the fastest draw I have ever seen,'' said Sam,
continuing to speak to the judge. "I understand why he
always wins.''

"He is the best *pistolero* I have ever seen,'' the judge said.

Sam silently agreed. The man showed no fear. He was
relaxed, appearing to be actually enjoying himself. "Who
was the man?'' Sam asked.

"Ramos Paz. He is the most deadly fighter in all the state
of Durango. Probably in all Mexico.''

At the sound of the church bell calling sunrise services, the
cuidadero de muertos, the undertaker, rose from his chair and
went out of his establishment to stand in front on the wooden
sidewalk. He raised a hand to shade his eyes from the sun and
looked along the thoroughfares and out over the houses of the
five thousand citizens of Torreon.

People in ones and twos and whole families left their
houses and walked in the direction of the large whitewashed
church on the plaza. Long, dark shadows, cast by the new
sun, kept pace beside every person.

The undertaker absently watched the religious faithful duti-
fully wend a course until they and their mimicking black
shadows climbed the time-worn steps and disappeared into
the open door of the church. His thoughts were not on the
happenings in the town, but rather beyond it on the bank of
the Nazas River, where a most irreverent event should have
begun with the striking of the bell.

Two horsemen at a gallop entered the town from the west.
The heavy hoof falls of their mounts echoed between the
sides of the buildings and reached the undertaker. He twisted
around to stare.

Without slowing, Ramos Paz held up two fingers for the
cuidadero de muertos to see and rode on with his comrade.
The man on the street gave no indication he understood. He

did not like this man who ruled the town by the fear of his sword and pistol—and his gold. Very recently Paz had persuaded the governor to appoint him *alcalde*, mayor. Now, as the highest city official, Paz had complete control.

A single rider leading a second mount came past at a slower pace. He was very gaunt, and dust lay thickly on his worn and faded clothing. His horses were lean and looked to need a good feed of grain. The youth must have some urgent reason to travel so hard and fast.

The young man was heavily armed with rifle and pistol. His glance roamed the streets and alleys with a quick, wary sweep. He settled his gaze on the man on the sidewalk.

The undertaker felt the penetrating inspection. Then the fellow nodded a short greeting and shifted his view to the sign above the door of the building. He seemed to understand the wording.

His course was exactly the same as that of Ramos Paz. The undertaker wondered if the *norteamericano* might be following the master duelist.

As the rider moved on, the bright rays of the sun caught the red hair protruding beneath the battered hat and seemed to set it all aflame. Strange to see a face so fair so far south in Mexico, thought the undertaker. Stranger still if he were truly pursuing Ramos Paz.

The undertaker's attention was drawn to a buggy approaching him. Two mounted men trailed close behind the vehicle. They led two horses with empty saddles.

Sam glanced to the rear and saw the procession halt near the man at the funeral parlor. After a brief conversation, the buggy and horsemen moved on and the man on the sidewalk went into the building.

Ramos Paz took his place at the long dining table that was lavishly spread with breakfast for two. Immediately a male servant entered and poured him a piping hot cup of coffee. Paz methodically placed two level spoonfuls of sugar into the black liquid and began to stir. The servant remained motionless, waiting. He knew the exact sequence of things that would occur.

"Ask the Señorita Sarah to please have breakfast with me," directed Paz.

"Sí, patrón," replied the servant, and hastily left.

Paz drank a quantity of coffee, savoring the flavor. It tasted immensely delicious after the morning's contest of skill. He had felt himself in little danger from his opponents; still, unforeseen accidents could happen. A slip on the grass, or the *pistola* to hang for a fraction of a second in the holster, could mean death.

He heard a sound and looked up. His pulse speeded. The most enjoyable occurrence of the day was beginning.

A young woman with striking white skin and yellow hair had come into the room. She stopped just inside the door and watched the man.

"Good morning, Sarah. Please be seated and take breakfast with me." Paz stood erect and smiled at her.

"If you insist," said Sarah, coming forward.

"No. No. Not insist. I mean it as a most kind invitation."

Sarah found a chair at the far end of the table and picked up the napkin at the plate. She had once rejected an invitation to eat with Ramos Paz and had walked from the room. After three days during which every particle of food had been withheld from her, she had grudgingly accepted his order to breakfast. She reasoned that her strength must be maintained, for one day her father and brother would rescue her from this hated captor and she would travel the long distance home.

Paz ate slowly, his eyes often upon the girl. He enjoyed observing her feminine movements, the curve of her fair cheek, and the swell of her young bosom.

Sarah's blue eyes swept over him in a challenging manner to show she was not afraid. Yet she knew she was.

Paz smiled in pure delight at the touch of her eyes, and in his anticipation of completely possessing her body and keen spirit. In two more days she would be fourteen, and among the women of his family that would be considered a mature woman. He would marry her and share his land and gold with her. Never would she want to return to the north.

She was worth the ten thousand pesos Bastamente had demanded for her, or ten times that amount. In reality, it had made no difference what he paid the kidnapper. For Ramos Paz had followed after Bastamente as he left the hacienda and killed him before he could talk and brag of the large fortune he had received for the girl.

Paz lingered over the meal, drawing Sarah into conversation. She answered in short Spanish sentences. He was pleased with her rapidly growing knowledge of his language.

Sarah found a hesitation in the talk and stood up. "May I leave now?" she asked.

Paz would have liked to extend the pleasant time with her. However, a troubling thought had crept into his mind and would not go away. "Certainly, Sarah. Thank you for the pleasure of your company. Perhaps we can go riding this evening."

As Sarah walked away, Paz intently evaluated her features. Satisfied with what he saw, he strode out into the courtyard.

"Jacobo!" he called loudly.

"Sí, patrón," sounded a voice from a room on the far end of the hacienda.

"Venga aquí," orderred Paz.

A short, swarthy man came outside and hurried toward Paz. *"¿Qué quiere, mi patrón?"*

"There is a tall, young *gringo* in the town. He has red hair. Go find him and follow to see what he is doing here. Report back when you know."

"Sí, muy pronto."

"Jacobo, do not feed the guard dogs today."

The man nodded his understanding and grinned agreeably. Hungry dogs made mean dogs. The *patrón* must be expecting an unwanted visitor. Jacobo hitched at his gun belt. Some gunplay would be welcome.

After Jacobo left, Paz remained standing and looking out over the city of Torreon lying in the valley below. Along the river and stretching for miles were thousands of acres of irrigated farmlands and orchards. A huge band of his sheep, a flower white patch far off on the right, was moving in the direction of the high mountain peaks to the east. Early pasture should be found, for the winter had been mild. Perhaps Sarah and he could ride up there on the morrow.

He leaned forward slightly and savored a splendid feeling, dwelling upon the thought that all this was his domain. It was good to own much land and have power over people.

The moon came up full and bright and, to Sam's dismay, much too early. A very bad beginning.

He remained hidden on the brushy crest of a ridge half a mile distant from the walled hacienda of Ramos Paz. He had been there all day evaluating the stronghold, three acres on the crown of a hill, and observing the activity of the inhabitants. At dusk the strong gates had been swung shut. Not one thing had been discovered that would make his entry easy.

In the early hours of the morning, he arose and, treading noiselessly, went down into the wooded swale through the silver moonlight and climbed the slope beyond. He found the wall, made of smooth adobe and higher than his outstretched hands. He hugged in close, seeking the deepest shadow.

Many minutes he crouched there. A dog growled near him, then was quiet.

Sam climbed erect and, springing upward, caught the top of the wall. He hung there listening, then drew himself up to lie tightly along the narrow top.

To his surprise, a second wall blocked his way beyond a space of ten feet or so. However, it was somewhat shorter and would be easy to scale. He dropped down inside and stood very still, has ears cocked for any sign of alarm.

The giant wolf dog came with a rush from his left. Sam dodged to the side and the gaping mouth and sharp teeth missed his throat. But the heavy body of the brute crashed into his shoulder and sent him rolling.

Sam was up instantly. The dog was faster. He growled and leaped in attack.

The dog could kill him in the confined space, or the men that heard the struggle would. Sam drew his six-gun and fired at the large, dark body hurtling through the air at him. The animal struck the ground beyond him in a loose-jointed tumble.

A roar of voices exploded inside the walls. A man bellowed, "To the west wall. The dogs have caught someone at the west wall."

Sam heard something closer and more imminently dangerous. One short bark, a snarl, and a second savage dog bounded through the deep shadows of the alleyway at him.

He jammed his pistol into its holster and jumped for the top of the wall. He levered himself upward. He was going to make it to safety.

A powerful clutch caught him by the boot and stopped his advance dead. The mighty grip yanked downward.

Halfway on top of the wall, Sam strained every muscle to prevent the growling beast from dragging him back to the ground. He drew his free boot up and rammed the heel down upon the head of the dog.

In ferocious response, the animal lunged backward, almost pulling Sam from the wall. He kicked again and again, raining crushing blows upon the head of the beast.

The bite of the animal came loose. Sam went up over the wall, jumped down on the outside, and landed running.

Sam had failed. Now Ramos Paz would double and triple the number of guards to protect his hacienda and what it contained. In all likelihood, he would station lookouts outside the walls on the high ground. Come daylight, these men could find Sam if he remained nearby. If Paz had guessed the identity of the intruder, he would dispatch tough *pistoleros* into Torreon to search for him.

Within three minutes Sam reached his horses. Behind him lanterns flickered inside and outside the walls of the hacienda. The angry shouts of the men came faintly.

Sam swung astride and rode to the south. An hour upriver from Torreon, he found cover in a dense tree-clogged ravine. He spread his blankets, but sleep would not come. He had failed Sarah again.

A new plan must be devised. He had not the slightest idea what that might be. How could one man beat a master duelist who commanded a hundred *pistoleros?*

CHAPTER 22

Sam dreamed of the duel he had witnessed. Time after time, his mind replayed the deaths of the two men. How outrageously outclassed they had been. Ramos Paz's draw of his six-gun had been fast beyond belief. So swift that it appeared his hand had reached for the weapon before the bell sounded. But that was impossible.

Sam awoke from his sleep with a jerk. He sat bolt upright, his mind thundering with a startling thought.

Slowly, deliberately, he ran the idea through his alert, conscious mind. Sometimes the sleeping senses got things confused and that would never do. He examined the idea, testing it from every angle—striving to find the flaw.

Not one weakness in the concept could he find. He bared his teeth and growled to the night, "Ramos Paz, I have discovered a way to steal a tiny fraction of a second from your gun hand."

In reply to the sound of his master's voice, the black stallion nickered from the darkness. The horse stirred Sam's memories of his father. Oh, what he would give to have that strong man here with him in this strange land to help battle the cunning fighter, Ramos Paz.

Early in the morning Sam rode up a narrow street and halted at the side door of the office of the *cuidadero de muertos* of Torreon. He tied his mount and entered the building.

The undertaker glanced up. A slightly puzzled expression spread over his face when he saw the *gringo* youth. "*Buenos días.* How may I help you?"

"Señor, I need some information, *por favor*. What is the

214

name of the old man that acted as judge of the duel yesterday morning?''

"Emilio Juardo. Why do you want to know?''

"I have questions that he should be able to answer. Where can I find him?''

"He has a house on the bank of the river. That street there will lead you to it.'' The undertaker pointed out the side door Sam had entered. "Follow it to the water's edge and go to the very first house on the right.

"Be very careful as you come close and call out to tell him you are a friend. Though he is very old, he still has enemies from long-ago times when he was a master duelist. He is an excellent shot. Is there anything else I may do for you?''

"No, there is nothing. I only want a little talk with the dueling man. *Adiós.*''

Emilio Juardo turned from inspecting his visitor and dropped two small lengths of wood on the coals in the corner fireplace. He spoke as if talking to the flames that leaped up. "So, you want to know about the rules for dueling.''

"Yes, I would like to learn what I can,'' Sam responded.

Emilio spun around. "The first rule is never to fight a duel,'' he cried out violently.

Sam backed up a step at the unexpected outburst. He looked into the aged eyes of the man. "Sometimes there is no other way,'' he said in a low voice.

"There is always an alternative,'' answered Emilio in a calmer tone. "Simply walk away. I do not want to see more dead men.''

"Suppose it is not for yourself that you fight. Suppose there is no other way to get justice.''

"Ah! You believe you must right some great wrong?'' Emilio showed his toothless gums in an ugly smile.

"Will you answer my questions, or must I ask someone else?'' Sam took a pace toward the door.

"I was once a great duelist,'' said Emilio in a muttering tone. "I have a hundred scars on my body. Look, see all my weapons of slaughter.'' He motioned a hand at several swords, pistols, and knives hanging on a wall. "Now I only use one weapon.'' He pulled a pistol from its holster on his hip and hefted it in his hand. "We are civilized men, so we have developed rules for killing. What we call dueling. I would use this to shoot any man that breaks those rules by beginning the contest before the signal or kills after his opponent is helpless.''

Emilio shoved the pistol back into its holster and cast his faded brown eyes up at Sam. ''The second rule is to survive and at the same time slay your adversary.''

''I understand that rule very well,'' said Sam. ''Who has the pick of the weapon to be used?''

''The man that is challenged.''

''How far apart do they stand when pistols are used?''

''Depends on the length of the duelists' strides. Each man paces fifteen steps in opposite directions. That would equal approximately eighty feet in your American way of measuring.''

''Does the challenged person have the say in where he stands for the fight?''

Emilio came out of his half-reverie. His eyes widened and shone at Sam. Some thought passed over his face; then he subdued it. ''Yes, that too, if he so wants. Do you have more questions? I grow weary.''

''Just one. Would you be my second?''

The man's eyes widened and shone again. ''And who would you fight?''

''Ramos Paz.''

Emilio cackled a shrill laugh and doubled over, chortling and pounding on his thighs in glee. Finally he controlled himself and straightened up. ''He will kill you without half trying.''

Sam did not like the man to laugh at him. But he asked again, ''Will you be my second?''

''I am the judge of all the duels in Torreon. No, I cannot be your second. However, you must have one so that if you are wounded and cannot speak for yourself, your second can stop the duel and perhaps save your life.''

Sam shoved the door open. ''This is a fight to the death, so I do not need anybody to help me.''

The door closed behind Sam.

The long, gangly man sat propped against the front wall of the hardware store across the street from the establishment of the *cuidadero de muertos*. The high collar of his coat was turned up around his neck, and his battered hat was pulled far down over his face. He had been there since early morning. He appeared to be sleeping.

Sam was thirsty and hungry. Still, he did not stir. From a hole in his worn hat, he watched the people on the sidewalk and the carts, wagons, and horsemen on the streets. This was the main thoroughfare of Torreon. A man such as Ramos Paz would appear on it sooner or later. Sam hoped none of the man's *pistoleros* found him before that happened.

The sun reached its zenith and began the long, sliding fall to the west. A water vendor came past with his burro carrying two bulging hides of the liquid. Sam called to him and bought a drink for *un centavo*.

The day wore away. In the middle of the afternoon, a group of four *caballeros* came along the street on prancing, spirited horses. Ramos Paz rode in the lead.

Sam climbed erect. The time was now and he must do this thing correctly. He unbuckled his six-gun and laid it on the sidewalk. His coat and hat were removed and dropped atop the weapon. He stepped out into the street.

A gust of wind flared Sam's red hair and sent it flicking about his face. He brushed it from his eyes with a swipe of his hand. "Ramos Paz," he shouted, "I want to talk to you."

The Mexican *caballeros* reined to a halt to examine the strange youth standing spraddle-legged in their course to bar the way. Ramos Paz looked for a weapon on the bony *gringo* and located none. He walked his mount forward.

"I see my dogs did not eat you," Paz said and laughed. "How did you like my pets?"

"You are a dog like your pets," Sam snapped back in a scalding voice. "You must steal your females. You cannot win them as other men do."

Paz blanched at the hard words. His features tightened. He raked his horse with spurs and the beast lunged at Sam.

The iron-shod feet barely missed Sam as he sprang aside. He bellowed out, "Are you a coward that you must run a man down? What will your friends think of that?" He must goad Paz into making the challenge.

"That is all you are worth," responded Paz. "If you had a pistol, I would kill you now."

"You have my sister a prisoner up there in your hacienda.

Free her so I can take her back home with me. Then I will fight you."

"You are a nuisance that annoys me." Paz's teeth were clenched and gleamed cruelly white. He moved upon Sam.

With a lopsided, mocking grin, Sam glared into the black eyes of the angry man. Paz lashed out and struck Sam a rough blow to the side of the head.

Sam rubbed his smarting cheek. That was the best hurt in the world. His grin broadened to a full smile.

"Go get your pistol," hissed Paz.

Before Sam could speak, an old man's voice cried out from the doorway of the office of the undertaker. "Did I hear a challenge given?"

Emilio Juardo came out into the street. Inside his head, he admired the young *gringo* for his skill in provoking Paz into the duel. "This challenge must be handled correctly," said the judge of duels. He spoke to Sam. "What weapon do you choose?"

"*La pistola.*"

"Where?"

"The place of yesterday's duel."

"The time?"

"Tomorrow. At the sound of the morning church bell."

The judge turned to Paz. "Are these conditions satisfactory with you?"

"More than acceptable," said Paz. "It will be nothing more than practice to shoot him." He sprang astride his *caballo* and spurred away.

Emilio Juardo spoke to Sam. "I have been waiting in the place of *el cuidadero de muertos* all day for this to happen. But you are mad. You cannot beat Ramos Paz with a *pistola.*" Emilio shook his head sadly.

"Then, old man, help the undertaker find a nice spot for my grave."

Sam rested on a point of the mountain above Torreon and watched the sun hurry to the west and the sky grow red and bloody. Some people believed such sunsets portended bad things to come. Sam did not dwell long on that thought. He raised his head and smelled the rock hills cooling in the evening.

The dusk came and went. The last shred of light drained from the heavens, spilling over the rim of the earth and leaving a black sky speckled with stars. On the eastern horizon, a yellow-eyed moon rose to orb the earth. Up on the mountainside an ill-tempered wind came to life to drone through the brush.

Doubts about his strategy for fighting Ramos Paz crept through chinks in Sam's resolve. He fought them down. There was no turning back now. Sarah's freedom or his death would come with the morning.

He thought of Zimmer. A friend to talk with would be very enjoyable at this time. But then again, a man could only die alone and it was perhaps proper he spend these last hours without friend or family.

With the first paling of the stars, Sam came awake. He immediately saddled and rode down toward the river. He must be the earliest arrival at the dueling place. In his heart he felt joyous in a ferocious sort of way.

He secured his mounts to a bush and unhurriedly went into the woods on the border of the meadow where he had seen Paz kill two men. The trees were rigid and dark and a fragile quietness lay everywhere. Sam leaned against the black bole of a giant tree and waited.

Soon the soft thuds of walking horses sounded, and Ramos Paz and two others moved into the edge of the clearing. One of the animals tossed its head and metal jingled.

A voice Sam did not know spoke. "The *gringo's* horses are here, but I do not see him."

Paz did not answer. He looked at the small form of Sarah sitting her mount beside him. She was casting glances all about. Let her see the brother, Paz thought, then see his death. After that she should be more pliable.

A buggy carrying the judge and the *médico* arrived. The judge climbed down and walked a short distance out into the dueling ground.

Under the trees where Sam stood, only shadowy remnants of the night still remained. In the meadow, dawn held sway. It was time to begin the ritual of the duel.

Sam came from the east toward the men. This was the crucial portion of his scheme. Was he correct? Did he truly have a tactic that would help him destroy his enemy, who was faster with a six-gun?

Sarah spied Sam stepping out of the woods and into the more lighted clearing. She waited for a second figure, her father, to appear. There was no one else. She spun to rake her eyes at Paz. A confident smile was on the mouth of the master duelist as he looked at Sam.

Sarah believed she was responsible for the peril her brother was in. Now she must save his life. She spoke quickly to Paz in a promising voice. "Let him go safely and I will do whatever you want."

Sam heard and called to her in a firm tone. "Sarah! No! I'm not afraid." He felt the wolf rising in his heart, bolstering his defenses. "Sister, do not shame me."

"He must die," Paz said, as if Sam had not interrupted.

A sob escaped Sarah. She rested her gaze upon Sam. His face was taut and his eyes savage. Then he winked and grinned in that certain mischievous way he had when, as children, they were about to pull a prank. Oh, brave, foolish brother, I love you so. And you will soon be dead.

"It is time," called the judge, beckoning for the men to come closer.

Sam stripped off his coat and dropped it to the ground. He approached the judge. Paz walked up from the opposite direction. He handed his cloak to his second. The master duelist was dressed in all white.

"Is there any argument I can make that will persuade you to forgo this duel?" asked the judge.

"No," Sam said.

"No," Paz answered.

The judge saw that Sam already wore his holstered pistol. He spoke to Paz's second. "Present your principal his weapon."

Paz strapped the gun around his waist. Then he drew and handed the weapon to Juardo. Sam also passed his six-gun to the judge.

"Shall one cartridge suffice?"

Both men answered in the negative.

The judge flipped open the cylinders of the weapons and examined the loads. "They are satisfactory." He returned the handguns to the duelists. "The contest will commence at the first stroke of the church bell. Take your places at fifteen paces.''

Paz holstered his pistol and started to step past Sam. With a hard hand, Sam stiff-armed Paz roughly in the chest, stopping him abruptly.

''I choose that position,'' Sam said, his hot eyes grinding into Paz. He pivoted and began to pace to the east in the direction of Torreon.

The face of the master duelist twisted with rage. The judge saw the fury in the man and his hand disappeared under his cloak to rest on the butt of his pistol. ''That is his right,'' warned the judge.

Paz's eyes were suddenly devoid of emotion, as noncommittal as a blind man's. ''I can beat him easily wherever he stands.'' He whirled and stepped off to the west.

Juardo believed the same. The *gringo* youth was mad.

Sam cocked his hearing to the rear and riveted his view upon Ramos Paz, facing him across the grassy meadow. He awaited the impending action. There was a flutter in his stomach he did not like.

Was a one-fifteenth-of-a-second advance start in drawing his six-gun sufficient to allow him to beat the master duelist? Or was his advantage shorter than that?

Sam calculated he would hear the church bell before Paz. Once from a quarter mile or so, Sam had observed his father chopping wood. Something very odd had happened—the sound of the ax hitting the log had reached Sam when the implement was raised above his father's head, halfway into the next swing. ''Sound takes time to reach you through the air,'' his father had told him. ''It can travel about a mile in five seconds.'' Thereafter, they had often measured the distance of storms from them by counting the seconds between the flash of the lightning and the arrival of the thunder.

The sun exploded over the mountain horizon. Sam heard the sound of the church bell speeding over the land from Torreon. He stabbed a hand for his six-gun.

Ramos Paz was alert, ready. He would not listen for the bell. He would pull his pistol at the very instant the *gringo* moved his hand. This should be an easy killing.

How had the fellow figured the man standing closest to Torreon would hear the bell first? Had Juardo known that fact and told him? Perhaps neither knew it. Sarah's brother might want that spot simply because he had seen Paz use it with success. None of this made any difference now.

Paz realized he had slipped into the old habit of listening for the sound of the bell to signal the beginning of the battle. Better stop that.

Even as Paz caught his error, the hand of the *gringo* brother dipped down and came up with a six-gun. The master duelist drew, never more swiftly.

Paz triggered his pistol. His opponent's weapon flashed red flame at the same instant. Paz saw that clearly. A bone-breaking blow slammed his chest. The ring of the church bell registered on his mind as he died.

Sam felt the hot punch of the master duelist's bullet tear into him. How could a man be so quick?

Though he tried mightily to keep his feet, Sam found himself falling. The ground rushed up to meet him. He cried out through his shocked numbness. He had failed Sarah again. Then the pain came and a whirling, black tornado sucked him up and the world vanished.

Sam crawled laboriously up out of the black hole of unconsciousness. His eyes came open to bright daylight and a sword, two-edged and very sharp, hanging an arm's length away.

Other weapons—pistols, knives, and more swords—were fastened to the same wall. Sam recognized the display of killing implements. He was in the home of Emilio Juardo.

Pain shot through his chest as he slowly rotated his head to look about. A slanting shaft of sunlight came through an open outside door to fall upon Sarah seated in a rocking chair. Her chin rested on her chest as she slept.

Sam viewed his courageous sister. She seemed much older, and weary. The sun was caught in her tousled hair, turning it into woven gold about her face. He remembered the last time he had seen it like that, when she had danced to protect him from Bastamente and his gang on the banks of the Rio Grande. She was a sister truly worth risking his life for.

"Sarah," he called. His voice was a hoarse croak.

She was awake immediately. "Sammy," she cried and sprang up to run to him. "Emilio, he is conscious. Come quickly."

Sarah smoothed his red hair and kissed him lightly on the forehead. She held his hand and the tears came, glistening clear droplets coursing down her cheeks.

A shadow fell over them and the dueling judge looked down. His wrinkled old face was grinning widely. "I told you he would not go into the land of the dead."

Sam glanced past Emilio and through the doorway. "Paz? What about Paz?"

"Ah! He is the one that went into the land of the dead. He will find many enemies waiting there. I believe that will not be a pleasant place for him."

"How about his *pistoleros?* Will they give us trouble?" questioned Sam.

Emilio shook his head. "Without a leader they were nothing. They were run out of town by noon yesterday. There were many citizens of Torreon who had old grudges to settle."

Sam was perplexed. "How long have I been unconscious?"

"A day and a half," said Sarah. "Rest now. I will fix you some broth." She wiped at her tears.

"Your strength will soon return with a nurse such as she," Emilio said.

Sam was very tired. And very happy. "Sarah, I have been to a faraway place called California. It is a rich land and there is a great and beautiful ocean. How would you like to travel there and help me build a large *rancho?*"

"I would like that very much, Sam." Sarah clasped his hand more tightly.

"Good." Sam smiled. He drifted off into a peaceful sleep.

About the Author

F. M. Parker has worked as a sheepherder, lumberman, sailor, factory worker, geologist, and a manager of wild horses, buffalo, and livestock grazing. He and a large staff currently manage five million acres of public rangeland in eastern Oregon. He is the author of two other Signet Brand Westerns, *Coldiron* and *Skinner*.